The Mystic Arts of Erasing All Signs of Death

The Mystic
Arts of Erasing
All Signs of Death

a novel

Charlie
HUSTON

BALLANTINE BOOKS   New York

The Mystic Arts of Erasing All Signs of Death is a work of fiction.
Names, characters, places, and incidents are the products of the author's
imagination or are used fictitiously. Any resemblance to actual events,
locales, or persons, living or dead, is entirely coincidental.

Published in the United States by Ballantine Books,
an imprint of The Random House Publishing Group,
a division of Random House, Inc., New York.

BALLANTINE and colophon are registered trademarks of
Random House, Inc.

Library of Congress Cataloging-in-Publication Data

Huston, Charlie.
   The mystic arts of erasing all signs of death : a novel
   / Charlie Huston. — 1st ed.
          p.   cm.
   ISBN 978-0-345-50111-0 (hardcover : alk paper)
   1. Crime scenes—Cleaning—Fiction. 2. Los Angeles County (Calif).—
Fiction. I. Title.
   PS3608.U855M97 2009
   813' .6—dc22   2008035293

Printed in the United States of America on acid-free paper

www.ballantinebooks.com

9 8 7 6 5 4 3 2 1

First Edition

Book design by Jo Anne Metsch

Sweet Virginia
again
on the sharp edge of a flat world

ACKNOWLEDGMENTS

By necessity there was more research involved in the writing of this book than in any other I've written before. Which is not to say I'm not a lazy bastard who happily made up a great deal of BS that flies in the face of many of the true facts as related to me by people who are experts in their fields. For instance, while the profession of trauma cleaning may not be well regulated, and competition may be intense, the range of warfare described herein is not at all factual. All errors and liberties are mine, and should not reflect in any way on the people who helped me.

Many details about the operations and history of the Port of Long Beach were shared with me by Art Wong, that port's assistant director of communications and public information officer. A man whose enthusiasm for his place of work is truly infectious.

Such workings as could be revealed about customs and border protection and security at the Ports of Los Angeles and Long Beach were illuminated by CBP press officer Michael Fleming and his associates.

Above all I am indebted to Mike and Carol Nicholson, owner-operators of Clean Scene Services, Inc. Trauma cleaners of Los Angeles. Their warmth and honesty as they talked to me at length about the often gruesome, and just as often blackly hilarious, nitty gritty of their work was without stint. Companionate human beings, and experts in their field, they share only the best possible traits with the fictional characters in this book. They are the only people I could imagine anyone wanting to have show up at the door should life take a sudden and violent U-turn.

PROLOGUE

I'm not sure where one should expect to find the bereaved daughter of a wealthy Malibu suicide in need of a trauma cleaner long after midnight, but safe to say a trucker motel down the 405 industrial corridor in Carson was not on my list of likely locales.

—Ouch. That looks painful.

I touched the bandage on my forehead.

—And if that's what it feels like to look at it, imagine how it feels to actually have it happen to you.

The half of her face that I could see in the chained gap at the edge of the door nodded.

—Yeah, I'd imagine that sucks.

Cars whipped past on the highway across the parking lot, taking full advantage of the few hours in any given Los Angeles county twenty-four-hour period when you might get the needle on the high side of sixty. I watched a couple of them attempting to set a new land speed record.

I looked back at Soledad's face, bisected by the door.

—So?

—Uh-huh?

I hefted the plastic carrier full of cleaning supplies I'd brought from the van.

—Someone called for maid service?

—Yeah. That was me.

—I know.

She fingered the slack in the door chain, set it swinging back and forth.

—I didn't really think you'd come.

—Well, I like to surprise.

She stopped playing with the chain.

—Terrible habit. Don't you know most people don't like surprises?

I looked over at the highway and watched a couple more cars.

—Can I ask a silly question?

—Sure.

I looked back at her.

—What the fuck am I doing here?

She ran a hand through her hair, let it fall back over her forehead.

—You sure you want to do this, Web?

That being the kind of question that tips most people off to a fucked up situation, I could very easily have taken it as my cue to go downstairs, get back in the van and get the hell gone. But it's not like I hadn't already been clued in to things being fucked up when she called in the middle of the night and asked me to come to a motel to clean a room. And there I was anyway. So who was I fooling?

Exactly no one.

—Just let me in and show me the problem.

—Think you can fix it, do you?

I shook my head.

—No, probably not. But it's cold out here. And I came all this way.

She showed me half her smile, the other half hidden behind the door.

—And you're still clinging to some hope that a girl asking you to come clean something is some kind of booty call code, right?

I rubbed the top of my head. But I didn't say anything. Not feeling like saying *no* and lying to her so early in our relationship. There would be time for that kind of thing later. There's always time for lying.

She inhaled, let it out slow.

—OK.

The door closed. I heard the chain unhook. The door opened and I walked in, my feet crunching on something hard.

—This the asshole?

I looked at the young dude standing at the bathroom door with a meticulously crafted fauxhawk. I looked at bleached teeth and handcrafted tan. I looked at the bloodstains on his designer-distressed jeans and his artfully faded reproduction Rolling Stones concert T from a show that took place well before he was conceived. Then I looked at much larger bloodstains on the sheets of the queen-size bed and the flecks of blood spattered on the wall. I looked at the floor to see what I'd crushed underfoot, half expecting cockroaches, and found dozens of scattered almonds instead. I listened as the door closed behind me and locked. I watched as Soledad walked toward the bathroom and the dude snagged her by the hand before she could go in.

—I asked, *Is this the asshole?*

I pointed at myself.

—Honestly, in most circumstances, in any given room on any given day, I'd say, *Yeah, I'm the asshole here.* But in this particular scenario, and I know we just met and all, but in this room here?

I pointed at him.

—I'm more than willing to give you the benefit of the doubt and say that *you're* the asshole.

He looked at Soledad.

—So, yeah, he's the asshole then?

She twisted her hand free and went into the bathroom.

—He's the guy I told you about.

She closed the door behind her.

He looked at me.

—Yeah, you're the asshole alright.

I held up a hand.

—Hey, look, if you're gonna insist, I can only accept the title. But seriously, don't sell yourself short. You got the asshole thing locked up if you want it.

He came down the room in a loose strut I imagine had been meticulously assembled from endless repeat viewings of Tom Cruise's greatest hits.

—Yeah, I can tell by the way you're talking. You're the one fucked with her today. Made jokes about her dad killing himself. You're the asshole alright.

The toilet flushed, Soledad yelled over it.

—He didn't make jokes!

The dude looked at the closed door.

—You said he made jokes.

He looked at me.

—Asshole. Fucking go in someone's home, there's been a tragedy, go in and try to make money off that. Fucking vulture. Fucking ghoul. Who does that, who comes up with that for a job? That your dream job, man? Cleaning up dead people? Other kids were hoping to grow up to be movie stars and you were having fantasies about scooping people's guts off the floor?

I shifted, crushing a few more almonds.

—Truth is, mostly I had fantasies about doing your mom.

He slipped a lozenge of perforated steel from his back pocket, flicked his wrist and thumb in an elaborate show of coordination, and displayed the open butterfly knife resting on his palm.

—Say what, asshole?

Say nothing, actually. Except say that maybe he was right and I was the asshole in the room. Certainly being an asshole was how I came to be there in the first place.

JEALOUS, BITTER, CYNICAL,
HOSTILE AND PRETENTIOUS

Chev was getting in my ass.

—Give me a hand here.

—Just a sec, I wanna finish this.

—A sec my ass, get the fuck over here and give me a hand.

I got up and walked across the shop, the copy of *Fangoria* folded open to an article about a new wave of bootleg Eastern European ultrahorror DVDs.

—Put that down and hold this.

I lowered the magazine, looked at the girl lying frozen on the table, her shirt pulled up, one tit untucked from her bra, tension in every muscle of her body, a thin stream of tears running from her eyes, flipped him off and took hold of the Glover Bulldog clamp locked on the tip of the girl's nipple, stretching it taut for the needle.

The girl banged her heel on the table.

—Don't pull on it, don't pull on it.

—I'm not pulling on it.

She squirmed.

—You're sooo pulling.

—I am not, you're moving.

I looked at Chev.

—Did I pull on it or did she move?

Chev turned from his kit, a large needle between the fingers of his left hand.

—Just hold it steady, both of you.

The girl froze.

I looked back in my magazine and read about a scene in a movie called *Amputee* where a guy has his eyes gouged out and his toes are amputated by the bad guy and sewn into his empty eye sockets.

—I'm holding steady.

The clamp vibrated slightly as Chev ran the needle through the girl's nipple and she jerked.

I peeked at her over the top of the magazine.

—Not too bad, huh?

Part of a smile crossed her face and she shook her head.

—No, not too bad.

I nodded.

—Yeah, here comes the bit that really sucks.

Chev twisted the jewelry into the hole he'd just put in her nipple, and gripped the ends of the open hoop of surgical steel with two pairs of needle-nose pliers, torqued until they lined up, popped a tiny bead between them and pinched them together so they held it tight. The girl's mouth flew open and she made a long whining noise and a little urine stained the crotch of her way too fucking expensive for their own good jeans.

I looked at the photo spread in the magazine.

—See, hurts like a motherfucker.

Chev took the clamp from my fingers.

—Asshole. Get the fuck away.

—What? I was helping, you said I should come over here and help.

He released the clamp and the girl's nipple snapped back.

—Just get out of here, will you? Go get me some smokes.

I twisted the magazine into a tube and stuffed it in my back pocket.

—Give me some cash.

Chev looked up from the blood he was swabbing off the girl's tit.

—No.

—Fine, I'll tell them we're not using money anymore, that we've moved beyond outdated concepts like commerce and that they should just give me your American Spirits because it's a goodwill society now.

He placed a gauze pad over the girl's nipple and had her hold it there while he taped the corners down.

—I gave you money for breakfast this morning and you never gave me the change. Use that in lieu of goodwill and go buy my smokes.

—Thought the change was a tip.

—It wasn't. Go. Get out.

He took a card full of cleaning instructions from his work table and handed it to the girl and started telling her how to care for the piercing, blotting her eyes for her with a Kleenex.

—You're gonna want to take the bandage off in a couple hours, in the shower with water running over it so it doesn't stick to the dry blood. Then you gotta clean it, rotate the jewelry under the water.

She made a face and he stroked her hair and she leaned her head against his hand.

—It'll be cool. It'll hurt, but not bad. The hard part is over.

I leaned against the wall by the door.

—Until mom sees it and you have to explain why the hell you let some creepy tattoo artist poke a hole in your tit.

Chev stepped away from the girl.

—Go be useful. Now.

I slid my shades over my eyes.

—I am useful. I serve a constant reminder that you're not as cool as you think you are and that you used to run home early from school every day so you wouldn't miss *Star Trek* and it wasn't till you shaved your head and got inked and opened this shop that chicks like her would even look at you.

—Now, out, the fuck out!

I pushed the door open.

—And you have the whole original series on deluxe DVD and an autographed William Shatner picture that you got at a convention when you were fifteen and had chronic acne.

The door swung shut behind me as I walked into the sunlight, whatever Chev was saying to me muffled and lost.

I didn't need to hear it. I'd heard it all before. Anything Chev has to say to me, I've heard it. Most of it starts with *asshole* and ends with *such a dick.*

I dug in my pocket and found the six odd bucks left over from the breakfast run I'd done over to the Denny's on Sunset. I'd planned on using it for some tacos later.

—Crap.

I stuffed the money back in my pocket and headed out.

Mostly Chev is cool. Until a chick he thinks is hot comes around. Really, it's not any different from our whole lives. Only difference is, back when we were kids, Chev turned into a worse stuttering dork around hot chicks than he already was and tried to make up for it by being a dick toward me. He doesn't get nervous anymore, mostly, but he still acts like a dick toward me. Which, sure, sometimes I deserve it, but mostly he's just trying to be cooler than he is. So who's the dick?

I walked up Mansfield, cut east and made for the big red Las Palmas Market. I could have just gone up Melrose from the shop and gotten the smokes from the gas station at La Brea, but everything's cheaper at the

Market. Save some money on Chev's smokes and there'd be enough for a soda and some gum. Chev can't ask for change I don't have.

Well, he can, but I can't give it to him. So that gets us both off the hook.

Coming back to Melrose with the smokes, I saw the girl coming out of the shop, Chev holding the door open, thumbing the digits of her phone number into his cell. I stood there and watched him watch her ass as she walked to the 2008 Z her mommy and daddy bought for her. She climbed in and waved and pulled into traffic and Chev held up his phone. *I'll call.*

I waved at her as I crossed the street and she punched it and almost ran me over.

Chev laughed and I walked past him and into the shop.

—Jailbait.

He let the door swing shut and caught the pack of smokes I tossed him.

—Asshole.

—Total jailbait.

He stripped the cellophane from the pack.

—Just turned eighteen. Her folks gave her the car as a birthday present.

—Bull. They gave her that car as a bribe to keep her from dropping out of high school and going up to the valley to become a porn star.

—Dude, she's eighteen. I carded her when she came in.

—Fake.

He dropped into one of the two old barber chairs customers sit in for easy arm and leg pieces.

—I know a fake when I see one. She's eighteen. Legit. And smokin' hot.

I unwrapped a piece of gum and stuck it in my mouth.

—She's a spoiled piece of high-maintenance ass that thinks it'll be cool to fuck a tattoo rocker because she's already taken it in the ass from every rich boy in Beverly Hills and variety is the spice of life and her family's money makes her life boring so she has to slum with losers like us.

He lit up and blew smoke at me.

—Losers like me, Web. Losers like *me.*

I took the magazine from my pocket and opened it back up.

—Well I hope you enjoy the fatal case of cockrot you're gonna get if you nail that chick.

—Jealous.

—Gonna be like this movie *Corrosion.*

—Bitter.

—Your flesh being eaten away.

—Cynical.

—Consumed by the billions of infected sperm monkeys that have been pumped into her by the Beverly Hills High football team since she was thirteen.

—Hostile.

—Excoriated to a nubbin with a shriveled sack hanging off it.

—Excoriated?

—Look it up.

—I know what it means.

—No you don't.

—Pretentious.

I threw the magazine at him.

—I am not fucking pretentious.

He caught the magazine and rolled it tight and counted points off his fingers with it.

—Jealous, bitter, cynical, hostile and pretentious.

I got up and grabbed at the magazine.

—And I'm not jealous, not of a rag like that.

He jerked the magazine away.

—Excoriate my ass.

—You wouldn't say that if you knew what it means.

I slapped the cigarette from his mouth into his lap and he jumped from the chair, whacking at the embers on his crotch with the magazine.

I shoved him.

—Cool it, that's a new issue.

He swatted the top of my head with it.

—You are such a dick.

—Fuck you.

I grabbed him around the middle and pushed him back into the chair and he smacked me across the ear with the magazine.

—Dick.

The string of bells hanging from the door jangled.

—Interrupting something intimate?

Chev shoved me away and got out of the chair and tossed my magazine on the couch against the wall.

I adjusted the tail of my shirt.

—Just trying to keep the romance in the relationship, man.

Po Sin stood in the doorway, using every bit of his huge roundness to blot out the sunlight behind him.

—Couple that's been together as long as you two, guess you must have to resort to the rough stuff. Me and the missus, we can mostly get by with a little dirty talk and Kama Sutra Oil.

I fell onto the couch, put my feet up on the arm and opened my magazine.

—Yeah, but you guys are pretty much newlyweds compared to us. I mean, me and Chev, we've been together like over twenty years, like since we were five or so. You guys been married how long?

—Hardly thirteen years, man. Like yesterday.

Chev lit a fresh cigarette.

—Don't listen to that fag, Po Sin, he's always creeping in my room at night, but he never gets any.

I turned a page.

—True, he is a bit of a tease.

Po Sin nodded and moved from the door, came to the middle of the shop and occupied it.

—Well, that's enough fagging around for me. You got your canister?

Chev started cleaning up the paper towels and bloody swabs from the nipple piercing, and jerked his head at me.

—Go get the can.

—Fuck you. 'M I your slave?

He stuffed the garbage into a red biohazard bag and pulled the sealed plastic magazine from the sharps disposal on the wall.

—You're my burden. You're my cross. My goddamned albatross and you haven't paid rent in two months and I fed you this morning, again, and you abused another one of my clients today and you can get off your ass and go get the can or get the fuck out and go look for a job.

I threw the magazine on the couch and pushed myself up and made for the back of the store.

—Your wife rag like this, Po Sin?

He shook his head.

—My lady, she beams messages to me through her eyes. She don't got to rag on me.

—Lucky man.

—So says you.

I went in the back of the shop and got the red biowaste canister and brought it out front. Chev handed me the bag he was holding. I went to drop it in the canister and a wad of bloody paper towels fell on the floor. I bent to pick them up.

—Not with your bare hands, not with your bare hands.

I looked at Po Sin.

—It's no big deal, it's just dry blood.

I grabbed the wad and dropped it in the canister with the rest of the waste.

He pulled at the waistband of his navy blue Dickies.

—Could have been a needle in the middle of that.

I slid him the canister.

—There wasn't.

—And you never know what's growing in blood. Living in it.

I showed him my hands.

—Too late now.

He looked at Chev and Chev shrugged. He shook his head and lifted the canister and considered.

—Ten pounds.

Chev shook his head.

—Eight, man, at the most.

Po Sin set the canister down.

—Got a scale handy?

—A scale? It look like I got a scale around here?

—Well, in the absence of a scale, I'm the expert. And the expert says this is ten pounds of biohazardous waste and at two bucks a pound you owe me twenty bucks.

Chev picked up the canister.

—Telling you, this is eight, tops. Sixteen bucks.

Po Sin adjusted his tiny oval wirerims with his thick stubby fingers.

—Chev, do we have a contract?

Chev scratched the stubble on the side of his head.

—No.

—So, I don't charge you a weekly rate, then, for picking this shit up, I don't charge you the same forty-nine fifty a week minimum I charge every-one else on my route. Is that right?

Chev looked at the ceiling.

—Yeah.

—I charge you a pound rate that I usually charge only to people that bring their own shit by and drop it off themselves, right?

Chev reached for the big leather wallet attached to his belt by a dangling steel chain.

—OK, OK.

—I mean, if I'm not doing you a solid here, if you'd rather do business in the manner of most of my clients, we can draw up a contract and I'll be here rain or shine on my appointed rounds every week and you can pay the pickup rate whether you have waste or not.

Chev opened the wallet and started pulling out bills.

—Got it. My bad.

—If you'd prefer that over, say, busting my balls for the sake of four bucks, I can go out to the van and get the paperwork right now. That suit you?

Chev held out two tens.

—No, man, no, here, here it is, it's cool, my bad.

Po Sin reached out and pinched the bills between his thumb and forefinger and tugged them from Chev's hand.

—Why thank you for your prompt and courteous payment.

Chev stuffed the wallet back in his pocket and pointed at the koi tattooed on Po Sin's forearm.

—Shit, man, not I like don't hit you with a discount on your ink.

Po Sin tucked the money into the breast pocket of his unbuttoned Clean Team Trauma work shirt.

—True. And it's also not like I ever *beef* with you about what you charge when *I* get the bro rate.

Chev nodded his head, put out his hand.

—No, man, you're right, I was out of line.

Po Sin folded his hand around Chev's.

—It's cool, just the ways and means of business. Four bucks is just four bucks, but, then again, it's four bucks. If you get me.

Chev looked at the number on the face of his vibrating cell.

—Yeah, don't got to tell me. Small business owners of the world unite.

He hooked a thumb at me where I'd sprawled back on the couch with my magazine.

—Wish you could teach some economics to the freeloader over there.

I didn't look away from the magazine.

—Indentured servant is more like it.

He ignored me, answering the phone and flipping open the appointment book on the counter at the front of the shop.

—Yeah, what did you want?

He rolled his eyes.

—A dolphin? In the small of your back?

He stuck a finger in his open mouth.

—Yeah, no problem. How about tomorrow afternoon?

Po Sin came over and peeked at my magazine.

—That guy got toes for eyes?

—Yeah. Cool, huh?

—He a monster?

—Nah, just a guy gets all fucked up by a psycho.

—What you see in that shit, man?

—I don't know.

—Doesn't bother you, all that gore?

—Why should it?

He looked at Chev.

—*Why should it?* He always been like that?

Chev put his hand over the phone.

—Actually, no. The taste for horror is kind of a new thing.

I looked up from the magazine.

—Hey, is there a problem here I'm unaware of? Am I not allowed to develop new interests and tastes? So I never really got into horror before, so it's a new thing, is that supposed to *mean* something? I mean, fuck, it's just fun is all.

Po Sin grunted.

—People getting hacked up and tortured and mutilated is fun. Shit's disgusting.

I put the magazine in front of my face.

—Says the man with a van full of bloody rags and dirty needles and shit-stained sheets and used condoms and wads of tampons.

He pulled the magazine from my hands and flipped through it, looking at the pictures.

—Some nasty stuff in here.

—Doesn't bother me.

He looked at me, nodded, and kicked the side of the biohazard canister.

—Give me a hand with this. Come out and get the empty.

I rolled off the couch.

—Like I'm everyone's slave today.

Chev was scribbling in the appointment book, back on the phone.

—With a sunset behind it, yeah, sure.

I followed Po Sin out the door.

—Ask her if she wants the dolphin snagged in a gill net or drowning in an oil spill.

Chev showed me his middle finger.

Outside, Po Sin was at the back of the Clean Team van, opening the doors. I set the canister on the edge of the curb.

He waved me closer.

—Bring it here.

I picked it back up.

—Maaan.

I brought it over to him and caught a face-full of the reek pouring out of the sun-baked rear of the van.

—Holy Jesus! Motherfuck.

He took the canister from me and snugged it in with several others and snapped a bungee cord around them to keep them from shifting.

—How's that for a gross-out?

I waved a hand in front of my face.

—Dude, that's some nasty shit.

He took an empty canister from a rack and passed it to me.

—Things are supposed to be airtight.

—They're not.

—No shit.

He slammed the doors closed and leaned his back against them, the polarized lenses of his glasses darkening.

—So. Still no work.

I lifted the empty canister.

—Working plenty.

Chev came out of the shop and lit up.

—Don't listen to him, he ain't worked in over a year.

Po Sin looked up at the sky.

—Been that long?

I spat in the gutter.

—It's been awhile.

I pointed at Chev.

—And don't listen to his bullshit. I work all the time. I mean, who's been doing the laundry? Cleaning the dishes? Cooking? Who's been running all your errands and fetching lunch and taking your truck to be washed?

Chev knocked ash from his smoke.

—Yeah, and who's been paying your rent and covering the groceries and the PG&E and the cable and the water and the gas and every other little thing that comes up?

—I've been kicking in.

Chev watched a couple Korean girls in midi tank tops walk out of the French café up Melrose.

—Mean your mom's been kicking in.

—Any of your business?

The girls disappeared into a shoe store and he looked back at me.

—Only that she's not gonna carry you forever and you need to get a fuck-ing job because the IOUs are piling up on the fridge.

—I'll get a job.

Po Sin tugged the end of his thin drooping moustache.

—Can't believe you can't get a job the way the schools need teachers.

Chev flicked his butt.

—He can get a job, they call him all the time. He could sub five days a week. He could go full-time again whenever he wants.

—Only I don't want to, asshole.

—You want to make a couple bucks, I got some work for a guy with a strong stomach for messed up shit.

I looked at Po Sin and squinted.

—What kind of work?

He looked at Chev and pointed at me.

—Know why he doesn't have a job? Because he's the kind of guy you offer him one and he asks what the work is.

He started for the cab of the van.

—He don't want to work.

I followed him around the van.

—I didn't say I don't want to work, I just asked what the job is.

Asking what the job was, that was actually a really smart idea. If I'd pursued that line of questioning a bit further, things would have been considerably less complicated. Dug a little deeper into that line of inquiry, and I might have avoided the whole *Who's the Asshole in the Motel Room* contest that would crop up later.

But Po Sin wasn't interested in filling in blanks.

He stopped and faced me.

—It's cleaning shit up, is what it is. We got a packrat gig and one of my sets of hands is flaking on me and there's a load of shit to haul.

I squinted again.

—You mean literal shit?

—I mean stuff. Ten bucks an hour for hauling stuff. You want or not?

Chev came around the front of the van.

—He wants.

—Hey!

Chev put a finger in my face.

—He wants because the fridge is empty and it's his turn to fill it and I'm gonna start eating all my meals out so there's nothing for him to graze on, so if he wants to eat this week he'll take the job.

Po Sin took a notepad from his back pocket and started scribbling with a nub of pencil from behind his ear.

—Good. Here's the address.

He handed me the paper.

—Seven in the AM. No later.

—No problem, just swing by and pick me up.

Midway pulling himself up behind the wheel, Po Sin stopped.

—Pick you up? My ass. Drive yourself.

Chev shook his head.

—He doesn't have a car.

—I have a car.

—No, you don't.

—Yes I do. I have a great car. I have a classic nineteen-seventy-two Datsun five-ten.

—You have car parts. You do not, in fact, have a car.

—Yes I do. I have parts in sufficient quantity and variety that when assembled in their proper order they will constitute a car. I have, de facto, a car.

—You have a de facto pile of scrap in the driveway is what you have, dude.

Po Sin turned the key and the van started up.

—The bus is a buck fifty. You got a buck fifty?

I stuffed my hands in my pockets, looked somewhere else.

—I don't ride the bus.

Po Sin pointed at the number 10 stop, up at the corner.

—Public transportation is a wonderful thing. Saves money, saves the environment. Gets you to a paying job. Take the bus.

I started to open my mouth and Chev stepped in.

—He's not riding the bus, Po Sin. He doesn't like the bus.

Po Sin looked at him. Looked at me. Looked away.

—Right. My bad. Thought maybe that had changed.

He looked at his watch.

—OK, I got a guy on the job, he can pick you up on the way. Be out front at six thirty and he'll grab you.

Chev butted me with his shoulder.

—Yeah, I'll get him up and make sure he has his sack lunch and everything.

Po Sin pulled the door closed and put the van in gear.

—So, see you tomorrow. And wear your boots, there tend to be sharps all over the floor on these jobs.

The van pulled from the curb and we walked back up to the front of the shop.

Chev put his arm around my shoulders.

—Your first real job. Me and your mom are so proud.

—Fuck you, I'm not going. I'll call Po Sin later and tell him not to send the guy.

—Yes, you are going. And to celebrate, me and your mom are gonna fuck like bunnies tonight.

I shrugged his arm off.

—Don't, man, that's not cool.

—Gonna fuck and fuck and fuck all night long.

—Dude, you're grossing me out.

He stopped at the door, pumping his groin at me.

—Gonna git our fuck aaawwwnnn.

I walked past him into the shop and locked the door. He grabbed the handle and shook it.

—Let me in, dick.

On the counter, his phone began to buzz and I picked it up.

—Want me to get it?

He stuck his finger against the glass.

—Do not answer that.

I looked at the number.

—Caller unknown. Probably a customer. Let me get this for you.

—Do not pick that up.

I flipped the phone open.

—White Lightning Tattoo.

Chev jammed a hand in his pocket, going for his keys.

—Asshole!

I nodded my head, phone at my ear, backing from the door.

—A string of barbed wire? Around your biceps? Yeah, sure, we can do that.

Chev turned the key.

—Do not say another word.

I covered the mouthpiece with my hand.

—No, it's cool, I can handle this.

He pushed the door open.

—Give me the phone.

I took my hand from the mouthpiece.

—Sure, sure, we can do that wire around your arm. We can also tattoo *lameass poser wannabe* on your forehead.

Chev came at me, grabbing for the phone.

I held it over my head, screaming.

—Or how about you just get a unicorn on your hip so people will know what a real man you are!

Chev snagged my wrist.

—Asshole.

I jerked my hand free, yelling at the phone.

—Or a rainbow on your ankle!

And it flew from my hand and hit the polished cement floor and cracked open and the screen shattered into five pieces.

We stood there and looked at the phone.

I toed one of the pieces.

—So, I guess I won't be blowing off Po Sin in the morning.

THE LAST TIME I'D SEEN HER

Chev's mom and dad are dead.

Which is why I can't make jokes about fucking his mom when he starts making jokes about fucking mine. It's also why he's constantly in my ass about calling my mom and being nicer to her and being more responsible so she doesn't have to worry about me. Like my mom worries. Like she can retain a single coherent thought long enough to work up a good worry. Not that I want to rag on her or anything, I mean, she's my mom. But life hasn't disrupted her mellow since, like, 1968. How is anything I do or say gonna break that trend?

Chev doesn't see it that way. Which makes sense. You take someone who doesn't have something themselves, they're always gonna put more value on it than the person who does have it. So, sure, I love my mom. But Chev may love her a little more than me. Which is maybe not as fucked up as it sounds like at first.

—Hey, Mom.
—Who is it?
—It's me, Mom.
—Web? Is that you?
—It's me, Mom.
—Cool. That's cool.
    There was a pause. A long one. This might mean she was:

    A) Waiting for me to tell her why I was calling.
    or
    B) So stoned she had forgotten I was on the line.

—So, Mom.
—Who is this?
    Which was pretty much a dead giveaway that the answer was B.
—It's Web, Mom.
—Heeey, Web. How you doing, baby?
—I'm cool, Mom, how about you?

—Alright, alright. The blackberries are ripening nicely.

—That's cool.

—Yeah. I could send you a couple quarts. Or some pies. Should I send you some pies?

Every time I talk to Theodora Goodhue of Wild Blackberry Pie Farms, she offers to send me some of her world-famous, all organic, bush-ripened blackberries. Or some of her equally famous pies. Then she hangs up the phone and, her short-term memory impeded as it is by the intake of her far more famous Wild Blackberry Cannabis Sativa, she promptly forgets.

—No, that's cool. I still have some of the last batch you sent.

—The crop's gonna be something special this year.

I never have any illusions about which crop she's talking about. Mom may have dropped out and headed to Oregon to pursue her dream, one in a long line of dreams, to start an organic berry farm, but it was only when she started cultivating some of her land with seedlings supplied by a friend from upper Humboldt County that her operation showed a profit and became self-sufficient. Not that she cares about the profit part of the equation.

—I'm sure it is. Hey, you know, I got to roll here soon, but I wanted to ask you something.

—You go on. We can talk later.

—Sure, but I wanted to ask something first.

—Sure, baby, sure.

—Chev got in a little fender bender and he's, you know, embarrassed to ask, but I knew you'd want to help if you could, so I wanted to ask if you could help him out with the repairs. And stuff.

I sat at the kitchen table, playing with the phone cord, looking at the bills stuck to the fridge with magnets, my share of each bill circled heavily in red. A thick sheaf of IOUs clipped to a magnet all their own. My signature at the bottom of each.

Mom inhaled deeply, exhaled long and slow. A cloud of smoke no doubt drifting to the ceiling.

—What about Chev, baby, is he OK?

—Yeah, he's fine. But his truck, you know.

—Yes. I know. I know, Webster.

Webster. The name my dad picked. As opposed to the name she wanted. Fillmore. Not for the president, mind you, for the rock venue where they met. Webster, the name she hates to use now. Because it's a reminder that they ever met anyplace at all. .

Crap.

—If you could help it would really . . . help.

—Webster.

—Yeah, Mom.

—Do you need money?

—Well, yeah, I can always use. But that's not why, I mean, Chev is the one. I mean.

—Webster Fillmore Goodhue.

Oh, double crap.

—Yes?

—Do you need money?

Stoned as a sixty-year-old Deadhead, berry growing, commune founding, transcendentalist yogi pot cultivator can get, Mom still sees right through me. Part of the science of being a mom.

Again, crap.

—Yeah. I do.

—Well. I wish you would just ask.

—Yeah.

—Well?

More crap.

—Mom. Can you send me some money?

—Of course I can.

—Thanks, Mom.

—Web, Web, I wish you'd call me Thea.

—It's weird. I don't like it.

—Chev does.

—Chev's not your son.

—Not biologically.

I looked at the photographs stuck on the fridge next to the bills. Looked at the one of me and Chev up in Oregon with Mom three years ago. Me on one side, Chev on the other, Mom, almost as big as Po Sin, between us. A joint between her lips. Three years ago. The last time I'd seen her.

—I just don't like calling you Thea, Mom. That's not gonna change. I'm almost thirty and it's not gonna change. OK?

—Of course it's OK. I just wish you would.

—I know. So. OK. I'm gonna go. I gotta go . . . do something.

—Web.

My turn to pause.

—Yeah.

—I could send you a ticket. A plane ticket, I mean. You could come up. For the harvest. Spend some time. Get a break from that place. Breathe some different air. Be away from all the unbalanced energy still floating around you.

—I don't need a break.

—But if you're not working anyway, you should think about shifting your position over the center point. You know, the earth, she knows where you are, and you can change her attitude toward you just by changing your physical location on her skin.

—Yeah. Sure, Mom, I know that, but the thing is, I am working. I'm working for a guy me and Chev know. Just that the job's just starting so I need some extra cash.

—You can have whatever you want, baby. You know that.

Sometimes it's hard to know if she means that literally. Like as a philosophy or something. The kind of thing she would tell me when she tucked me in at night when we lived in the house in Laurel Canyon, before she took off. *You can have anything, Web, anything you want. You just have to want it, wish for it, dream it, and it will happen. That's how I got you. I wished for you and there you were.* A story that ignored the fact that she got pregnant with me one night when she was so fucked up she forgot to put in her diaphragm. At least that's what my dad told me.

—I know.

—I'll put some money in the mail. And those berries. And a couple pies.

—Great, Mom. That's great.

—I love you, Web.

—Love you, Mom.

Another long pause.

—Love you, Mom.

And the sound of the phone hanging up.

She never forgets the money. Not sure why that is. Some part of the mothering instinct that won't let her fully relax until the cub is cared for. Or something. I mean, it may be a month before it shows up, and there's no telling what she'll send (could be whatever is in her purse when she drives past the post office on a trip into town, or it could be a rubber-banded roll of twenties in a FedEx envelope, no note, just the cash), but she'll send it.

But no berries or pie. Which will bum Chev out more than it will me. That's him missing things he didn't have.

I put the phone back in the cradle. It's a big yellow Bakelite phone with big old push buttons. I'd found it in a pile of garbage someone left at the curb when they moved out of the building, and took it inside and tinkered with it till it worked. The timing had been excellent because the night before Chev had come home with a girl he'd been seeing and after they screwed he had broken up with her and she'd thrown our cordless at him and it'd broke. She wasn't so much pissed at being dumped as that he'd waited till he got off, but before she did, to do it. Anyway, the way we go through phones, a heavy-duty model is the best bet. As long as it doesn't get thrown at anyone.

I looked in the fridge and the cupboards, but there wasn't really anything to eat. Just half a box of oatmeal, some brown iceberg, a big can of coffee beans, a bunch of takeout condiment packets of catsup and mayo and soy sauce and duck sauce, a frosted bag of Green Giant peas, and some crusty brown rice left over from a Genghis Cohen doggy bag.

I thought about putting the rice in the microwave and mixing it with the duck sauce, but did the dishes instead. Then I emptied the wet grounds from the coffeemaker, ground some fresh beans and put them in the hopper and filled the reservoir with water. The linoleum in the kitchen was gritty so I sprayed window cleaner on it and gave it a mop. Then I got the vacuum from the hall closet and ran it over the brown wall-to-wall semi-shag.

I really do take care of the cleaning and the cooking.

Then I sat in the canvas director's chair in the living room and cycled through the 157 TV channels a few dozen times without watching anything for more than two or three minutes at a time. Then it was close to six. The sky was still bright and the air hadn't started to cool yet and I'd gotten a little sweaty cleaning, so I unbuttoned my shirt and walked around the apartment. I rearranged some books on the shelves that covered two of the livingroom walls. Chev had borrowed a couple of my biographies, Houdini and Groucho, and put them on his shelf, and put some of his volumes of *ReSearch* on mine. I put them where they belonged.

Then I stood there and flipped a few pages of one of his back issues of *Gearhead* and looked at the clock, but it was just a few minutes after six now. I put the magazine back and went in the bathroom and stared at the tub and thought about cleaning it. It was gonna be a biiig job and I didn't feel like it. But I thought about it for awhile.

I looked at the clock again. Just a few more minutes had passed.

It would be getting busy at the shop soon. I could walk over and give Chev a hand shooing out the kids and keeping the drunks in line. I could go down to my parking space in the driveway and uncover the 510 I bought last summer and take the boxes of parts out of the backseat and the trunk and start working on it. I could turn on my computer and play a game.

I looked at the clock and it was just about six thirty.

So I brushed my teeth and got undressed and lay down on the futon mattress on the floor of my room and read the rest of my *Fangoria* and then it was seven and I turned out the light. The homeless couple living in the alley behind our building were drunk and screaming at each other, so I listened to them for a little, and then I fell asleep and I slept for eleven hours straight.

Which was several hours less than I'd slept in months.

CODE ENFORCEMENT

I forgot to set my alarm clock. Which was OK because Chev didn't forget to set his and snuck into my room and put it on my pillow when he came home from the shop.

After I spent a minute banging it against the floor to get it to stop buzzing, I swore revenge and crawled back under my covers. Then the phone started ringing. Very loud and just outside my bedroom door. It rang. And it kept ringing. And it kept ringing. And I got up and opened the door and picked it up.

—What? What the fuck?

—Is this Web?

—Yeah, what the fuck?

—Yeah, my name is Curtis.

—What do you want, Curtis?

—Nothing. I was in White Lightning last night and I got this boss Tasmanian devil on my shoulder and the guy, Chev, he said he'd knock twenty bucks off the price if I got up at six and called you and made sure you were up. So?

—What?

—You up?

I hung up the phone and threw it across the hall and it put a dent in Chev's door and I heard laughing behind it.

—Fuck you, Chev. Fuck you!

But I was up so I turned on the coffeemaker and got in the shower.

The Cutlass Cruiser station wagon idled at the curb, all gloss black paint, buffed chrome and dark tinted windows. One of the windows slid down and a driver just a shade lighter than his car looked out from behind mirrored sunglasses.

—Web?

I pulled my hoodie tighter around my body, the morning air still carrying a chill.

—Yeah.

The driver tilted his head at the passenger seat.

—Let's get rollin'.

His window zipped up and I walked around the car. He pushed the door open and took a black suit coat from the passenger seat so I could sit. I climbed in, glancing at the rear of the cruiser where the back seats had been removed to make room for a gurney. And stashed just behind the front seats, a tightly packed bedroll and three milk crates filled with various pieces of camp gear tucked neatly on the floorboards. Coleman stove and lantern, hand generator emergency band radio, tent bag, ground tarp, a coffee can of rattling iron stakes, four small red fuel bottles, shrink-wrapped bundle of flares, boxes of waterproof matches, a hatchet with a well-worn leather handle, binoculars, a large plastic canteen, an Army surplus mess kit in a nylon pouch, a black cast-iron skillet with a heat-warped bottom. And more.

I pulled the door closed.

—Going on a trip this weekend?

He dug a finger behind one lens of his glasses and rubbed an eye.

—Do me a favor and buckle up, OK?

I pulled the seatbelt over my shoulder and lap and clipped the silver tongue into the buckle.

He stuck out his hand.

—Gabe.

I took his hand, calluses on his palm scratching my skin.

—Web.

He loosened his black tie and undid the top button of his white short sleeve shirt.

—Some coffee there if you want it.

I took the large white cardboard cup from the holder clipped to the dash.

—Thanks.

He put the car in drive and pulled from the curb.

—No problem. Didn't know how you liked it. Some creamers in the glove box.

I opened the glove box and found a couple creamers bouncing around on top of registration papers weighted down by a huge ring of at least a hundred keys, and a thick flipper of leather with a little plastic handle jutting from it. I closed the box and peeled back the top of my creamer and poured it in my cup.

Gabe pointed at the paper bag in the middle of the front seat.

—Garbage in there.

I dropped the empty creamer in the bag.

He drove us a couple blocks up Mansfield, past several two-story apartment buildings stacked like stucco cakeboxes in pink, aqua, terracotta, yellow and mint. Across Fountain the street gentrified slightly into a sprinkle of trendified craftsmans and renovated 1930s Spanish revival apartment blocks that were going to be squeezing out the drifters at the BHS Hollywood Recovery Center in due course. He stopped at the corner next to the Off Broadway Shoe Warehouse, and I watched some skater kids across the street working the steps of the Liberal & Household Arts Building at Hollywood High. He found a hole in the commute traffic and turned right, the Hollywood Hills rising just north of us, early summer smog settled on their tops. We started and stopped our way down past a few motels and strip clubs and stopped for the light at Highland.

A school bus crossed the intersection.

I closed my eyes for a moment, when I opened them it was gone. I looked down the street, knowing it must have just turned the corner, but unable to keep myself from thinking other thoughts. Thinking about the Flying Dutchman. Ghost ships. Haunted freighters, lost souls that manifest and dissolve, unbidden. Just the usual.

The light changed and I sipped my coffee.

—So where we headed?

Gabe glanced at his right blind spot and changed lanes.

—Koreatown. Code enforcement. Second day. Guy had stuff piled floor to ceiling. No egress. Blocked himself out of his own bathroom. Been filling gallon milk jugs with piss. Shitting in little individual ziplock bags.

—Ah, man, Po Sin said it wasn't a real shit job!

He looked at me, my face reflected in the mirrored lenses below the deep, horizontally scored forehead and cropped graying hair.

He looked back at Sunset.

—He lied.

Po Sin was waiting when we got there, studying several large red splotches of paint on the back and sides of his Clean Team van.

He watched us get out of Gabe's wheels and pointed at the van.

—Motherfucker.

Gabe walked over, pulling the tie from his neck and folding it into a neat roll that he tucked in his pocket. He touched the paint with the tip of his finger, leaving a slight imprint.

—Couple hours after midnight. Maybe three or four AM.

Po Sin kicked one of the van's tires.

—Motherfucker.

I took a look. The paint covered the name of the company on both sides of the van and dripped down over the phone number and web address.

—That sucks.

Po Sin turned his face to the sky.

—Motherfucker!

Gabe picked a scrap of yellow rubber that was stuck in the paint.

—Water balloon.

—Motherfucking water balloon!

—Where was it parked?

Po Sin pointed north.

—At the shop. Around back. They didn't just drive by and heave one out the window, they parked, got out, walked around, and pelted it. Only reason they didn't get the windshield was because I had it nosed in against the fence back there.

—No one at the shop?

Po Sin walked to the back of the van, taking a set of keys from his pocket.

—Someone was supposed to be at the shop. Someone was sure as hell supposed to be at the motherfucking shop!

He pointed a finger at the sky.

—They're asking for it. There is no denying they are asking for it! And they are going to fucking get it!

Gabe hooked a thumb in a belt loop of his black slacks.

—How you want to go about it?

Po Sin looked down from the sky.

—Eye for an eye.

Gabe took the sunglasses from his face. Crease-cornered eyes, the faded black outline of a tear tattooed beneath the left. He nodded.

—OK, I'll make some calls.

Po Sin looked again at the van.

—Motherfucker.

He unlocked the van and opened the rear doors.

—Let's get to work.

He pulled out three white packets and handed one to me and one to Gabe. I watched them shake theirs out until they unfolded into paper jumpsuits. Po Sin's the size of a mainsail, Gabe's meant for a normal human. I did the same and stepped into mine and watched how they tied the flaps on theirs. I was tying mine closed when I heard a long loud rip and watched Po Sin pull a huge roll of duct tape around and around his ankle, sealing the leg of the Tyvek suit to the top of the plastic shoe cover he'd slipped over his boot. He did the same with his other ankle. And then both wrists. And then the neck. He passed the tape to Gabe who did likewise.

Gabe offered me the tape.

—Do it yourself, or need a hand?

I got taped up and hooded and Gabe showed me how to fit the goggled filter mask over my mouth and nose and I followed him into the hotel, Po Sin trailing behind us, glancing back at his vandalized van.

—Motherfucker.

The roaches swarmed me. The first bag I shifted disturbed their routine and they swarmed me, simultaneously revealing what my feet had been crunching on when I walked into the dark apartment, and what the constant background rustling sound was caused by.

So I freaked a little.

A couple hundred cockroaches come spilling out of the shit-encrusted nooks and crannies of a dead shut-in's festering den and start racing each other up your legs to see which can be the first to crawl in your facial orifices and see if you don't freak.

Po Sin watched the freaking. Stood there with his arms folded, framed by towers of piled trash and bundled newspapers and plastic gallon milk jugs filled with urine, and watched all the cockroaches in creation crawling on me trying to find holes they could climb into.

—Can't handle this, you can't handle the job.

He stood in front of me, his torso being populated by swarms of roaches combining into continents, pieces breaking off and drifting and forming with other masses. The geophysical history of the earth enacted by roaches on a globe of a man.

He extended an arm and elegantly brushed a few from the sleeve of his Tyvek.

—Worse things to be covered in, man. Let me tell you.

Gabe walked past me, edging down the open corridor between the piles of refuse, making for the dim light at the back of the place where they'd excavated a couple windows the day before.

—Lots worse things.

He disappeared, lost in bugs and towering waste.

Po Sin watched me.

And, not wanting to at all, I thought about worse things.

Po Sin crunched over.

—OK?

The legs of one of the roaches tickled the exposed rim of skin running between my filter mask and the edge of the Tyvek hood. I flicked it to the floor and stomped on it. And, incidentally, about a dozen more.

—Yeah, I'm fine. You're a dick, but I'm fine.

He nodded and pointed toward the back of the apartment.

—Then head back there. Gabe is bagging the shit. Start hauling it down to the service elevator.

I started down the hall, the smell of rancid crap already seeping through the mask.

—You suck, Po Sin!

Appearing in front of me, Gabe shook his head.

—Here's the thing. You don't want to yell like that. It will break the seal of your mask around your chin and jaw. They'll get in. You take off the mask to get them off and they'll be all over your face. Be in your nostrils.

Roaches in your nostrils. Pretty bad. But still, like I say, there are worse things.

So I got to work.

I hauled shitbags. A lot of them. The shut-in who lived in the place, he must have shit like a dozen times a day. He must have eaten nothing but beans and broccoli and topped it off with Müeslix.

Hauling the big black garbage bags filled with little bags filled with shit between the teetering masses of putrefying garbage, the smell of ferment-ing waste in my nose hairs, I tried to do some math. I tried to figure out how many years the guy must have been shitting in bags to create this kind of poundage.

I took another load of the bags down in the service elevator and out the back to the bin Po Sin had rented for the job and had parked in the alley. My face itched under the mask and I wanted to take it off, but I knew the reek coming off the bags would kill me without some kind of protection. I started taking bags from the dolly I had piled them on and began flinging them over the side of the bin.

I tried to remember how much Chev said a new cellphone was gonna cost. Almost two hundred. At least twenty hours of shit-flinging to pay that off.

Crap.

One of the bags snagged a flange of steel at the top of the bin and tore open and little ziplocks of shit spilled down onto the asphalt.

—Crap!

I bent and started picking them up.

Three hours in, and my back and knees and arms and shoulders were killing me. I remembered my dad and his cronies sitting out on the porch behind the Laurel Canyon house, sipping bourbon and water and playing *Worst Job Ever*. All trying to one-up the others.

Gas-pump jockey.

Bellhop.

Stable boy.

Cabby.

Janitor.

Cow inseminator.

Night watchman.

High school teacher.

That last one from my dad. The trump that beat everyone and ended the game in laughter. Nearly all of them having been public school teach-ers at some time or other before they got involved with the movie busi-ness.

Wish I could get a round of that game going. Put some money on it. I'd clean up.

Shitbag flinger.

—Ho, who's that on shitbag duty?

I looked up at the guy coming down the alley tying himself into a Tyvek.

—Who's the man behind the mask?

He came close, tugging at the shoulder seams of the Tyvek, trying to get the garment to give some breathing room to the thick muscle wadded around his neck and arms and torso.

He stopped.

—Hey. Who? Who the fuck are you?

I tossed a bag of shit into the bin.

—Who the fuck are *you*?

He ducked his head back.

—What?

I pointed at my face.

—Sorry, I got this mask on, it must have garbled my use of the spoken word. Allow me to employ sign language.

I crooked my index finger into a question mark.

—Who.

I held up my middle finger.

—The fuck.

I pointed at him.

—Are you?

He pushed his head forward.

—The fuck you think you are?

I shook my head.

—No, see, we're still having communication problems here. It must be because I'm speaking English and you're speaking Dickanese.

He grabbed the finger I had aimed at him and pulled up on it.

—What?

Pain shot up my arm and my knees started to fold. I quickly calculated how much harder it would be to fling shit with one of my index fingers snapped off, and how much longer it would take to pay off Chev's new cellphone, and made a strategic decision about how to handle the situation.

—Whoa, whoa, man! Whoa, my bad! Just foolin' around! That hurts, man. Easy, big guy, my bad. Uncle. Uncle!

He gave my finger a twist and let go.

—That's right you call uncle. Fuck with me, smart ass.

I flexed the finger, making sure it would still fling shit.

—Yeah, that's me, smart ass. It's a habit.

He tilted his head as far as his neck would allow.

—You still trying to be funny?

I shook my head.

—No, man, I'm not. Seriously. I mean, I wasn't trying to be funny in the first place, I was just trying to communicate on your level. Sincerely.

He grabbed my finger again and I went to my knees in the little bags of shit, many of them popping open under me. From the corner of my eye I saw several roaches that had been clinging to me bailing off, abandoning the ship that was clearly going down.

He added torque to the back pressure on the finger and I fell to my side in the shitbags.

He stood over me, straddling my body and the crap piled beneath me.

—Man, you are funny. You are so fucking funny, you know what I did, you're so funny?

I writhed, trying to take some of the tension off my finger.

He gave it a jerk.

—I said, *You know what I did, you're so funny?*

—No, no, man, I don't. Please, please tell me.

He leaned down, putting his pocked face in mine, his breath fogging the lenses of my goggles.

—I forgot to laugh, that's how funny you are.

—Knock that shit off.

The guy looked at Po Sin, coming out the service exit at the back of the hotel, pushing a hand truck stacked with rotting cardboard boxes.

—Uncle, who the fuck is this?

Po Sin pointed.

—Let go his finger, Dingbang.

He let go of my finger and turned.

—Man, Uncle, don't call me that. Told you my handle's Bang. Just Bang.

Po Sin lifted the mask from his face, flicking a couple roaches from the exposed skin.

—OK, Just Bang.

—No. Just. Bang. Not Just Bang. Man.

Po Sin looked at me.

—Just Bang Man. It's like he's asking for trouble.

I laughed.

Bang turned.

—What you laughing at, shitbag? Lying in a pile of shit. What's so fucking funny about that?

Po Sin came over and offered his hand to me, looking at Bang.

—Go home, Nephew.

—What the fuck, man. I'm here. I'm ready to work.

Po Sin gave my arm a tug and it almost came clear of its socket as he hauled me up.

—Job started three hours ago.

—Told you I was gonna be late.

—No you didn't.

—I did. I called Aunt Lei and she said she'd tell you.

—No you didn't. And don't bring your aunt into it.

Po Sin pointed at the bags scattered at our feet and looked at me.

—Get these in the bin and change into a Tyvek with no shit on it, Web.

Bang pointed at me.

—Who the fuck is he?

Po Sin put a hand on his shoulder and turned him toward the end of the alley.

—He's the guy who got here on time this morning.

Bang stood his ground.

—Bullshit, man. That's bullshit. This is my job.

Po Sin leaned slightly, putting his weight behind his hand, and moved Bang off his ground and down the alley.

—That *was* your job, until you didn't spend last night at the shop like you were supposed to. That *was* your job until the van got plastered with paint because no one was there keeping an eye on things.

—I was in court yesterday. I told you. I had a violation. Fucking cop pulled me over because I'm Asian. Total profiling.

—He give you a DUI because you're Asian?

—Fuck does that matter? That's not the point. He had no reason to pull me over in the first place. I was driving fine. He wasn't profiling for Asians, he never would have known I had an open container. And that's not the fucking point anyway. I had court. I told you I had court.

Po Sin propelled him farther down the alley.

—You didn't tell me.

—I did! I did! I called! And after court I had to go explain it to my mom and she got upset and didn't want me to drive because she didn't understand that it was OK, that I hadn't been suspended and I called to tell you I couldn't be at the shop, man.

—No you didn't.

Bang dug in his heels and shrugged off his uncle's hand.

—Fuck your hand off me anyway. I do all the shit work! All of it! You, that fucking round-eye Gabe, you never pull your weight. Not that anyone could pull your weight.

—Nephew.

—No, fuck you! Fuck you and this shit job. I fucking quit! See how long that scrawny fucker lasts doing the heavy lifting for you. See how long he lasts when there's trouble. Fuck you and fuck your fucking wife who can't take a fucking phone message and.

Whoever else was meant to be fucked had their name deleted by Po Sin's hand wrapping around his nephew's throat and shoving him into the graffitied brick wall of the hotel.

Po Sin held him there. Bang turned red.

I took a couple steps.

—Po Sin.

He looked at me. Looked at his nephew. And let go.

Bang slumped, gagged and wheezed. Po Sin put a hand on his chest.

—Dingbang? I. Dingbang.

Bang knocked the hand away.

—Don't call me that!

He pushed from the wall and ran to the end of the alley.

—Gonna pay for touching me, man! No one touches Bang!

He took a step, stopped, and pointed at me.

—You too, shitbag, you're dead!

And he rounded the corner of the alley and was gone.

Po Sin stood there for a second, turned and walked toward me.

—Sorry. He's my nephew. But. He.

—He's a dick, Po Sin.

He pulled the end of his moustache.

—Well. Yes. Like father like son. Nothing like working with family to bring out the best in a man.

—Or to make him want to strangle them.

He smiled.

—Don't know about you, but some of my family, I don't need to be any-where near them to want to strangle 'em.

—I find it helps that my mom lives out of state.

—Never had a problem with my mother. My dad I could have throttled a couple times.

—My dad spends all his time in a bar out in Santa Monica. That far west, may as well be another state. He's safe from me.

—Yeah, distance makes the heart grow fonder.

—I didn't say that.

He started for the service entrance.

—My mother and father are both permanently out of reach. And my brother. Well. We're out of touch. Last thing I need at this point is less family.

He stopped and stared at the end of the alley where Bang had disap-peared.

I bent and picked up a shitbag and tossed it in the bin.

—He was asking for it, Po Sin.

He kept looking down the alley.

—He's a boy, I'm a man.

He turned his head to me.

—A man should be able to retain his composure.

I looked at the shit at my feet.

He made for the entrance.

—It's about lunch. Finish up with that and we'll go grab a bite.

—Where?

He waved a hand over his shoulder.

—Doesn't matter. With a job like this, wherever we eat it's gonna taste like shit.

I watched him go inside. I massaged my finger and rotated my wrist and swung my arm around, making sure it all worked. Then I started. Putting more shit in the bin.

He was right about lunch.

What with the smell of well-marinated crap in our hair and on our clothes and up our noses and down our throats, lunch didn't have much appeal for me. Not so, for the more experienced hands. I watched Po Sin tear into his third cheeseburger, and Gabe scrape the last of his chili from the bottom of the bowl.

Po Sin washed down a bite of burger with chocolate milkshake.

—Different things bother different people.

I picked up one of my fries and took a bite of it. It still tasted like shit.

—So you're saying I shouldn't be disturbed by the fact that having my nasal passages smelling like dung ruins my appetite? What relief. I was worried it was me, I was worried I might be some kind of deviant not wanting to eat when all I can smell is ass butter. What a load off, knowing that I'm not alone and everyone has their own problems.

Po Sin wiped his mouth.

—Thought that'd make you feel better.

I dropped the fry and pushed the unfinished bulk of my meal to the middle of the table.

—So what bothers you?

Po Sin grabbed some of my fries and shoved them in his mouth.

—Me? Nothing.

Gabe rubbed his nose.

—Nothing but kids.

Po Sin looked at me.

—Kids are hard. No one likes kids.

I looked away from Po Sin, watched some teenagers at the Fatburger counter shove each other around, laughing, and chose to ignore whatever the fuck point he was trying to make.

—I like kids. Kids are OK.

Gabe drained the last of his ice tea.

—Dead kids. No one likes dead kids.

Po Sin threw me another look, I refused to catch it, and he ate another fry.

—On a trauma job. When it's a kid. That's rough.

Gabe leaned back, the table warped in the lenses of the sunglasses he hadn't taken off since coming out of the hotel.

—Doesn't really count anyway. Kids bother everyone. None of the other stuff bothers you.

Po Sin shrugged.

—Do the job long enough, you see it all.

He dipped his head at Gabe.

—Gabe can't stand the smell of mold.

—Mildew.

—Right, mildew. Water damage. Doesn't like it.

I looked at Gabe.

—Mildew?

He didn't look at me.

—Yeah.

—Rancid mounds of feces are cool, but mildew freaks you out.

He scratched a scar that ran down the top of his left forearm.

—I don't like it much. That's all.

Po Sin's phone rang. He looked at it and answered.

—Clean Team. Uh-huh.

He felt his back pocket, found a notepad, and reached behind his ear for his stub of pencil.

—Sorry to hear that. Uh-huh. I'm sorry. Yes. Yes we do. Uh-huh. Well, we're on a job right now, but we could be there tonight. Or tomorrow morning. Uh-huh. I'm sorry to hear that. Yes it is. Yes it is. I'll. Yes. Well, I'd like to ask a few questions if I may. Well, it gives us an idea of what's involved. How many of us might be needed and such. Uh-huh. Well, most important is, have the police and the coroner released the scene? Good. OK. And can you tell me what room it happened in?

I watched him write *bedroom* on the notepad.

—Sure. And if I may, can I ask how? Right. I know.

Gunshot.

—And if I may, the type of weapon?

Handgun.

—Do you happen to know the caliber of the weapon?

9mm.

—I know. I know.

He took the phone from his ear and rolled his neck around. I could hear crying, cut off as he put it back at his ear.

—Can you tell me if any doors or windows were open? Can you tell me how many?

2 doors.

—Uh-huh. No. Well, it's pretty much impossible to give an estimate on the phone. Sure. What we'll do is, we'll come out, tonight or in the morning, whichever you prefer, and we'll take a look and we'll do an assessment and we'll tell you just how much time it will take and how much it will cost. No, free of charge, we do that free of charge.

He talked a little more, wrote down an address in Malibu and a phone number, and hung up and dropped the phone in his pocket. He picked up the last of his cheeseburger and put it in his mouth.

—Nine millimeter in the mouth. Gonna be an earner, that one.

Gabe nodded.

—The bigger the gun, the bigger the mess.

I knew that already. That bit of wisdom about guns and the messes that they make.

TILL HIS NEIGHBORS
SMELLED HIM

After lunch we brought the last of the boxes down to the bin, followed by the few pieces of spavined furniture. With the floor cleared throughout, the one-bedroom apartment didn't look half big enough to have contained all that we had hauled out of it, and the stench seemed worse than ever.

I pointed at a stain on the carpet that seemed to be the epicenter of stink.

—What the fuck is that?

Po Sin came over, holding the mask to his face.

—That's where the decomp was.

—Huh?

—The guy who lived here, that's where he died and rotted till one of his neighbors smelled him.

I stared at the stain.

—What's the? Why's there a stain?

—Fluids, Web. A body dies, sits in a hot room in L.A. in July, you get a lot of fluids coming off it.

I stared, and the stain's Rorschach shape arranged itself into sprawled limbs and a bloated trunk.

—What's that black stuff?

Po Sin took a collapsible pointer from the pocket of his Tyvek, snapped his wrist and it shot open and he put it to use.

—Blood here. All this. A body decomposes, it starts to swell up, fills with gases. Eventually, it's gonna pop. Blood comes out of that, it's like dirty motor oil. Same color and consistency. This yellow, that's where the fat has started separating, that's tallow.

I squatted to look at something and the reek slapped me in the face. I turned my head and stood and took a couple steps back.

—Jesus.

—Yeah, he was ripe.

I pointed at the little lines wiggling off the stain; traceries, like veins under the skin.

—What are those?

—Maggot trails. They hatch in the corpse then go looking for a better life. All those little black things are the dry maggot shells.

He slapped his palm over the end of the pointer, collapsing it, dropped it in his pocket, and pulled out a carpet knife.

—Let's get this shit up off the floor.

We began cutting, peeling away flat industrial weave patterned in precise geometries of grime that outlined where boxes had once been stacked. And on the wood floor, just under the stain left by the decomp, a larger stain. More abstract. And in need of scrubbing.

So I scrubbed.

The apartment stripped and bare, cockroaches fleeing through every crack, seeking refuge in the neighboring apartments, Gabe brought up an ozone generator and plugged it in.

Po Sin took off his mask and wiped his forehead and pointed at the machine.

—It'll bond oxygen to oxygen. Essentially purify the air. Eliminate the odor, not just mask it.

I was looking at the stain on the floor. Fainter now, but there was no way to get rid of the entire smear of the man's death.

Po Sin followed Gabe to the door, leaving the ozone generator behind to do its job. He stopped and looked at me.

—You OK?

I scuffed at the stain with the toe of my paper-covered boot.

—Sure.

—Never seen that one in a horror movie before, huh?

I stood there for another moment before following them out.

I hadn't. I hadn't seen that kind of thing before.

Not exactly.

—He does accommodations at night.

My head was out the window of the moving van, blowing some of the stink out of my hair. I pulled back inside to hear better.

—Accommodates what?

—Bodies. For the coroner. He picks them up. It's what they call it. Accommodations.

—No shit?

—Sure. Some wino goes stiff on Skid Row, who ya gonna call? His buddies gonna take up a collection, get him a nice casket, a mausoleum at
Hollywood Forever? Damon Runyon don't live here no more, man. Once
they grab his last can of Sterno and his shoes, if he's got any, they walk
away. Sooner or later, someone at the mission or one of the treatment cen-
ters, or a cop cruising by because he took the wrong fucking turn, will see
the body. Sometime after that, the coroner gets a call. They have a service
they call to do the pickup. Gabe works for one of those services. It's his
night job.

He took a bite out of a Slim Jim he got from the box beneath the driver's
seat.

—That's why he can't drive you home.

—So what's up with him? Know he keeps a sap in his glove box? And
what's with all that camping gear?

—Gabe's between places of residence just now.

—What, he's homeless?

—He prefers to have no fixed address at this time.

—Uh-huh.

I tapped my cheekbone.

—And that tattoo, that tear under his eye, that's gang shit, right? He some
reformed O.G. or something?

He shoved that last six inches of the Slim Jim in his mouth.

—Don't talk shit you don't know shit about, Web. 'Sides, you got a problem with him if he has a history? You don't want to ride with him? You'd
rather ride the bus?

We rolled on Beverly, the street bending east at the ramps to the 101.

—I don't ride the bus.

He crumpled the empty wrapper and threw it under his seat.

—I know.

Traffic crawled to a full stop for no visible reason. It being in the nature
of all L.A. drivers to be suddenly seized en masse by retardation and start
hitting the brake pedal when every light in the immediate vicinity is a nice
bright green.

Po Sin, taking advantage of the respite, removed his hands from the
wheel, stretched, looked at me.

—But you should, you know, ride the bus. Might be good for you.

I stared up at the giant red sign for the Ambassador Dog & Cat Hospital. A beacon for wounded animals everywhere. Or something. I mean, there has to be a reason why the sign is so fucking tall, right? I always picture some old lady out walking her Maltese when a sharp pain starts radiating down its left front leg. She crouches next to the stricken dog, screaming for help, cars passing by, no other pedestrians in sight. Desperate, she looks to heaven, and there it is, visible from a mile away, the Ambassador. Thank Jesus for that fucking sign!

—You listening?

I looked at him.

—Yeah. I'm just failing to hear anything that has anything to do with anything I give a shit about.

Traffic moved. Po Sin drove.

—You give a shit alright.

—Says you.

He adjusted the rearview.

—Xing's back on the bus.

—How proud you must be of her.

He grunted, a phlegmy and no doubt Slim Jim flavored sound that was meant, I suppose, to indicate his disgust.

We passed Jollibee. I stared at the red and yellow fiberglass Jolly Bee out front.

—What's with the paint on the van?

Po Sin flicked on the headlights.

—Nothing. Just business.

—Just business? Paint bombs?

—There's some competition out there. Trauma scene and waste cleaning is a growth industry.

—Competition for cleaning shit. I'm trying to make that work in my head. What kind of people are drawn to that kind of work and fight for the honor?

He reached over and punched me lightly in the shoulder. Lightly for Po Sin being sufficient to slam me into the door and leave me rubbing both shoulders.

He jabbed me with his forefinger, each jab deepening the shade of purple that would no doubt be spreading across my shoulder in the next hour, if it survived his onslaught.

—Kind of people who are fighting over cleaning shit and blood and assorted bodily fluids are people who need a job. People who need money.

Now I don't know about you, but I know a few people who fit that profile. You know anyone like that? Ring any bells?

I pulled out of his range.

—Yeah, yeah, I get it. Sure, I'm no better than anyone else. I'm just saying, seems weird to be fighting over who gets to pick up the shit.

He took a right on Highland.

—There's money to be made, people will fight. And seeing as this is a nasty area of commerce to be involved in, it sometimes attracts a pile of assholes.

—Like your nephew.

He took advantage of another halt in the traffic to stare at me.

—Web, you know the one about the pot and the kettle and what one called the other and what that story is supposed to mean?

—It's not a story, it's more of a saying. And yeah, I know that one. And what it means. Need an explanation?

—No. My point is, shut the fuck up.

In front of my building he counted twenties from his wallet.

—Eighty bucks sound right?

I looked at the driveway, Chev's '58 Apache parked in front of my parts receptacle/car in our stacked parking slots under the building's overhanging upper story.

—Sure, sounds fine.

He held out the money and I took it and put it in my pocket.

He folded his wallet.

—Not gonna count it?

I pulled open the door.

—No.

—What if I'm ripping you off?

—You're not.

—How do you know?

I stepped out of the van.

—Well, if you are, it's only money, man. How upset am I supposed to get?

He stuffed the wallet deep in one of his front pockets.

—*I* spent the day hauling crap, I'd be pretty pissed if someone tried to rip me off.

I closed the door and leaned my forearms in the open window.

—Yeah, but you're a money-grubbing pig.

—You want to do some more work for the money-grubbing pig sometime? Tomorrow maybe?

I looked at the rack of silver mailboxes riveted to the beige stucco wall at the base of the stairs.

—Well, not really. But I got to buy Chev a new phone.

He put the van in gear.

—One of us will pick you up at seven.

He started to pull out. I walked alongside as he backed into the street.

—Yeah, but I was kind of thinking I might get a check today. And if I do. You know.

He stopped the car.

—Web, your mom sent you some money and you don't feel like working, that's fine. She didn't, and you want to work, call me in the next couple hours. I haven't found anyone else by then, you can work. Good night.

And he drove away.

I watched the van to the corner. Pulled the money from my pocket and counted it. Eighty bucks even, folded around a Clean Team business card. I let down the tailgate of the Apache and sat on it and dangled my legs, riffling the edge of the card along my knuckles, thinking about things.

A truck drove slow down the middle of the narrow street, a windowless Dodge Ram van, freshly sanded and primered across the hood and down one side. It paused while some kids rode by on their bikes in the opposite direction, and then eased down the street while I watched the kids pedal to the corner and whip into the alley. I could hear the homeless couple screaming at each other down there, calling each other names.

—Whore.

—Asshole.

—Bitch.

—Fuckface.

—Cocktease.

—Cocksucker.

—Cunt.

—Shithead.

The glorious spoken-word street poetry of Hollywood.

I listened to them and looked at the Clean Team card and tried to re-member the first time I met Po Sin. I could remember the first time I'd *seen* him. Dropping off his youngest, Xing, walking across the chain-link-enclosed playground, the kids stopping in their tracks to watch a leviathan amongst them, holding the hand of his round-faced daughter, her Sponge Bob backpack dangling from his free hand. He'd made an impression.

But the first time I'd met him? School play maybe. Po Sin leaning against the back of the auditorium because the little folding chairs were too small. Me standing back there keeping an eye on the rowdy kids who like to sit as far from the front of a room as possible.

I'd been one of those kids at the back. Spitballs. Whispering. Elbow digs. Giggles. Passed notes about boogers. But mostly sneaking a book out of my back pocket to hide in my lap and read, tuning out whatever was happening up on the stage at the front of the hall.

Pretty much the same shit going on with the kids I was eyeballing. Except there was a greater chance that the notes being passed around would include the word *fuck,* and that anyone looking at something in their lap was going to be playing a Gameboy or PSP, not reading a book.

Po Sin had smiled when Xing, an infamous back-stabbing two-faced queen-bee, universally hated by all the second-grade girls and the entire female faculty, came on stage as a fairy or a tree or a rainbow or something, and applauded after she got out her line.

I'd leaned close and told him how cute she was, and he'd looked at me and shook his head.

—She's a terror, an absolute bitch. But yeah, she's cute as hell.

We talked a little during the cookies and punch segment of the evening. He'd told me his business. I'd mentioned that my roommate needed someone to dispose of his biowaste.

He and Chev hit it off, and Chev would come home and give reports about what Po Sin was cleaning while I corrected papers. Tales of hand-scrubbing each piece of ballast along two hundred yards of rail bed after a train strike on a junkie, delivered as I put small red marks in the margins of phonics tests and *What I Did for Kwanzaa* essays.

He looked me up after I quit. To say what, I don't know. I didn't answer the phone or listen to the message he left. Something about Xing, I imagine.

Later, when he'd come by the shop to pick up Chev's waste, and see me hanging, he'd say some nice things. At first. Then he started making some suggestions about how I might want to, I don't know, get some help or some other kind of daytime talk show bullshit. When that weed didn't take root in me, he stopped talking about it. For a long time. Then he got used to the idea of me being a dick and started treating me like normal and telling me I was acting like an asshole fuckup, which was a whole hell of a lot easier on both of us.

And now I was working for him. Acquiring new job skills. The mystic arts of erasing all signs of death. These things, these things you do to get by when need arises, they sometimes equip you for the rest of your life. However long that turns out to be.

There was a rattle overhead. I looked up and watched a small flock of sparrows as they hopped and scratched across the fronds of a palm tree growing from the neighbor's dense yard, pecking at some kind of tidbit that had come to rest up there. A crow flapped down from the power line, scattering most of them, cawing, its action drawing the attention of several members of the murder that made the street home. I leaned over and picked up a rock and pitched it into the tree and watched the crows wing off to look for easier fodder in the alley dumpsters down the street. The sparrows came back.

I got up and closed the tailgate and went upstairs, dragging my hand over the stucco wall of the complex as I walked down the second-floor ex-terior walkway, listening to stereos and TV shows and arguments and yip-ping dogs behind the doors of our neighbors. I unlocked the front door and walked in and looked at the girl whose nipple I'd stretched the day before at the shop, sitting on the couch in her panties and Chev's favorite Misfits T, with one of my books open in her lap.

She looked up.

—Oh, it's the dick.

Chev walked in, pulling on his boxers, tattoos scattered over his body, thickest at the ends of his limbs, thinning as they approached his torso.

He hoisted a tallboy of Miller at me.

—Hey, it's the breadwinner.

He dropped on the couch next to the girl.

—This is Dot.

Dot made room for him next to her.

—Yeah, I already said hi.

She held up the big purple and gold book she'd been flipping through.

—So did you really teach over at Hollywoodland Elementary? These kids are so cute.

I walked over and took the book from her and closed it and went to the shelf and found its space with the other yearbooks and slipped it in where it belonged and turned and stared at Chev.

He rubbed his shoulder.

—Sorry, man, I didn't know she was looking at that.

Dot looked at him, at me.

—What? I like kids. What?

Chev got up and walked toward the kitchen.

—Hey, good news, working man, you got a FedEx package from Oregon. And it's not berries.

He grabbed a FedEx envelope from the table and scaled it to me. I caught it and headed for my room.

Dot smiled.

—Sorry about looking at your book. I just finished my first year at UCLA in the education department. I was curious. I didn't know you were a teacher.

Chev opened the fridge.

—Told you she was eighteen.

She made a face as I walked past her.

—Oh. My. God. What the fuck is that smell?

I took a long shower. A very long shower. And then I took another one. Longer this time. And then I splashed myself with some of Chev's Old Spice. And a little more. Then I went in my room and turned on my fan and opened my window and tried not to breathe through my nose and prayed that the stink wouldn't get into my bedding and the carpet. And after about a half hour I finally grew something resembling a brain and gathered my dirty clothes and bagged them and took them down to the laundry room, ignoring the various squeals and grunts coming from Chev's room as I passed his door.

Back in my room I opened the FedEx envelope and shook out the bills and an assortment of change.

$567.89. And, true to form, no note. Not that I'd asked for one.

Under certain circumstances, the odd amount would mean Mom had sent whatever was lying around, but that wasn't the case here.

Five hundred.

Sixty.

And seven dollars.

Eighty.

And nine cents.

Five six seven eight nine, an ascending numerical sequence. Sent specifically to bring me luck, to raise my spirits, to lift my fortunes.

I'm lucky there wasn't a crystal pyramid in the envelope.

Five hundred sixty-seven and eighty-nine cents. Enough to cover the new phone, buy some groceries and pay off some of the IOUs on the fridge.

I thought about what I'd do the next day. Sleep in. Have some coffee. Pick up around the place, clean the tub. Go do some grocery shopping. Maybe hit the bookstore for a few novels. Get the latest issue of *Femmes Fatale*. Stop by the shop. Have lunch. Buy a couple DVDs. Come home and have some dinner. Watch a movie. And in bed by seven. Just like pretty much every day this last year. Any day when I had money, that is.

I thought about it. How nice and mellow it would be. A day to myself after having to be around people and be at Po Sin's beck and call and hear all his shit.

Yeah, a *me* day as a reward for all that hard work.

I picked up the handset from the phone I'd brought into the bedroom.

—Clean Team.

—Hey, it's Web.

—Yeah?

—You find anyone for tomorrow?

—Why?

—Nothing.

—Didn't get any money from mommy today?

—No.

—Well, you want to work, all you got to do is say so.

—I want to work.

PIPE BOMB IN THE ASS

There was a lot of blood at the Malibu beach house. And it was everywhere. Really everywhere.

Gabe studied the thick maroon blotch at the center of a lighter red eruption splashed over the wall and headboard, all of it studded with gray and yellow and pink gobbets of dangling matter.

He fingered a strip of yellow tape, marked like a yardstick, that ran up the edge of the wall. Near the top it intersected with another piece that ran horizontally just over the highest point of the mess. He looked at that point.

—That wasn't a nine.

The deputy coughed in the doorway.

—Yeah, what we thought. But it was. He did it with a mouth full of water.

Gabe looked again at the dry blood.

—That would do it.

I thought about high school science classes. How shock waves travel through water. I thought about what would happen if you filled a soda can with water and stuck the barrel of a gun in the hole and pulled the trigger. And then the deputy filled in the gaps in my imagination.

—The water shredded his cheeks. Crushed his nasal passages and ripped his nose off. Some of it was forced down his throat and it turned his tongue inside out and punched a hole in the bottom of his stomach. Goes without saying it took the whole back of his head off. Everything behind the ears.

He rapped his knuckle on the wall opposite the bed.

—Created so much pressure in his sinuses, his eyes popped out. We found one of them over here.

I looked through the open door that led to the master bath. Blood spackled the white tile and porcelain and bath towels. My reflection in the mirror over the twin sinks was glazed with dried streaks of red. Beyond, through a door at the far end of the bathroom, and let me just say that it was a really big fucking bathroom, I could see more blood spattering the carpet, chair and desk in what looked to be a small den. Small by the standards of this house, that is.

But those rooms were nothing compared with the bedroom. The bedroom looked painted in blood, but not well painted, mind you. Painted, in point of fact, by a collection of one-armed troglodytes employing bundles of reeds rather than brushes and rollers. Painted in dripping and splotchy reds, maroons and purples punctuated by bits and clots of gray and white and black, and the occasional twisted knot of tendon.

—This is unfuckingbelievable.

Gabe and the deputy looked at me.

I held out my arms, bugging my eyes.

—What? Am I wrong? I mean, this is unfuckingreal. This is. Water in the mouth? Water in the mouth gets you this? Myfuckinggod.

The deputy looked at Gabe.

—Where'd you find him?

Gabe picked at something imbedded in the wall, his fingernails rimmed with dry yellow paint.

—Po Sin knows him.

—You tell him about the pipe bomb?

Gabe took a Leatherman from the nylon case on his belt and unfolded it into pliers.

—Be my guest.

The deputy put his hands on his hips.

—Guy was ex-military.

He looked at Gabe.

—Right?

Gabe closed the tips of the pliers over whatever was in the wall.

—I think so, yeah.

The deputy looked back at me.

—OK, ex-military guy wanted to off himself. So he made a pipe bomb.

I put my hand to my forehead.

—No.

—Yeah. And to do it, what he did was, he sat on it. And I don't mean sat on it, I mean he *sat* on it. Full insertion.

I put my other hand on my forehead.

—Oh no.

He nodded.

—Yeah. Pipe bomb in the ass. And, here we go, he does this while seated on his water bed.

—Oh shit.

—You'd think. But here's what happened. The, what, the *internal dynam-ics* of a bomb in the rectal passage were such that the force of the explo-sion went straight up. Not only did the bed not burst, but by giving slightly while still offering resistance, it helped to focus the blast upward. Thing went off, it scoured his viscera, guts, lungs, everything, shot them up through his head and out the top of his skull. Like a fountain. The whole room got sprayed, but other than looking a little bloated, and, you know, his head being gone from the eyebrows up, he was intact. And the bed was peachy.

He made pistol fingers and pointed at me.

—That was a fucking mess.

Gabe twisted the pliers and pulled something free of the wall and in-spected it.

—Yeah. It was a big job.

He dropped the object in his palm and walked to the deputy, folding the Leatherman away.

—You need this for anything?

I walked over and looked at the large silver-filled molar he was showing the deputy.

The deputy shook his head.

—No. We finished in here. No way to fake a scene like this. Don't need teeth in the wall to tell us what happened. He made it easy. Note. All that.

I walked to the door and looked down the hall. I could see Po Sin on the couch next to the girl who'd let us in. The two of them going over papers on a clipboard, the girl signing her name. Po Sin taking a travel pack of Kleenex from his breast pocket and handing it to her as she set the clip-board aside and wiped her nose with the back of her hand.

I looked back in the room.

—So why'd he do it?

The deputy looked at me.

—Brain tumor.

He pointed at what had been a head, now gored all over the wall.

—Guess he showed it who was boss.

In the driveway Gabe and I put on our Tyveks and I watched Po Sin palm the deputy a fifty.

—Thanks for the referral, Mercer. Hope we can do some more business over here.

Mercer pocketed the cash.

—No problem.

He opened the door of his patrol car.

—Far as I'm concerned, Aftershock's off the referral list. Last job I put them onto, a teenager did her wrists in the bathtub, right. Found out she was pregnant or something. Anyway, door closed. Hardly any splatter at all. Plastic shower curtain. Couple towels. Easy as hell. A month after they were in there, the girl's brother uses the tub for the first time, to wash the family dog, right. Has Fido in there, running the water to get it warm how his best little friend likes it. What happens is, the water starts backing up, starts filling the tub, and it's fucking red. Drain was choked with dry blood and feces from the girl. Those Aftershock rocket scientists, they poured some Drano in there and called it a day. Little boy is already traumatized from his sister having to take *a real long nap,* and now bloody water's gushing up from the drain and his dog is spazzing out. Family calls Aftershock, pretty justifiably upset, and Morton tells them it's not his problem. Tells them he did his job and they signed off on the work. He'll be happy to send someone over, but he'll have to draw up a new invoice. Fucking prick. And guess who gets the next call? They have my fucking card 'cause I was first on the scene. Want to know why the people I suggested to them to clean up after their *tragedy* won't take care of their responsibilities? Want to know what I can do about it, right? Well, last thing I need is these people getting upset with me and putting in a call to the Civil Litigation Unit and end up with those fuckers asking me what the hell I'm doing giving referrals for private contractors. So I call fucking Morton and tell him to get his ass over there and take care of it before I call a friend in Parking Enforcement and see that his fucking van has a ticket on it every time it's on the street.

He took his hat off and tossed it inside the car.

—So fuck them and fuck the guild. From now on, you're top of the list west as well as east side. And I'll spread the word.

Po Sin gave him a thumbs-up.

—Much appreciated.

—My pleasure. I refer you guys, you get the job done. And you've never stiffed me.

He got in the car and pulled down the short drive to the PCH, waited for a hole in the traffic, and headed south.

Po Sin came over to the van, stripping off his Clean Team shirt and reaching for the Tyvek Gabe held out to him.

—To protect and to serve, Web, to protect and to serve.

I scooped brains.

I scooped them with a wide plastic paint scraper from a ninety-nine-cent store, and I wiped them onto blue industrial paper towels, I dropped the towels in red biohazard bags and dropped the bags in a fifty-gallon plastic garbage can with a Clean Team sticker on the side.

Po Sin watched.

—Spray some more up there.

I took the spray bottle from tool belt and sprayed some hydrogen peroxide, and specks of blood and brain I'd missed on the counter foamed white.

Po Sin nodded, pursed his lips.

—See, you miss stuff. No matter how close you look, there's always more.

He took a step toward the bedroom where he and Gabe were dealing with the real environmental disaster.

—And stop taking off your mask.

I blew out my cheeks.

—What, it doesn't smell or anything, there aren't any cockroaches trying to crawl in my mouth.

—No, but there's dry blood, and it will flake and go airborne and you'll inhale it.

I pointed at the fogger in the bedroom.

—I thought the Microban killed everything.

—It does. It should. But it's still considered a bad idea to breathe other people's dry blood. Trust me on that one.

—Fine, fine.

I put the mask over my mouth and went back to scraping and wiping. Cleaning the blood and brains. Throwing away the ruined terry-cloth towels and bathmat and a thick robe that had been draped over the shower rod, and the fuzzy cover on the toilet seat. Opening the cabinet doors and looking inside and spraying hydrogen peroxide, in case one of them had been open when the guy did it. Doing the same with the drawers. Checking the back of the shower curtain liner. Peeling the liner from the curtain and looking between them. Finding spots of blood in the grout between tiles and getting down on my knees and working at it with a toothbrush, trying to scrub it from the porous material. Spinning the roll of toilet paper on its spindle and finding a dry pink blot soaked through dozens of layers. Tossing the roll in with the other hazards. Finishing. Standing in the middle of the huge bathroom and turning in place, finding no sign that death came here.

And liking that feeling. Things back as they had been. Better than they had been. Like nothing had ever gone wrong.

Clean. Blank. New.

I nodded to myself.

—Never know the stupid fucker was too lame to just eat some pills or stick his head in a plastic bag or some shit like normal losers.

—Oh my God.

I looked over at the open door of the den, and found the girl who had signed the contract with Po Sin standing there.

She stared at me, both hands covering her mouth.

—Oh. Oh, my Gaaawd!

She turned, shoulders shaking, and ran.

I looked up where heaven is supposed to be kept.

—Crap.

Po Sin appeared at the other door.

—What? What the hell was that? Who was that?

I pointed at the den.

—The girl. I didn't know she was. She snuck up on me.

From the den we could hear muffled, choked sobs.

He stepped into the bathroom, pulling his mask from his face, hissing.

—What the fuck, Web? What did you do?

—Nothing, man. I was talking to myself. I was. I didn't know she was there.

He stared at me, looked at the door the girl had stood in, tiptoed to it and peeked in the den. He looked over his shoulder and waved me over. I crept to his side and looked in the room. The girl was standing in the corner where two walls of bookcases converged, her back to us, shoulders jerking, sounds hitching in her throat.

Po Sin stuck his index finger in my chest and then pointed at the girl.

I shook my head.

He balled his hand into a fist, put it close to my face, pointed at the girl again.

I shook my head.

He leaned down, put his mouth to my ear.

—You get your ass in there and apologize for whatever asshole comment came out of your mouth right now or you will never work a day with me again.

He straightened, glaring down at me, mouthing words.

Grow the fuck up!

And he turned and walked back into the bedroom, back to helping Gabe cut away the blood-soaked portions of the mattress so they could be bagged for disposal.

I stood in the pristine bathroom. Cleaner now, no doubt, than it had been since the day the house was built. I looked at the gleam and shine on every surface. I looked at what I had done to make things look normal again. I thought about maybe being able to do that some more, make things the way they were.

And then, for some reason, I thought of the Flying Dutchman bus I saw the other morning. Thought of it ghosting the streets.

And shook it off.

I looked at the girl's heaving back and shoulders.

—Crap.

I crossed the room, pulling the mask from my face, lifting the safety glasses to my forehead.

—Um. Excuse. Um. I didn't mean any.

Her shoulders shook harder.

I peeled the rubber gloves from my hands and wiped sweat off my forehead.

—Look. I really. I didn't mean anything personal. I didn't know you were there. I mean, I know that doesn't make it OK for me to say shit like. To say stuff like that, but I didn't mean anything by it, it was just. It's a little tense, doing . . . this. And I guess I have a fucked up . . . a lame sense of humor sometimes.

—Oh God. Oh gaaawd! Stop! Stop, Ho, my God, stop, you're killing me.

She turned, tears running down her face, gasping, waving a hand at me, trying to kill the laughter forcing its way up her throat.

.   .   .

—Oh, man, so completely inappropriate.

—I said I was sorry.

She shook out her match and dropped it off the deck to the sand below, watching it get caught in the wind and tumble into some rocks.

—No, it was just so perfect. Totally inappropriate. Exactly the kind of thing he would have said.

She pushed her glasses a little higher on her nose.

—Except he wouldn't have apologized.

I looked over my shoulder through the open sliding glass door and caught a glimpse of Gabe coming back into the house with another pack of scrapers.

I looked down at the tide as it washed over the rocks.

—Well, left to my own devices, I wouldn't have apologized either.

She choked on a lungful of smoke, more laughter combining with a few hacks.

I watched for a second then gave her a couple light pats on the back.

—You OK?

She coughed into her fist.

—Oh, sure, I'm fine.

She wiped the damp corners of her eyes with one of the Kleenexes Po Sin gave her.

—My dad killed himself in one of the more deliberate and grotesque manners imaginable and I'm laughing about it with one of the guys I'm paying to clean his brains off the wall. I'm doing great.

I turned and leaned my back on the deck rail and shrugged.

—Well, as long as you're OK then.

She smiled.

—Totally inappropriate.

—At least he left a note.

I didn't say anything, too occupied at the moment with working my Scotch-Brite pad over the speckles of blood on the surface of her dad's desk.

She picked another almond from the large bowl of them on the table next to the wingback chair near the hallway door.

—I mean, I knew he was sick. But. But I'm glad he left the note anyway. So I know for sure why he did it. Sort of.

She dropped the almond back in the bowl, picked out another.

—You think anyone would lie about that? I mean, no one would lie on their suicide note, would they?

I replaced the lamp I'd taken from the desk, minus the silk shade that had been sprayed, and looked over at her.

—You want to be a little more enigmatic with your questions? Seriously, if you try a little harder I might get curious or something.

She studied the almond between her fingers, rotating it.

—No. I don't mean anything. He was sick. He was going to die. Soon. Painfully. I know why he did it. I just never read a suicide note before. It made me wonder. I guess. But no. It all makes sense.

I adjusted the silver pen-and-pencil set on the desk and lined it up with the antique in-and-out box and an absurdly detailed model of a freight vessel, its deck stacked with tiny cargo containers, Chinese characters on their sides.

She tossed the almond in her mouth and chewed.

—Makes sense as only a person making their head explode can make sense, I mean.

I walked to the section of bookcase that was in line with the open bathroom door.

—He had some nice books.

She watched me.

—Yeah. He loved his books. Well, he loved having a den with lots of books on the walls anyway. He never actually read them. He loved how they looked, but if it wasn't business-related or on the topic of fishing, Dad didn't have time to read much.

She dropped her voice an octave.

—*Too much to do, sweetheart. Why bother reading about some made-up life when you can live it yourself?*

She brushed curly dark hair from her forehead, bit her lip.

—Is that bad, that it kind of makes sense to me? What he did? Should I be worried?

I misted the spines of the books and watched white speckles appear over dozens of them.

—Fuck do I know. I just work here.

—Right, I forgot, you're the retard who doesn't know how to say the right thing.

She picked up another almond, moved it toward her mouth, stopped.

—Should I be eating these things?

I looked at the bowl of nuts, well out of line with the bathroom door.

—Um. Truth?

—No, lie to me, that would make me feel so much better.

I wiped my cheek on my shoulder.

—I doubt they could get hit with anything over there.

She started to put the nut in her mouth.

I turned back to the bookcase.

—But then again, this is my second day on the job and I'm the same lame fucker who made fun of how your dad wasted himself. So you might not want to listen to someone so clearly retarded.

She dropped the nut back in the bowl.

—Yeah, you got a point.

She got off the chair and walked over to me and looked at the books.

I misted them again and she reached out and touched the tip of her finger to a white spot that had appeared on a photograph on one of the shelves: a sunburned man with a thick moustache, large arms and shoulders, standing on a dock next to a striped marlin, well over 200 pounds, hanging from a tackle rig.

—Damnit. Goddamn it.

—What the fuck are you doing?

I helped Po Sin muscle the bagged and gutted mattress down the hall to the front door.

—Working.

He stopped, pausing in front of the door that led into the den, watching the girl as she took several books down from the shelves and boxed them.

—Looks to me like *she's* working.

I looked at me again, shook his head, and backed toward the front door and out into the sun.

We leaned the mattress against the van and I pointed back at the house.

—She wanted to go through them herself. She said she didn't want to keep the fabric-covered ones because she could see some of the marks.

Po Sin rested his ass in the open back door of the van and it dropped on its shocks.

—Fuck *that*. I mean, what are you doing *talking* with her?

I raised my hands over my head.

—You said talk to her!

—I said apologize, I didn't say engage in a damn *tête-à-tête* with her.

—She wanted to talk, man. What am I supposed to say? *Oh, miss, so sorry, my boss is a total prick and will freak out if I have a conversation with you in your own house while you're grieving the loss of your father who just killed himself. Maybe you should take this dime and go call someone who's allowed to give a fuck.*

Po Sin turned his head and looked through the ranked cedars to the clogged traffic on the PCH.

—Gonna take forever to get home.

I kicked a rock.

—Yeah.

He pushed himself up, the van bounced, free of ballast.

—Giving a fuck, Web, that's not exactly the MO you've been working under for some time now.

I watched traffic.

Po Sin watched it, too.

—And people in her situation, they are prone to acting in ways they would not under normal circumstances. Start doing shit like talking to the help about their personal tragedies. Situation like that can become quickly awkward. People can all of a sudden realize they are not acting like themselves and freak out on everyone around them. And people employed to eliminate evidence that their loved ones ever existed can make attractive targets when they lash out. And that can make the job much more difficult than it needs to be. And this is my livelihood here. My business that I built from the ground up. And I don't need to have it getting all fucked up because some shell-shocked young woman mistakes your disinterest in pretty much anything for some kind of blasé charm, and ends up getting more deeply injured than she already is and has an inevitable emotional detonation and refuses to pay her fucking bill. I have enough problems, thank you.

—Don't worry, I know he's a disaffected asshole. No danger of me getting sucked into his emotional black hole or anything.

We turned from the traffic.

She stood at the top of the driveway, wind blowing her hair across her face and rippling the hem of her knee-length black jersey dress, a box of books in her arms.

—So you guys want to look and see if you want any of these?

. . .

—You sure?

—Yeah, of course. No, wait.

I stood away from the box of books I was sliding into the back of the van and she reached in and pulled one out.

—Not this one.

I looked at the title.

—You like that?

She looked at it herself.

—No, I'm keeping it because I think it sucks.

—Well that makes sense then, because it really does suck.

She bit her lip.

—My dad loved *Sister Carrie*.

—Oh fuck, I'm sorry, I.

She clutched the book to her heart and threw her wrist across her forehead.

—He treasured this book and called me his little Carrie. This book was a bond between us. A treasure we shared.

I stuffed my hands in my pockets.

—Yes, please fuck with me some more, I like it so much when you make me feel like an asshole. And it's such an obvious challenge to you, I can see how you can't help yourself.

She dropped her arms and smiled.

—Sorry. You're just so funny when you try to apologize. You're so bad at it. You can't hide the fact that you don't think you should have to do it.

—Again, I'm glad my being an asshole is a source of entertainment.

—It is, it is.

Gabe came out of the house, carrying the fogger and a half-empty jug of Microban. He walked between us and set them in the back of the truck.

—All done.

He looked at the box of books, the girl pointed at them.

—Help yourself if you want.

He shook his head and peeled his Tyvek off, stripping to his black slacks and white short sleeve.

—No, thank you.

He walked to his Cruiser.

—See you around, Web.

And he got in the car and rolled.

The girl looked at me.

—What's his story?

—I'm not allowed to ask.

Po Sin came from the house, the clipboard in his hand.

—Ready for the walk-through?

She looked up at the house.

—No, it's fine. I looked. It's fine.

She reached for the clipboard, but he held it away.

—We should really do a walk-through. Have you look at everything on the invoice and check it off.

She took the clipboard from him.

—No, I don't want to do that.

She signed her name and put her initials next to several ballpoint Xs on the contract.

—It's fine.

Po Sin raised his shoulders.

—Just if there's a problem, something we might have missed, and you don't see it now. You know? The home owner's insurance can get tricky.

She handed the clipboard back.

—If there's a problem, I'll pay to have it taken care of.

She looked at the house.

—Or I'll light a match and burn the place down.

Po Sin turned and slammed the rear doors of the van.

—Just so you know what's what.

She held out her hand.

—I know what's what.

He shook her hand, nodded, and started around the van.

—Come on, Web, time to hit it.

I looked at the girl, pointed at the van.

—Well, I gotta. You gonna be? In there?

She tapped me on the shoulder with her book.

—Go on, Web. Sensitivity doesn't suit you.

I scratched my head.

—Yeah. And I thought I was doing so well with it.

She smiled, turned, and wandered back toward the house, drifting from one side of the sandstone path to the other, slapping the book against her thigh as she went.

In the van, I watched her as Po Sin jockeyed for an open spot in the traffic. I watched her go to the open door of the house, stand there, then turn away and sit on the edge of the porch and open the book and flip slowly through the pages till she found one she wanted to read.

The last sight I'd have of her for some time, without bloodshed being involved anyway.

Cherchez la femme.

THE SON OF A BITCH HE RAISED

Bumper to bumper down the Pacific Coast Highway. The feet of the Santa Monicas on our left dotted with custom luxury homes; losing bets placed against inevitable mud slides and quakes. The stilted houses on our right, overhanging the beach and the ocean, equally stupid money placed against the tides.

But Jesus they have great views.

I thought about the girl back at her father's beach house. Her beach house now, one could assume. I eyeballed the clipboard on the dash in front of Po Sin, and he caught me and shook his head.

—No fucking way.

—Why?

—Because that is private information that a client has shared with me for the purpose of doing business and you are not allowed to look at it.

I reached for the clipboard.

—But I am an employee of the firm and should be trusted with this information if I am to do my job in an efficient manner.

He placed a weighty fist on the clipboard.

—But you are not a *trusted* employee. You are a ten buck an hour fuckup day laborer who is not allowed to cherry pick the phone numbers of attractive female clients so that you can harass them and get me sued.

I leaned back in my seat and folded my arms.

—Fine. Whatever you say, *jefe*.

He stuck his hand under the seat and came out with a Slim Jim and unwrapped it.

I looked out at the Pacific Ocean.

—What was that about the guild?

Po Sin cocked an eyebrow.

—What?

—The guild. That deputy you bribed mentioned a *guild* and something about *aftershocks* or something?

—Don't worry about it. It's not your problem.

I threw my hands up.

—Shit, man, I know it's not my problem, I'm just curious. I'm just trying to make conversation. I'm not allowed to ask about the damn girl back there. Fine. You don't want to talk about the business. Fine. So let's talk about the diet you're supposed to be on and how that's going. How are your cholesterol numbers looking? Triglycerides? How's the blood pressure? Your wife know you're munching sticks of pig ass seasoned with MSG?

He bit a hunk off the Slim Jim, chewed it once, and swallowed.

—Soledad.

—Say what?

—Her name is Soledad. And here's a tip, it means *solitude* in Spanish. As in, *Leave me the fuck alone.*

I held my arm out the window and felt the sun burning it red.

—She didn't pick her own name.

—Drop me over here.

Po Sin looked around.

—We're only in Santa Monica. How the hell you gonna get home from here?

—I'll get a ride.

—*A ride.* Chev gonna drive out here to pick you up?

—I'll get a ride. Pull over, pull over here, man.

He pulled the van to the curb on Ocean, just past the pier.

—Tell you one thing, you get stuck out here, I won't be coming to get you.

I opened the door and started to get out and he grabbed the tail of my old Mobil gas station shirt.

—Web.

I looked at him.

—You get stuck out here, you're gonna be riding the bus.

I tugged free.

—I can get a ride.

He held up his hands.

—As you wish.

I climbed out and pushed the door closed.

—That's the idea.

He pushed a button on his armrest and the passenger window slid down.

—Listen, there's no job tomorrow. You want to make some more cash, you can help clean the shop.

I shrugged.

—Sure. Sure. Sounds good.

—OK.

The window rolled back up and he drove off toward the 10 West.

I stood there for a minute and looked at the causeway to the pier and thought about walking out past the bars and the fried-food stands and the Ferris wheel all the way to the end so I could stand there and stare at the water. But instead I turned around and trotted across the street and walked into the late-afternoon darkness inside Chez Jay.

Dark, the only light coming in through the open upper half of the split front door and three portholes cut behind the bar. Fishing nets, life preservers and a ship's anchor on the walls, a tattered American flag hung in a single billow over the bar. I took a seat on the corner. The bartender looked down from the TV where he was watching a rerun of *Charlie's Angels*.

He came over.

—I was always a Kate Jackson man. You?

I glanced at the TV.

—Never watched it.

He stops in his tracks.

—Naw?

—Didn't have a TV growing up.

—No kidding. One of those.

—Yeah. One of those. No early childhood brain cancer to retard my emotional development.

—That's not funny.

—Not supposed to be.

He looked back up at the TV.

—Well I like the show.

—Yeah, I rest my case.

—Huh?

—Can I have a beer, please?

—What kind?

—Whatever.

He took a mug from behind the bar and drew a Heineken and set it in front of me.

—Four.

—I got that.

I looked at the old man tucked into the angle where the bar met the wall. Hunched over an open book, a stack of several more books at his elbow, thick plastic-rimmed glasses on the end of his swollen nose, a sweating glass of beer in front of him paired with a half-full shot glass.

He nudged a few dollars out of the pile of bills next to his drinks.

—That bother you, that no-TV thing?

I lifted my glass and took a sip.

—No. Not really. I read a lot.

The bartender took the money and went back down the bar.

—Well I like TV.

The old man gestured at his back.

—And here he is, tending bar.

I shrugged.

—It's a job.

The old man scraped his fingernails over his whiskers.

—It's a shitty job.

The bartender turned up the volume on the TV.

The old man dog-eared the corner of the page he was reading and closed the book.

—You still read a lot?

—Yeah.

He started going through the stack. He found what he was looking for and pulled it from the pile and offered it to me.

—Ever read this one?

I took the book and looked at the cover.

A Fan's Notes.

—Yeah, I read it.

He took the book back.

—That's a good book.

I took a sip of beer.

—It's good, I like it, but it's not that great.

He put the book on top of the stack.

—Did I say it was great? I said it was good. Try listening.

—Whatever.

He pulled at the collar of his red flannel shirt, the skin beneath beach-bum rough and brick red.

—A great book is a rare thing. What have you read lately that's great?

—Nothing.

—See what I mean.

He held up the book he was reading when I came in.

—*Anna Karenina.* A great book. Indisputably.

—Indisputably great trashy fiction.

He set the book down.

—Are you trying to upset me?

—No. I just think it's a great piece of popular melodrama, but not a great piece of art.

He turned on his stool, faced me.

—Who the hell? Where do you get off? This is one of the.

He backhanded the air.

—Why do I bother? You might as well have spent your childhood watching TV. Should have just wheeled one into your bedroom and plugged it into your eyes and let it brainwash you like the rest of society. You could be a bartender instead of a teacher. You could have a nice comfortable job pouring drinks and mopping vomit and watching TV. Wasted time. Wasted effort.

He picked up his shot glass and drained it.

—Wasted life.

I stared at the beer in my glass.

He knocked the base of the shot glass on the bar and the bartender came down with a bottle of Bushmills in his hand.

He topped off the old man's shot glass.

—L.L., how 'bout you take it easy on my customers. You buy the guy a drink, doesn't mean you have the right to browbeat him.

I raised a hand.

—It's cool, he's my dad.

L.L. wrote a novel.

It's on that shelf with the Nelson Algren and Bukowski and Kerouac at your local independent bookstore. If you have one of those. If not, you can find it on the Internet. But it will probably be the printing they did for the movie.

He wrote his novel before he met my mom. Really, he met my mom because he wrote the novel. It was a cult thing. Dozens of printings over the years, each of them a run of a couple thousand, well regarded enough to get him several guest lecture gigs in the late sixties as a not quite elder statesman of the counterculture. If not for that, he'd never have been at UC Berkeley in '68. Never gone to the Fillmore with some of his grad students to see a happening, and loudly denigrate it as bullshit, sounding off at the back of the hall, a bottle of mescal in one hand and a huge joint in the other, surrounded by the more reactionary wing of the peace and freedom movement. If not for that, he'd never been challenged by an attractive young undergrad from SF State, who proposed to show him how rock music, acid and free love could change the world. Never would have eyedroppered a dose of U.S. government pure LSD and ended up fucking the undergrad's brains out in Golden Gate Park at dawn, receiving along the way what he once described to me as, *The most sublime head known to man or Jesus. I saw the universe entire in that blow job, Web, the whole damn shooting match.* Never would have taken the undergrad to wife that week. Never would have brought her back to Los Angeles with him. And certainly never would have gotten stone fucked up with her twelve years later, on one of the rare occasions they had sex anymore, and forgotten to make sure she had in her diaphragm and impregnated her with a child she would refuse to abort, all of it ending with me as his son.

Or that's how he tells the story.

The old man rubbed a hand over his round belly.

—Would you have preferred that? If I'd just plopped you in front of the boob tube for your education? It could have prepared you for a menial life, it would have been no trouble at all. It would have been much easier than teaching you how to read when you were two. It would have been much easier than showing you the constellations or taking you to the Getty to see Rembrandts or the Hollywood Bowl to see Bernstein. It would have been much easier than giving you an education that you were able to use, something to share with your students. There's no nobler profession, no better use of a life than to teach, but I could have saved us both the trouble and given you a TV and that would have made you happy, it seems.

I looked at the old man.

—I'm not teaching anymore.

He blinked.

—Oh, and what kind of job have you turned your energies to?

—I'm. Cleaning stuff.

He picked at the tuft of gray hair sprouting from his right ear.

—A janitor.

—No.

—You're cleaning for a living?

—Well, for the last couple days.

—Then you are, my son, either a janitor or a housekeeper. Are you a housekeeper?

—No.

He swiveled on his stool and signaled the bartender.

—Do you have, by any chance, an application? My son, I think, might be looking to improve his employment situation.

The bartender blinked.

—We're not hiring.

My dad shrugged.

—Alas. Another beer then. He can use it to drown his useless dreams and sorrows.

I drained my glass and set it down.

—Thanks, Dad. But I think you're mistaking me for you.

He grinned, showing me the gap where his two upper front teeth used to be before he lost them in an Ensenada bar fight.

—Ah, now there's the little son of a bitch I raised.

Lincoln Lake Crows loves teachers and teaching. In theory. Which is to say, he loves the idea of teachers and of teaching.

The Noblest Profession, Web. No greater calling than the passing of knowledge from one generation to the next. A thankless task it is, to the outsider. The teacher, the true teacher, knows that the rewards of his calling are not properly measured in silver. They are measured in the achievements of the teacher's students. Respect, yes. Admiration, yes. A word of thanks, yes. All these are well deserved and appreciated. But the true and absolute payment comes in seeing a student learn and apply that learning. No matter how modest their accomplishments may be, that is the reward. That is coin of the realm for a true teacher.

And he should know. Old L.L. put his years in as a high school teacher. Toiling in the mines of public education for well over a decade.

He'd still be there now.

Except that he wrote a novel. And he lived in Los Angeles. And someone he knew knew someone who knew someone who passed the novel around to someone. And that someone turned out to be Dennis Hopper. And he showed it to Bob Rafelson. And *Bob,* as he was known around our house, took out an option.

And L.L.'s opinions about remuneration changed very rapidly thereafter.

At least that's how my mom tells the story.

—And what brings the fruit of my loins to the western precipice of this, our waning civilization?

I forked up the last of the sand dabs he'd ordered for me and wiped my mouth.

—Nothing.

I put the fork down and pushed the plate away. Dad hadn't bothered to eat, food inhibiting, as it does, the absorption of alcohol.

He flicked his eyes across a page of the book he had reopened while I ate.

—*Nothing.* Certainly. Why should a janitor be anything but aimless? The freedoms of the laboring class. Why fill the off hours with knowledge and investigation, with self-improvement? To what end, after all? *Nothing.* Indeed.

I leaned over on my stool and took a toothpick from the dispenser on the shelf next to the menus. The waiters were coming on for dinner service, I watched one use an ice cream scoop on a tub of refrigerated butter, plopping the perfect little balls into white dishes. Another slid trays of dinner salads into the stand-fridge. The manager chalked specials on a board. A couple regulars came in and the bartender started making their drinks without being asked.

I looked at L.L. reading *Anna Karenina.* I thought about Anna throwing herself under her train. I thought about the shower of blood and brain on the bedroom wall of the house in Malibu. I thought about the putrid stain the pack rat left on the floor in Koreatown.

I picked my teeth.

—Guess I was just thinking about you, L.L. Thought I'd come by and see how you're doing.

He glanced at me, eyes peering just over the top of his glasses. He signaled the bartender and looked back down at his book.

—A banner day. Another beer is surely in order.

L.L. wrote the screenplay, and it was a hit.

It was read by everyone in Hollywood. Dad became the hottest writer in town. Coppola tapped him to adapt *Travels with Charley.* Redford wanted to know if he'd brush up a remake of *The Heart of the Matter.* Michael Cimino was looking to do the life of Jim Thomson. Robert Evans thought he'd snagged the Holy Grail, the rights to *The Catcher in the Rye.* Did L.L. want first crack? Anything and everything with a whiff of the literary, L.L. Crows was at the top of the list to write, adapt, brush up, or take a pass at.

And he took every job. And he wrote some of the most consistently excellent and praised screenplays Hollywood has ever seen. And not a fucking one was ever produced. Nothing that he got screen credit for, anyway. But in the '70s, and through most of the '80s, his red pencil marks had decorated, and vastly improved, he'd be sure to inform you, the pages of a small forest's worth of scripts. Some good, some pure ass. Several Oscar nominees, and a few winners. Not that he gave a fuck one way or another. Because they weren't his stories. He was just the hired gun, getting richer than any human could pray to a fat and greedy Jesus to get.

His story, his admired and lauded screenplay of his one and only novel, walked up and down the runway and had its skirt lifted by every A-list studio/actor/director/producer in town with a yen to take on the what had become *the greatest movie never made,* and while it had more than a few dollar bills stuffed in its panties, no big spender ever stepped up to throw down for a trip to the champagne lounge.

A source, one might say, of some slight bitterness in years to come.

—And what are you reading these days?

I looked up from the copy of *Down and Out in Paris and London* that I'd taken from his pile. I'd scooted over to the stool next to L.L. to make room for a couple that was waiting for a table. Full dinner service in swing, Chez Jay went from elbow room empty to sardine can packed in less than an hour. I'd forgotten.

Sitting at his side, reading silently, sipping at a beer, it came back. Childhood revisited.

I closed the book.

—Horror mostly.

He rubbed his forehead, kept his eyes in his own book.

—Dare I ask by whom written?

—Whatever. Stephen King, Joe Lansdale, Clive Barker.

He winced.

—Web. Ambrose Bierce, Lovecraft, Stoker, for God sake.

I went on.

—Dean Koontz, Kellerman.

—Edgar Allan Poe, ever heard of him? J. S. LeFanu? Algernon Blackwood?

—James Herbert. Straub.

He slammed his book closed.

—Are you trying to kill me? Did you come here solely to antagonize me and rub my face in your ignorance? Certain tales by Mark Twain, Charles Dickens, Edith Wharton for fuck sake, all horror of the highest order. Dear God, Webster, Henry James! Shirley Jackson! Or in later years, Harlan Ellison, Bradbury, Matheson!

I slammed my own book.

—I'm not looking for fucking enlightenment, I'm looking to turn my fucking brain off for a couple hours!

He rose from his stool.

—*Turn your brain off?* Turn your?

He began collecting his books.

—Well, I have news for you, Web.

He cradled the books and put his face in mine.

—You have fucking well succeeded at that!

Heads had turned, the manager was coming over.

L.L. took a thick roll of bills from the hip pocket of his faded and baggy madras shorts and flipped a couple hundreds on the bar.

—Sorry about the fracas, Ernesto. My son is a mongoloid, and if I don't speak at a certain volume and pitch he can't understand human speech.

Exit, L. L. Crows, having added to his great legacy of closing lines.

I never heard about how great teaching was when I was a little kid. By then, the mid-eighties, he was one of the senior script doctors of the industry, a go-to guy when a little class was needed on a project, making an obscene living tweaking other writers' illiteracies. All I heard about was how vital the movies were.

People say escapism as if it were some foul bane. As if the denizens of this weary world were not deserving of some surcease and ease. They say it as if that is the only virtue the cinema might possess. As if it is not the great art form of the twentieth century. As if Godard and Fellini and Hitchcock and Cassavetes and Bergman and Altman and Wilder never walked the earth. One movie, one, of only moderate success, it touches more lives than I touched in nearly fifteen years of teaching. The years I toiled in that cesspool of incompetence and mediocrity called the public schools. I shudder, Web. My bowels turn to water when I think of what I might have accomplished. But no regrets, regrets are for small men with minor minds. We, my boy, we are for scaling mountains, you and I. We are for leaving monuments. A movie, a film, it is a testament in light and color and sound, a record of achievement, a projection of artistic vision penetrating directly into the brains of the audience. They cannot help but be touched, changed, when our words vibrate their eardrums, when the photons carrying our images strike the rods and cones of their eyes. Filmmaking, Web, let no one tell you other-wise, is a noble endeavor, the surest way for giant men to leave their marks upon the landscape of human emotions.

Delivered as he drove me around greater Los Angeles in his 560SL, after keeping me home from school so we could go to the NuArt together to see a Michael Curtiz revival, pointing from time to time with the hand that didn't contain a can of beer.

There, at Wilshire and Crenshaw, the house that served as exterior for Nora Desmond's mansion. There, the rest home Jack and Faye go to in Chi-natown. *There, the Ennis Brown House, Price's House on Haunted Hill. The Ambassador Hotel, where Anne Bancroft and Hoffman have their affair. Your mom and I fucked there once. Here in San Pedro, right there, they filmed the Skull Island landing in King Kong. This spot here, Hollywood and Sunset, where Griffith built his Babylonian temple and staged the single largest orgy of all time.*

Mom was spending most of her time in Big Sur by then, hanging with the Esalen crowd. Yoga and transcendental meditation and organic hummus and mud baths and, I assume, fucking men considerably younger and less caustic than her older and no longer looked-up-to husband.

So she wasn't around when L.L. got the call that his screenplay had finally been green-lighted. She missed the scene when his ghostwriter pals drove up the canyon to drink their way through the case of Krug he opened for the occasion. She missed the following morning when he got the final draft of the script from his agent and found that it had been rewritten five times in the year since it had been most recently optioned; thick batches of colored pages mixed into the script, indicating the many hands that had revised his work. She missed the evisceration he performed on the house after reading the rewrites, while I sat out front on my Big Wheel, and Chev and I listened to him creating a whole new lexicon of cursing. And by the time the movie was made two years year later, with Judd Nelson and Molly Ringwald in the leads, directed by John Badham, she had relinquished claims on communal property and left for Oregon to find her *true self, unencumbered by the artificial constraints of marriage and rigidity of bourgeois child-rearing concepts.* That final exit relieving her of the scene after L.L. went, hope springs eternal, to the premiere.

He sat through it. All one hundred and seventy-nine minutes of it. Sat through every tired cough and forced laugh from the audience, sat through the round of relieved applause as the credits rolled. Sat through the entirety of its mediocrity, and saw it as a movie guilty of the ultimate crime: forgettability. It wasn't even bad enough to be remembered for the incompetence brought to bear. Nor, after all the years and near-misses gone by, were the expectations, or the budget, high enough for it to be held out as a great flop. He sat in the theater, enduring the shoulder pats and congratulations of various sucker fish of the movie business. And I sat in the seat next to him the whole while.

The climax Mom missed by fleeing north was to come the following morning when L.L.'s agent informed him that his name could not be removed from the credits. *An Alan Smithee Film* would never grace the opening titles. So he began making a bonfire of every bit of movie memorabilia, every treasured celluloid print, stacks of laser disks, collected and bound editions of every screenplay in which his talent had played a roll, and his SWG membership card, and proceeded to burn down half the house, nearly sending an inferno through the canyon and over the entire range of the Hollywood Hills.

The next day, after L.L.'s lawyer got him out on bail for his arson charges, I was enrolled in private school, gifted with a collection of the *Great Western Works of Literature,* and received my first in a lifelong series of lectures praising the professional educator and condemning popular culture in all its forms.

But never condemning the movies. Which, to tell by their eradication from L.L.'s conversation, were an advancement in entertainment that had never existed at all.

I followed him out to the parking lot, to his current SL, the latest in a line of annual acquisitions. That residual money for the years of hackery still rolling in.

—L.L.

He dropped the books on the back seat of the open-top car, adding them to the small library jumbled there, and turned to me.

—What? What can I do for you that I have not already done? Having seeded you and nourished you and clothed you and educated you, what more is there that I can do at this late date?

I looked at the purple veins in his nose. The swollen feet stuffed into chef's clogs, the spindly legs sticking from the shorts, the sweat-stained fishing hat that covered the melanoma scars on his bald head. I thought about reminding him of a few details from our life. And then not seeing him again for another two years.

Instead I thought about the dead man's stain soaking through the carpet, maggot trails leading away from motor oil blood and greasy tallow.

I pointed at the car.

—I could use a ride.

He started to raise a pointing finger, and stopped.

—Yes. A ride.

He opened the driver side door.

—Get in then.

I walked around the car and got in and he drove to the parking lot exit and waited for a couple pedestrians on the sidewalk, and I saw him looking down at the pier, at the merry-go-round. He rubbed his mouth, opened it, closed it.

Leaving me to hear what he'd said many times, over twenty years gone down, in this same place.

There, on the pier, the merry-go-round Paul Newman runs in The Sting. *Do you want to ride it?*

.   .   .

In front of the apartment L.L. reached into the backseat and knocked through the books until he found the copy of *Anna Karenina* he'd abused me with at the bar, and flipped through the pages as I got out of the car.

He closed it and held it out.

—Take this.

—I've read it.

He leaned across the seat and shoved the book into my chest.

—Read it again. It will help keep you from getting any more ignorant than you have already become.

—Well, when you put it that way.

I took the book.

—Thanks.

He put the car in gear.

—Don't thank me. Just read the damn book.

And he was off, tires breaking traction as he squealed away, nearly running over my feet.

I watched him career around the corner, almost killing a man pushing a bicycle hung with plastic bags filled with empty bottles and cans.

—I'd say it was good to see you, L.L., but I'd be so fucking lying.

WHAT BEING A DICK GETS YOU

—I love *Anna Karenina.*

I looked at Dot, still on my couch, still in Chev's Misfits T, but now apparaled with low-rider jeans, several textbooks scattered around her.

—What the fuck are you doing here?

—Studying. What's your favorite part? Mine's when they tour Europe together.

I walked to Chev's bedroom door and looked inside, finding the usual piles of dirty clothes, overflowing ashtrays, Cramps and Black Flag and *Hot Rod* magazine posters, and liberally sex-stained sheets. But no Chev.

—What I meant by my question was, *what the fuck are you doing here?*

She reached under her shirt and scratched at the nipple Chev had pierced.

—I'm taking summer term so I can graduate in three years and they cram like five months of work into like five weeks and I have to study for like three tests and my sister is having her sweet sixteen at the house and she's been watching those shows about those huge birthday parties girls throw and she's doing a theme that's supposed to be Studio 54 but it looks like it's going to be more like Adult Film Stars of the Future and the place is infuckingsane because she's being an utter and total rag and I have to have quiet so I can pass fucking developmental psychology which is totally kicking my ass.

I put a hand to my forehead.

—But what the fuck are you doing *here?*

She picked up her notebook and tapped a pen with a fuzzy purple ball at the end against the lecture outline neatly printed on the open page.

—Chev said it was cool.

—Chev's not the only one who lives here.

She doodled a little kitty face.

—He said if you were a dick I should remind you that he's the only one paying rent right now.

I dropped the book at her feet.

—Fuck you. Have a book.

She picked it up with one hand, scratching her nipple again with the other.

—Cool! Thanks.

I walked to the kitchen, pointing at her chest.

—And don't do that, it'll get infected and your nipple will fall off and the rich, shallow and handsome afterbirth you're destined to marry will reject you and you'll end up a crack whore.

I opened the fridge and looked at the shelves stuffed with groceries; fresh, organic, very healthy groceries.

—What the fuck?

She settled into the couch, opening the Tolstoy in her lap.

—I took some of the money you left this morning and went shopping.

I closed the door and looked at her.

—Chev is going to shit when he sees food in here that didn't come from the Arby's or the In-N-Out.

She flipped pages.

—No he's not. He likes me a lot. He said so.

I took a package of tofu from the fridge.

—He say that before or after you bought this?

She flipped more pages.

—Doesn't matter. He likes me. I can tell.

—He likes to fuck you.

She looked up from the book.

—Well, duh! I'm a great lay.

I put the tofu back in the fridge and looked for something I could actually eat.

—How would you know, you been fucking yourself lately?

—Hey!

I took my head out of the fridge and looked at her.

—What, did I say something to offend?

She shook her head.

—Fuck no. I just wondered, if I get the book, do I also get this?

She held the book up, showing me the sheaf of hundreds hidden in the pages.

I walked over and looked at the money, tucked into the scene where Levin discovers the joys of physical labor.

—My dad put it there.

—Why?

I picked up the cash.

—I don't know. To apologize for being a dick maybe.

She flipped the pages of the book.

—Well if that's how your family apologizes for being a dick, how much do I get?

I folded the bills and put them in the breast pocket of my shirt.

—You get to stay here and study.

She closed the book, ran fingers over the cloth cover.

—Hey?

—Mmm.

She looked up at me.

—I'm sorry about that thing.

I looked around, trying to find the thing she was talking about.

—What, the tofu?

She shook her head, pointed at the bookshelf.

—No. That thing. The yearbook. I recognized the name of the school, of course, but I didn't, like, know you were there or anything. But Chev told me. I didn't mean to, like, stir shit up.

She put her fingers on the back of my hand.

—That sucked. I remember when it happened and it totally sucked. I cried all night. So. I'm sorry. You know.

I looked at her fingers on my hand.

—Stop touching me, you stupid plastic bitch.

She pulled her hand back.

I pointed at Chev's bedroom.

—Don't get too comfortable around here. Chev is just going to fuck you until he gets bored, and then stop calling you except for maybe once or twice over the next couple months when he's drunk and needs a booty call.

Her lips thinned, she started collecting her books.

I kept talking, walking to the door.

—And you'll tell your friends that's cool, you can use the hookup, but when you call him to get the same action, he won't even bother to answer. He'll see your name on his phone and put it right back in his pocket and say something about how it's *some chick I was hooking up with and now she's strung out on the dick.*

She shoved the books into a knapsack and stood.

I waved her down.

—No, no, you stay here, make yourself at home, I'm sure Chev will be back soon for a pit stop.

I went out the door, the copy of *Anna Karenina* hitting it just as I slammed it behind me.

I stood there, thought about going back in and apologizing. Thought about going back in and telling her some lies about how Chev told me she liked to be pissed on. Thought about staying right where I was and never moving again in my life.

But what's the point? Apologies don't make things better. And you can only hurt someone so much before they stop caring what you do to them. And if I stayed where I was, sooner or later the weird cat lady from down the hall would come out and ask me to help her get that mean calico from behind the dryer in the laundry room and I've been clawed enough by that rabid fucking feline.

So I went down the stairs and around the building and cut down the alley that ran east to Highland, taking the shortcut toward the shop, with a few choice words left in my vocabulary to be directed at my best friend.

In the alley, the homeless couple stood outside their tent, sorting recyclables between the three barrels mounted on their cart.

—Cocksucker.

—Bitch.

—Fucking loser.

—Fucking whore.

Their matching Mohawks bobbing as they dipped in and out of the barrels, coming up with glass and plastic and aluminum.

The girl glanced at me.

—Hey, hey, got any change today?

I put my head down and walked past, skirting the row of cars parked behind the apartments that shared the alley.

I heard her spit.

—Fuck you, asshole! We just live here! We're just alive! Just like you! You don't have to ignore us because we're homeless!

I turned and walked backward away from them.

—I'm not ignoring you because you're homeless. I'm ignoring you because you scream at each other in the middle of the night when I'm trying to sleep. And also because I hate that Santa hat you wear every Christmas because you think it's gonna make people give you more money or something. I'm ignoring you not because I don't like homeless people, but be-cause I don't like you, personally.

I bumped into something, smacking my head hard into whatever it was.

The homeless couple's eyes bugged.

I turned around and got shoved to the ground by a big motherfucker in a ski mask.

He kicked me in the ribs.

—Don't fuck with the guild, asshole.

I curled around the pain.

—What?

He got down on one knee and grabbed the front of my shirt and pulled my head from the ground and slapped my face back and forth.

—Don't! Fuck! With! The! Guild!

Snot and blood ran from my nose as I started to cry.

—OK! OK! OK! No guild fucking!

He took me by the throat and shook me.

—I'm fucking serious!

I choked.

—I know! I know! I know! I can tell by the way you're strangling me!

Two more guys in ski masks appeared behind him.

—Come on, man, let's go, people are watching.

The big one took his hand from my neck and looked at the gaping homeless couple.

—They're just fucking crackheads.

I rubbed my throat.

—Hey, just because they're homeless doesn't mean they're crackheads. They could be junkies, asshole.

He grabbed a wad of hair.

—Still so funny, still making me forget to laugh.

I coughed up some bloody phlegm.

—Dingbang?

He made a fist.

—Bang, motherfucker!

The fist came at me.

—Just Bang!

BANG!

I remember a sideways view of Bang and his two buddies getting into a van with bright yellow paint splotched over a smoothly primered front and side. I remember the van hauling ass down the alley. And I remember the homeless couple coming over and squatting next to me, the girl pouring some water from a bottle onto a rag and wiping at the blood on my face.

—See, that's what being a dick gets you.

And I remember thinking she just could be right.

Then I took a little nap.

—I can stitch it up.

—No fucking way.

—Dude, seriously, I can totally stitch it up.

I slapped Chev's gloved hand from my face, knocking the needle and thread from his fingers.

He shook his head.

—Gonna have to re-sterilize that before I stitch you up.

I covered the gash in my forehead, left when Bang bounced my noggin off the asphalt.

—You are not stitching me up. You aren't even sewing buttons back on my shirt. You are coming nowhere near me or my skin with that needle, man.

He started stripping the black rubber gloves from his hands.

—Whatever. I don't know why you're being such a puss about it. I use needles on people all the time.

I threw my arms out.

—Asshole, you use them to punch holes in people's genitalia! You wield needles for the purpose of inflicting voluntary bodily mutilations! You don't close holes, man, you make them!

He stuffed the gloves in the waste box on the wall.

—Look at it however you want, man. Way I see it, skin is my métier, flesh my milieu. Modifying the body is my art.

I looked out the open service window at the customers sitting in the waiting room listening to us fight. I looked at him. I closed the shutters over the window.

—Are you high?

He giggled.

—Really high, man.

I put my head in my hands.

—You're high and you were going to stitch my wound?

He took an American Spirit from the pack on the desk and lit it.

—Why not? I tattoo high all the time.

—Not the same, man. Not the same.

He blew smoke rings.

—Says you.

I lifted my head and stared at him. I opened my mouth, observed just how red his eyes were, and gave it up.

—Sure. Says me.

I stood up and made the room go sideways and Chev grabbed my arm and eased me back down.

—Whoa there, Hoss. Easy there.

—I'm cool, I'm cool.

I stood again, slower this time, and went over to the mirror on the wall and looked at my face.

—Crap.

There was a knock on the door. Chev opened it and his apprentice Dina stuck her pierced face in.

—Hey, I'm doing this.

She held out a stencil of a little pitchfork-wielding devil.

—What should I use?

Chev looked at it.

—Loose seven for the line work. Straight seven for the color. You need a machine?

She squinted, smiled a little.

—Can I?

He picked up a small plastic case from the desk, undid the clasps on the side and took out a chromed tattoo gun and handed it to her.

—Got to get your own gear, lady.

She took the machine from him.

—I know. I'm saving. Thanks.

She started to close the door, saw me and stopped.

—Fuck, Web, what happened? Looks like you got beat up.

I pointed at my split swollen lip, bloody nose and the gash in my forehead.

—Is that what it looks like, Dina? Because I'm afraid you're mistaken. Wounds like these, you only get them one place. Between your mom's thighs when she crosses her legs too fast.

She flipped me off on her way out.

—Fuck you, you dick.

The door closed and Chev faced me, flicking ash on the floor.

—Feeling all better?

I ripped the paper wrapper off a gauze pad.

—I'm getting there.

He stubbed his butt in a tin ashtray with a Hamms label enameled at the bottom.

—Good. Because seeing as the topic of your dickness has come up, I thought we might talk about you being such a huge fucking phallus to Dot.

I pressed the pad over the oozing gash.

—She call you or something?

He fingered another smoke from his pack.

—Yeah, man. She called me. She called to tell me the homeless couple was screaming in the alley for help and that you were all fucked up down there. She hadn't called me, you'd still be there, asshole. And, by the way, she added that you flipped out on her and said some fucked up shit about me.

I used another pad to wipe dry bloody snot from my upper lip.

—Yeah, well, I may have been less inclined to say fucked up shit about you if you hadn't been talking to her about shit that's none of her business and that you should know better than to talk about with chicks you're nailing and that you know damn well you're gonna kick to the curb next week.

He was quiet for a moment, listening to the high buzz of Dina hitting his machine, tuning the power. He put his head out the door.

—Dina, baby, no higher than ten volts on that machine. It'll get squirrelly.

He pulled his head back in and closed the door.

—I'm not gonna be kicking Dot to the curb next week.

—Fine. Week after next.

He lit up and blew smoke.

—I like her. I'm not kicking her anyplace. She's cool and she's gonna be around for awhile. Adapt to the concept.

I looked for my Mobil shirt.

—Fine. You adapt to the concept that you shouldn't be talking about *some things* to chicks you've been fucking for twenty-four hours. No matter how much you're deluding yourself about the longevity of your affections for her.

He leaned his back on the door and folded his heavily decorated, gym-enhanced arms over his chest.

—Web, with all due respect and love, you are not the only one who's dealing with that shit.

I stopped looking for the shirt.

—What?

He raised a hand.

—Look, man, I'm not saying it's the same thing, but we live together. You know? And you're my best friend. And this shit ain't easy. I mean, all this, this whole asshole of the year thing you're doing, it ain't easy. Someone, someone I like, asks me why you're such a dick, that's a complicated answer. Because I want her to know that you're not a dick. Well, not *just* a dick. That you're cool. So I have to tell her some things. And seeing as how we are best friends and seeing as how we live together and seeing as how because of that, what happens to you has a tendency to rain shit all over me, I don't feel too fucking bad about telling Dot what the hell the deal is.

I touched my swollen lip. It hurt.

Chev moved away from the door.

—Cuz the thing is, man, it's not just you. I mean, I may be about the only friend you got left willing to put up with your shit, and I got to tell you, man, it ain't fucking easy. It is trying, man. It is hard work. And I appreciate you leaving some of Thea's cash this morning. And I think it's great you're doing some work for Po Sin. And if you can't be fucking civil to my friends, I can *deal* with it. But you have to cut me some slack on *how* I deal. Cuz like I'm saying, this is not just your thing.

He put a hand on my shoulder.

—OK?

I nodded. I looked at him. I tapped the middle of my forehead.

—You got something here.

He put a hand to his own forehead.

—Here?

I nodded again.

—Yeah, you got a big weeping vagina that's whining *meeeeeeee, ooooooh meeeeeeee.*

He took his hand from his forehead.

—Not cool, man.

I brushed his hand from my shoulder.

—Where's my fucking shirt?

He went to the deer antler coatrack in the corner and tossed me my shirt. I snagged it from the air and the hundreds I'd stuffed in the pocket slipped out and fluttered to the floor.

He looked at the cash.

—Been slingin' dope?

I fiddled with my shirt, picking at some dry blood on the collar.

—No.

He pointed at the money.

—Where'd that come from? Thought your note said Thea sent an ascending sequence.

—She did.

—Thought your note said it ended in nine.

—It did.

—That's like a grand there.

—Yeah.

—So where's it come from?

I didn't look up.

—L.L. gave it to me.

He didn't say anything. I looked up. He stared at me, the muscles under the *MOM* and *DAD* tattoos centered on either biceps tensed.

I pointed at the money.

—I didn't ask for it or anything, man. He just, he gave me a book and the money was in there. I. I just went to see him. I needed to. Chev, I haven't seen him in two years. I wanted to see if he was alive for fuck sake. I just. Shit, man.

—Get the fuck out of my shop. Pick up that money and get out.

I squatted and started collecting the money.

—I need to use the phone. I have to call Po Sin.

He crossed to the door.

—There's a payphone on the corner.

I stood, the money in my fist.

—I wasn't gonna spend it, Chev. I was gonna give it away. I didn't even know I had it. He put it in a book.

—Web.

—Yeah.

—I love you, man.

—I know.

He opened the door.

—But if you don't shut up and get out of here right now, I'm gonna love you a lot less, you son of a bitch.

I could have said something else. I could have said something so unbelievably dicky it would have made him laugh. I could have torn the money into little pieces and went and flushed them down the can. I could have done a lot of things. But it was kind of a delicate situation. And I don't have a good track record with doing the right thing in delicate situations.

So I just got the fuck out.

Cuz down to one friend in the world, you tend to get anxious about how long you can hang onto him before you fuck up and do that one last thing that can't be forgiven and you get left all alone for the rest of your life until you die on the toilet in a stinking SRO apartment and no one finds your corpse till it swells up and tumbles from the can and bursts open and even the maggots have had enough of you and move on.

Besides, he had a right to be pissed.

After all, my dad did kill his parents.

It was an accident.

Does that go without saying?

Does it matter?

Does it matter that he didn't actually take a gun from his pocket and shoot them in the face? Does it matter that they were all close friends? Does it matter that they had a standing Friday night date at the Palm in the Beverly Hills Hotel from years back, from well before my mom took off, from before Chev and me were even born? Does it matter that three of them drove drunk back up the Canyon every week, year after year, always in L.L.'s latest Mercedes, always, even in the rain, with the top down? Does it matter that, despite L.L.'s blood alcohol level, the inquest showed that the true blame for the head-on collision lay with the driver who'd been coming down Laurel Canyon, screaming around corners on the wrong side of the road? Does it matter that L.L. was acquitted of vehicular manslaughter? Does it matter that L.L. did his utmost to adopt Chev, and that, when he couldn't fight the obvious objections, he lent every bit of financial support he could to Chev and his foster family?

No, it fucking doesn't.

Especially if you're Chev.

It might have mattered. It might all have made a big difference.

If L.L. could have kept his mouth shut and never gotten shitfaced one night and, in a classic bit of L.L. theater, decided it was time we knew *the true face of God,* and revealed to us that he *should never have been driving* that night. After years of lies.

Still, it might not have mattered, at nearly twenty years of age by then, Chev might have had enough perspective to see why L.L. had lied, and he might have had a big huggy moment with his crazy father figure.

Might have happened.

If L.L. hadn't also revealed that he was having an affair with Chev's mom and that, at the moment of the accident, Chev's dad had been passed out in the jumpseat, and her mouth had been in L.L.'s lap.

See, as was often the case with L.L., it wasn't so much the fucked up shit he did, as the fact that he had to talk about the fucked up shit he did.

So I understand Chev getting pissed at me for having L.L.'s money in my pocket. Cuz we're not supposed to take his money. Ever. For anything. It was an oath we swore. Nineteen, Chev dropped out of college because he didn't want anything to do with the trust L.L. had set up for him; didn't want his money, and didn't want the education L.L. had told him his mom and dad would want him to have. Didn't want anything to do with anything L.L. touched, said, or thought. And I joined him. Skipped out on UCLA and enrolled at LACC. Having kind of figured out by then that if push came to shove, I'd be better off with Chev in my corner than with L.L. My rare moment of wisdom, recognizing that blood is not in fact thicker than water.

That oath may have kind of been broken by not stuffing L.L.'s money down the garbage disposal the minute Dot showed it to me. But I was too busy being a dick to her to be bothered with that.

Crap.

So I thought about that kind of stuff, the kind of stuff where your dad is kind of responsible for the deaths of your best friend's parents, while I stood next to the payphone at the gas station on the corner of La Brea and Melrose waiting for Po Sin to come and pick me up.

Again, crap.

AS NORMAL AS IT GETS

—Motherfucker!

—So is this covered by workmen's comp?

—Motherfucker!

—I mean, if I get beat to crap by the competition, are my medical expenses taken care of? Missed wages? All that shit?

Po Sin drove one-handed, hammering his fist against the roof of the van.

—Mother! Fucker!

He pulled the van into the lot of a two-story strip mall, put it in park, got out and walked into a liquor store stationed between a nail salon and a Pilates studio, just under an auto insurance office. I watched him through the glass as he walked to the snack rack and started grabbing things, his lips ceaselessly moving.

Motherfucker! Motherfucker! Motherfucker!

He came out a moment later, got in the van, dropped a sack full of junk food between our seats, ripped open a bag of puffy Cheetos, put it in his lap and started shoving them in his mouth as we pulled back onto Santa Monica Boulevard.

—Moferfuther!

Orange crumbs sprayed the inside of the windshield.

—Mofufer!

I poked a finger in the sack of chips and beef sticks and snack cakes.

—Feeling a little anxious, Po Sin?

He wiped orange dust from his finger onto his pants.

—Fuck you, Web. And, yes, I am. I am a stress eater, OK. When I am stressed I lose composure and self-control and I eat compulsively. That's what happens. You've seen me, right? You see how fucking fat I am, right? You think this shit just happens? It doesn't. I don't have a fucking thyroid problem here, I eat too much and I eat junk food. And I eat more when stressed. And I'm stressed right now. OK? OK? OK?

I leaned away from the crumbs and the spittle filling the air between us.

—Yeah, OK, I get it. You're stressed. You got a right to be. I understand. Hey, I'm stressed, too. Which, you know, I think makes a lot of sense in this scenario. Seeing as I was the one who got his face beaten in by your goddamn nephew. Oh, and by the way, I couldn't help but notice that the van he and his friends took off in had been recently vandalized in the same shade of yellow paint that Gabe had under his fingernails this morning. Not that I think the two things are related or anything. Not that I think I've landed in the middle of some kind of dead-body-cleanup range war or anything like that.

He hammered the roof again.

—Fucking Morton! Fucking guild!

—Yes, the guild, interesting that you should mention that. So happens that Bang brought that up while we were chatting. I must confess that I was at something of a loss when the topic came about. Somewhat in the dark, as it were. Perhaps you might fucking enlighten my ass.

He jerked the van to a stop at a red light and turned to me.

—His name is Dingbang, not Bang. It was his grandfather's name. Dingbang, not Bang.

I folded my arms and put my feet on the dash.

—As long as he doesn't beat me up anymore, he can call himself whatever he wants.

Po Sin snapped his fingers.

—Feet, feet.

—Yes, they are, right there at the bottoms of my legs.

—Off the dash.

I shook my head.

—Uh-uh. Consider it getting my ass kicked for the job tax.

He put more Cheetos in his mouth.

The light changed and we moved forward and I looked at the road ahead.

—Hey, hey. Hey, where are we going?

—Sherman Oaks.

I took my feet off the dash and pointed at the road.

—But why are we going this way?

—Because it's fastest. Why do you care?

—No, Highland to the 101 is faster.

—No it's not. Not where we're headed.

—Here, turn here!

He kept going straight.

—Fuck, Po Sin, you needed to turn there.

He crumpled the empty Cheetos bag and dropped it in the grocery sack.

—Chill out, Web, this is the way to go. What's your fucking problem?

—Nothing. I just think my way is faster.

He pulled a tube of Pringles from the sack.

—Well you're wrong. Laurel Canyon is the way to go.

I didn't say anything, just put another mark down on the tally sheet, one more point scored by God in our ongoing game of *Who's the Bigger Dick*.

And we twisted up through the canyon of my childhood, passing the curve, the decisive landmark in Chev's life, me fingering the hundred-dollar bills in my pocket.

Casa Vega is dark as hell.

I'm only guessing about that, mind you, but I'm pretty certain that combination of blackness, dimly illuminated by red glass-filtered candlelight, is the precise effect that would really go in Hades.

Except I doubt they have nachos and margaritas there.

We felt our way past the bar and into the dining room, Po Sin apparently guided by second sight, or an interior compass that always reads true to hot ceramic platters heaped with chili relleno. At the back, under one of the nicer bullfighters on black velvet I've come across, we found Gabe in a red leather booth, his black jacket on against the blasting AC, tie knotted, sunglasses on his face.

We slipped into the booth and he gestured at the food.

—I ordered. ·

Po Sin grabbed a fork and started digging into a beef-stuffed bell pepper covered in melted cheese.

—Thanks.

Gabe looked at me.

—Eat something. It's good.

I pointed at my face.

—Yeah, I'm sure it is, but aside from the fact that chewing sounds like a bad idea right now, I just don't like eating in an environment where I can't see my fork coming at my face. This crazy fear of stabbing myself in the eye.

Po Sin grabbed my plate and pulled it in front of him.

—Fine by me.

I took a chip from the basket on the table and tried nibbling the corner and the salt got in the cut inside my mouth and I winced and picked up one of the margaritas Gabe had got for us and took a big swallow, but I didn't see the salt all over the rim because it was so fucking dark and that really hurt like a son of a bitch.

—Son of a bitch!

Gabe pushed a water glass my way.

—Sorry about that. Didn't know if you liked them with or without.

I filled my mouth with cold water and swished it around, and that hurt, too.

—Crap.

I looked at Po Sin as he mopped his first plate with a tortilla.

—So look, man, I don't want to be ungrateful for the dinner I can't eat or anything, but are we at the part where I get to know what the fuck, or what?

He scooped guacamole onto a chip.

—Yeah, we're there. We're there.

He ate the chip. And then a couple more. Gabe sat behind his sunglasses.

I slapped the table.

—So what the fuck then? What's the deal? What the hell is the guild? Whatwhatwhat?

Po Sin wiped his lips with a red napkin.

—Aftershock.

—Huh?

—Aftershock is the name of another trauma cleaner. They have a lot of contracts, mostly on the west side. Hotels, office buildings, property management. And they get most of the law enforcement referrals over there. Cops, sheriff's deputies, they're at the scene of a violent crime, someone asks them, *How do I clean this up? My baby Huey, my little boy was shot here, how do I clean it up?* Baby Huey, mind you, is six and a half feet and over three hundred pounds and he's bled all over the house after getting shot on the porch by the guy who used to be his best friend before one of them fucked the other one's baby mama or some such crap. So the law officer suggests a reliable trauma cleaner who will come in and take care of the situation.

I found a paper-wrapped straw on the table and unpeeled it.

—And he gets a bribe for doing it.

Po Sin waved a finger in the air.

—It's not a bribe. It's a referral fee.

—It's illegal as hell.

—It is that, but it is not a bribe.

I dipped the straw in my margarita and took a sip.

—And the guild?

He lined up the second plate of chili relleno.

—The guild is a racket. Guy who owns Aftershock, Morton, is trying to get all the cleaners to join a guild. Guild will distribute jobs and contracts. Set prices. Broker health coverage, that kind of shit. The more cleaners he can get to sign on, the more pressure he can put on the remaining independents. They don't join, they're gonna have to find a way to live off the scraps of jobs that don't go through the guild.

—And you don't want to join an organization that will help to set the market in your favor and allow you to pool resources because?

He licked his fork clean and set it in the middle of his equally clean plate.

—Because it's a scam, Web. Because the work won't be distributed throughout the guild equally. Because it's set up so that Morton is the president and administrator of the guild, which, seeing as he owns Aftershock, is a rather large conflict of interest. Because the jobs come in and he assigns two out of every three to his own fucking company. So, what, I join and give the guild access to my contracts and contacts, my 7-Eleven gig, my Hyatt contract, my Amtrak deal, all my public housing call-lists, I hand that all to the guild and then what? Fucking Morton takes the sweetest plums for himself and I have to wait and get some shit call to clean up in front of a gas station where a dog got hit by some old lady who couldn't see over the steering wheel.

He propped an elbow on the table and jabbed a finger at me.

—Clean Team is my business. I created it. I built it. I made the contacts and sweated the contracts. Someone calls me, they know what they're getting. Twenty-four hours a day that goddamn phone is on. Someone calls, they have trouble, they're in pain, someone they love has died messy and they are traumatized, I pick up that phone any hour of the day or night. I talk to them civil and gentle. I come as soon as I can. I tell them straight what is involved and what it will cost. The job is harder, takes longer than I thought, costs me more than I estimated, that's my problem, I eat the loss. That's my reputation. Doing the job the way it should be done, that's all I do. And that is worth something.

He leaned in, the tabletop tilting slightly under his weight. I remained very still, having, not for the first time, a sudden awareness of his crushing bulk.

—And I don't give that to anyone. What is in my house is mine. Who is in my house I take care of. My name, my reputation, those are in my house, those are for the well-being of my family. And I will not have my house fucked with.

He inhaled through his nose, a long wheeze, and leaned back into the depths of the booth.

—Especially not by an asshole like Morton.

I poked my straw into the melting ice at the bottom of my margarita glass.

—OK, then can you advise me as to how you will be making allowances to ensure I won't be getting beaten again? Because a police complaint is sounding like a pretty good strategy to me.

Po Sin looked at Gabe. Gabe looked at something, but I don't know what, all I could see was darkness and tiny red flames reflected in his glasses.

Po Sin picked up his margarita and drained half of it.

—The thing you have to remember here, Web, this isn't what you'd call a heavily regulated industry. They set the bar pretty low. Two hundred bucks, proof of a fixed address, and a contract with a licensed hazardous waste disposal company is all you need to be a certified trauma cleaner.

My eyebrows went up.

—Bullshit.

—No bullshit at all. You got employees, you have to pass an OSHA class, but that's it. So, see, you get a mixed bag of types drawn to the trade. At worst, mostly, you get people who are just fucking incompetent and lazy. They give the trade a bad name, but they also go out of business pretty fast. But there is a higher class of worst-case scenario, because some folks are just plain crooked as hell. Whether that means overbilling or maybe cutting corners on a job, whatever. Kind of stuff that Deputy Mercer was talking about with Aftershock. Worser case, you get some straight-up thieves. Go into a house, take advantage of being there while the family is staying in a motel because they don't want to look at the bloodstain that used to be daddy, and they clean it out. Family says, *Where's the TV, where's the stereo, where's my stamp collection?* These guys say, *Oh, that stuff, it was all contaminated, had to be disposed.* Contaminated? Shit was on the second floor at the back of a house where daddy did himself in the downstairs bathroom. Or maybe your aunt dies, chokes on her chocolate-covered cherries, lays there for a week with her Pekinese so hungry it takes a few nibbles. These guys come in, they do a great job with the cleaning, you're happy as hell with the deal. Two months later, new charges start showing up on auntie's credit cards. Stuff like that, we'd like it to stop. But we'd also like it not to have too bright a light shined upon it. Those kind of stories get too much coverage, that's bad for everyone's business.

I scooped some ice from my glass and put it in the middle of one of the red napkins and folded the material around it and pressed it to the knot on my forehead.

—Yeah, OK, no cops. So I'm still waiting for the part where you guys stop trading paint bombs and I don't have to be freaked about this shit happening to me again.

Gabe's phone beeped once. He took it from the clip on his belt, looked at the face, put it back on his belt and nodded at Po Sin.

Po Sin rubbed his nose.

—OK, you've got a handle on that first part. And yeah, there's also been some intimidation happening. Vandalization. Like the paint on the van. Also, job calls come in, you show up at the address and what do you find? Find a vacant lot, find a Chinese caterer where there's supposed to be a private residence. Don't have to think hard to figure who made the call, who's wasting your time and effort. Shit goes back and forth for a few months now. Some tit for tat. The guild trying to show us who's boss. Us showing them we don't work for no one. But you getting beat on, that was new. That was an escalation.

—Oh, lucky fucking me, breaking new ground.

He raised his hand and a waiter materialized from the gloom and placed a check on the table.

—I'm guessing that was my prick nephew at work.

I took the ice from my forehead.

—You're guessing? Man, I already told you it was him.

He placed some money on the check.

—I'm saying that was probably his own thing. Like he was pissed about being fired, went running to Aftershock. I know Morton, he was more than happy to hire the punk. See what kind of dirt he can dig up on how we go about our business. Maybe find out we cut some corner he can go to the Better Business Bureau about. Fortunately, the kid knows fuckall. But he probably took it personal you were working his old job. Probably decided he'd show his value to his new employer by going the extra yard.

He took his glasses off and rubbed his face up and down.

—So now we have to sort it out, make sure things don't get out of hand.

—Yes, yes, do that, sort it out before it gets out of hand, before, I don't know, before someone gets beaten up or something.

He put his glasses back on.

—You know, Web, you don't want to be involved in any of this, you don't have to be. It's as easy as saying you're done with the job.

I took a chip from the basket and broke it in half.

—I know.

He took one of his empty plates by the rim and rotated it a few degrees, back and forth.

—So are you? Done with it?

I thought about that; not liking it much when someone pounds on me, I thought about it pretty hard. I thought about chilling out, like I had been for a year. I thought about hanging at the apartment. Sleeping. A lot. I thought about the slender thread dangling my friendship with Chev. And what would happen when it broke. And how much strain I'd already put on it.

I thought about the things I'd thought about most that last year, and how little I'd thought about them the last couple days when I'd actually had something to do.

I crushed the chip and watched the crumbs fall into the basket.

—No, I'm not done with it.

He pushed the table away, making room to rise.

—So let's go then.

I got up and trailed them to the door.

—Where are we going?

Gabe opened the door on the relative brightness of Ventura Boulevard at night. Po Sin went out and passed his parking ticket to the valet.

—We're going to a sit-down with Morton and his Aftershock captains. Make sure we all understand there's limits here. Things we can't be doing without causing trouble for everyone.

I waved my hand.

—I don't want to meet those assholes. I sure as shit don't want to see Dingbang.

The valet drove up in the van and Po Sin slipped him a couple bucks.

—Not to worry, you're not invited.

—OK, so who's taking me home?

He stood aside from the van and gestured at the open door.

—You're not going home, you're going to my shop.

—What? I thought you said I could clean it tomorrow.

—I did. You can. Or you can start tonight. I just need you there.

The valet parked Gabe's Cruiser behind the van and Gabe got behind the wheel.

Po Sin held up a finger to him and looked at me.

—Dingbang has keys to the shop.

—So let *him* clean it tonight.

—Web, Dingbang has keys to the shop and I haven't had the locks changed yet.

It took a second. I like to think I'm smart, but still it took a second. Then I got it.

—Fuck that!

He ran a knuckle over his moustache.

—Listen. Listen up here. We're gonna go talk to these guys. Have a couple beers at a place not far from here. It's nothing. It's exactly what they say it is. A negotiation to make sure no one gets carried away. But Gabe, he's a little more cautious than I am, a little less trusting, and he thinks they could use this as a way to be sure the shop is empty. Go in there and mess shit up.

—I know, I get it. That's why I said fuck that.

—It's not gonna happen. OK? All you do is go in, turn on all the lights and hang out. Clean if you want, or watch the TV in the office. Dick around on the computer. Nothing is going to happen.

—Then I don't have to be there.

He looked over at Gabe, back at me.

—I know, you're right, but it will give Gabe a little peace of mind. And one of the things I pay him for is so he has peace of mind. Because when he has peace of mind, I know everything is cool with everything. Make sense?

I shrugged.

—Sure, makes sense. I'm still not gonna sit there and wait for Dingbang to show and kick my ass again.

—Dingbang will be at the sit-down. To be disciplined. That was part of the deal. And even if someone comes by, the second they see the lights on, see someone in there, they'll take off. No one is looking to hurt anyone. What happened to you was the exception.

—Maaaaan. Crap.

He took me by the elbow.

—Web, this isn't a regular job. This is not nine to five. We clean blood and brains. We scrub shit. We vacuum maggot shells. We inhale gas from rotting corpses. This is not a regular job. And you will rarely be asked to do regular shit if you hang around. Sitting watch on the shop for the night, that's about as normal as it gets. Make sense?

I looked at Gabe, waiting to roll. I looked at the valet, waiting for us to get the fuck out of the way so he could bring the next car around. I looked at Po Sin, waiting for me to do or be something I didn't quite get.

I nodded.

—Makes sense.

He let go of my elbow.

—Then get in the van and get over there.

I got in the van.

—Web!

I looked out the window, he stood in the open passenger door of the Cruiser.

—Anything *does* happen, call nine one one.

I shook my head.

—Yeah, that I can manage.

He waved and got in the car. Gabe nodded at me through the windshield, and tossed me a slight salute.

The man paid to have peace of mind.

Where do I get that fucking job?

NO WOMAN'S TOOL

North of Ventura Boulevard, on a street off Burbank Boulevard near the 170 on the edge of North Hollywood, there's a strip of light industrial zoning. Cinder-block buildings that work sheet metal, rent construction equipment, rebuild tractor motors, salvage copper wiring from scavenged conduit, or simply seem to provide nothing but a center point around which to wrap chain link and concertina wire for large barking dogs to patrol without cease. Beat-to-hell late-model pickups, the same ones seen circling West Hollywood loaded with leaf blowers and weed whackers on weekday mornings, line the curbs. Telephone poles drop power lines to the corrugated roofs of the buildings.

In the middle of this glory I perched on a workbench and stared at a row of three coffin freezers stuffed full of rags, bits of bedding, carpet, sofa cushions, paper towels, and all the other debris soaked in every effluvium of the human body that gets removed from trauma scenes. Biohazardous material awaiting transfer to Saniwaste, then to be trucked to Utah, where such things are burned en masse.

Or so I read in the Saniwaste brochure I'd found on a rack in the office. It was that or the back issues of *Entertainment Weekly* in the john. Is it a shock the brochures won out?

I slid off the edge of the bench and walked around. I poked at a machine that, according to another brochure, recycled formalin. I wondered what they did with the specimens they removed from the formalin before they processed it. The eyeballs, biopsy tissues, amputations, perforated intestine and whatever that had been preserved in jars of the stuff, the material the brochure referred to as *pathology*. I wandered to the window and looked across the street at one of the large dogs patrolling its patch of asphalt. Well, that would be one way of getting rid of the stuff. But they probably ship it to Utah with the rest of the waste.

I went back in the office and turned the TV on and flipped a couple channels and turned it off. I moved the mouse around on the computer, thought about looking at some porn, imagined the implications of jerking off in that particular environment, and discarded the idea. All I needed was another disturbing mental image running around my brain banging at the walls.

Thinking about disturbing mental images made me think about disturbing mental images.

That sucked.

I sat on the edge of the twin bed that was parked in the corner of the office doing duty as a cot. A regular cot being, one assumes, out of the question for Po Sin's needs. I looked at the clock. It was just after midnight. I tried to remember the last time I'd been up that late. Crap, I tried to remember the last time I'd been up past nine PM. It'd been awhile.

It's not like it's a mystery or anything, all the sleep.

Sleeping was just easier than being awake.

So why fight it?

I curled up and stopped fighting. A daily ritual of the last year. Giving up.

Hello, you've reached Clean Team. We're currently out of the office on a job. If you have an emergency we can help you with, please call 1-888-256-8326. That's 1-888-CLN-TEAM. We'll be there for you.

Beeeeeep.

—Um, hi, this is, uh, this is Soledad Nye. The woman in Malibu. You cleaned my dad's mess? I mean, oh fuck, that was horrible. You cleaned the house. Anyway. I was hoping I could get in touch with one of your employees. Web. I wanted to talk to him about . . . anyway. My number, well, he should call me on my cell. The number. Hang on.

I didn't quite kill myself when I jerked out of sleep and slammed my already damaged head into the shelf that hung too low over the bed, but I came close enough that I had to crawl across the floor to answer the phone on the office desk.

—Hello? Hello? Crap! Crap!

—Uh, Web?

—Yeah, yeah, it's me. Oh fucking crap! Jesus.

—Are you OK?

—Yeah, I just kind of, crap, banged my head really hard.

I sat on the floor, back against the side of the desk, phone to my ear, hand clapped over the brand-new lump rising from my head.

—Do you need some ice?

—Sure, yeah, that would be great.

There was some silence.

She cleared her throat.

—Web, you know I'm not there to actually get you the ice, right?

I blinked my eyes a few times, tried to bring the face of the liquid crystal clock on the wall into focus.

—Yeah, I know that. I was being funny.

—Or not.

—Yes, well, being not funny is more my forte.

—I noticed.

The clock straightened out for me. 12:32 AM.

—Yes, it's good of you to call my place of work to leave a message that, I can only assume, would have been meant to make clear my lack of humorousness. I'm flattered by the attention. Is there anything else I can do for you now that you have not laughed at me.

—Oh, I've laughed at you.

I took my hand from my head and looked at it. No blood. What luck.

—*At* me. Just not *with* me.

—You never know, stranger things have happened.

—Indeed.

I sat there and held the phone. She, I imagine, did the same. I have, I also imagine, less patience than she. Less patience, it's safe to say, than most normal people. Therefore, I cracked first.

—So, Soledad.

Note that the first time I spoke her name out loud I did it without stuttering or squeaking into a register higher than Tiny Tim's. A memory I treasure with some pride. A lesser man would have embarrassed himself with some verbal tic. Not I.

—So, Soledad. Why the fuck are you calling?

—Um, right. Well, I'd like to say I'm calling to ask if you want to go grab a coffee or something traditionally ambiguous and noncommittal.

Observe how I remain aloof and calm.

—But that's not the case?

—Nooo.

—The case is?

—The case is. I need a favor.

A favor? She's in need? And yet, not a tremor in my voice.

—The favor is?

—The favor is, well, I need something cleaned.

But of course. Was there ever any doubt. My janitorial expertise is re-quired. L.L. would be so proud.

But I'm no woman's flunky.

—What needs to be cleaned, when?

—A room. Now.

I looked at the clock again. *12:35 AM. Clean a room? At 12:35 AM. Is she out of her fucking mind? Does she think I'm an absolute tool?*

—Where are you?

Where she was, of course, was that motel. What was in the room, of course, was that blood. Who was with her, of course, was the guy trying to out-asshole me.

A title I was ready to relinquish in light of the butterfly knife he flashed at me.

If that all rings a bell.

HOW BREATHING WORKS

The guy with the fauxhawk showed me his blade, a slight crust of dry blood gummed at the hilt.

—Say that again? Say it. About to go Bruce Lee on your ass here, you keep talking about my moms.

I put my back to the door and shifted the carrier of cleaning gear so that I held it in front of me.

—Hey, no, all done, I'm not saying anything.

He took a step, twirled the knife.

—I fucking thought not, asshole.

—Did it hurt?

He stopped walking, the knife stopped twirling.

—What?

I spoke very slowly.

—When. You. Thought. Did it hurt? Like because you're not good at it, I mean.

He slammed his forearm across my throat, pinning me to the door, the point of the knife poking my cheek.

—Asshole! I said shut the fuck up! I said it was a wrap!

I thought about bringing up the carrier and shoving it into his gut, but the last time I'd fought anyone other than Chev was in junior high. And that was scrawny Dillard Hayes who'd made some lame joke about Chev not having a mom and I'd gone whacko about it. And I got the shit kicked out of me. And Dillard didn't have a knife.

So I tried diplomacy instead.

—No, you didn't actually tell me to *shut the fuck up*. And you certainly didn't say anything as lame as—GAH!

No, *he* didn't say GAH! *I* said GAH! Or, rather, I kind of barked GAH when he drove his knee into what was meant to be my balls, but was actually the carrier, which then hit my balls.

—GAH! GAH!

He did it twice more. If that didn't communicate.

The bathroom door swung open and Soledad came out toweling her hands dry.

—Jaime!

This seemingly directed at the fauxhawk dude about to put his knee on the money for the fourth time.

He let go of me and turned.

—What! What!

I dropped to the floor and tried to figure out how breathing worked.

Soledad came and kneeled next to me.

—What the hell, Jaime?

Jaime waved his knife.

—He was being an asshole, just like you said he would be!

She put a hand on the side of my face.

—I said he might *act like an asshole* and you needed to be chill.

He pointed the knife at me.

—Why do I have to be chill when he's being the asshole?

She shook her head, looked at me, her face all but hid in the long curls of hair falling around it.

—You OK?

I squirted more tears and kept my hands jammed in my crotch by way of an answer.

Jaime came and leaned over her and looked down at me.

—Besides, he deserved it for being an asshole at your house today.

She looked up at him.

—He wasn't. Fuck, Jaime, he was trying to make me laugh.

He raised his hands over his head.

—See! That's sick, man. Your dad offs himself, blows his fucking brains all over, and this asshole tries to make it funny? That's sick shit.

She stared at him, shook her head.

He raised his shoulders.

—What? What did I say? He's the one made jokes about your dad eating a bullet. Why'm I getting bitch looks?

She looked at the floor.

—Just shut up. Shut up and have a drink.

—What'd I do?

She put fingertips to her forehead.

—Please, Jaime. Just. Chill and have a drink. Please.

He reversed the gesture with his wrist and thumb, folding the knife and tucking it back in its sheath.

—Fine. Whatever. Just want people to remember, this whole production,

it's my deal. We got a schedule to keep to here and I don't like falling behind.

He walked to the room's lone chair, almonds popping under the heels of
his chrome-studded ankle boots, took a seat, and picked up a white plastic shopping bag from the floor.

—So you just get the asshole up to speed and on set. I want to roll this
thing and wrap.

He reached in the bag and pulled out an airline bottle of Malibu rum.

—Incidentals keep popping up and throwing my budget to shit.

I pointed at him.

—Let me guess, you're an actor, but what you really want to do is direct?

He drained the bottle and threw it across the room and it bounced off
my forehead.

—Fuck you, asshole, I'm a fucking producer.

Soledad closed her eyes, shook her head, opened her eyes, and looked
at me.

—Web, meet my brother Jaime.

—It's not as bad as it looks.

I sat on the closed lid of the toilet, the plastic bag of ice she got from the
machine by the motel office resting between my thighs.

—See, the funny thing about that statement is the fact that it looks so very
very bad, that there is ample room for it to be not as bad as it *looks* and still
be chronically fucked up.

She took the wet hand towel from my forehead.

—I know. Still. It's not as bad as it looks.

I looked at the blood on the towel in her hand.

—Well then, that explains all the relief pouring over me at this moment.

She bent and peered at the gash in my forehead, reopened when Jaime
kneed me and I bit the floor.

—This should be stitched up. Want me to take a crack at it?

—What? No. What the hell with people who don't have any medical training at all wanting to stitch my tender flesh?

She straightened and dabbed the towel on my head again.

—I don't know. Just something I always kind of wanted to try.

—Stitching up an open wound?

—Yeah. Weird, huh?

I didn't bother with an answer, the weirdness of such a desire going without saying. The sexiness of it not being something I wanted to get into. As it would suggest too much about my own weirdness. A quality already on abundant display in my current mode of employment. Also by the fact that I was sitting in a motel bathroom at one thirty in the morning with a bag of ice in my bruised crotch and a beautiful and bookish and emotionally complicated young woman tending to my hurts while her brother got tanked in the adjoining blood-splattered room.

Instead, I got straight to the most important matter at hand.

—You smell great.

She took the towel away again.

—It must be the rose petals I've been bathing in.

I inhaled.

—Could be.

She tossed the towel in the sink.

—Or the deodorant I've been spraying on myself to cover the fact that I haven't bathed since my dad died two days ago.

I nodded.

—So I am kind of an asshole, huh?

She boosted herself on the sink and dangled her feet.

—You do have some moments of impropriety.

I took the ice bag from my nut bag and touched my numbed genitals.

—Yeah, certain things bring it out in me.

She picked up a pack of cigarettes sitting by the basin and put one between her lips.

—Like having the future generations of your family name put at risk?

I dropped the ice bag in the tub.

—Like being asked to an apparent murder scene to clean it up.

She struck a match and placed the flame to the end of the cigarette.

—Oh, that.

She shook the match out and let it fall to the floor.

—Jaime didn't actually kill anyone.

She blew some smoke.

—He just cut him up a little.

I rose from the can, testing my ability to move with a dangling pendulum of agony between my legs.

—Oh, is that all? Well then, let's get to work.

—He was being an asshole, asshole.

—One assumes.

—What?

I took my head from under the bed, where I was shining a flashlight looking for stray blood, and looked at Jaime.

—One assumes he was an asshole. Otherwise, one assumes, you would not have *cut him up a little.*

I looked at Soledad, standing by the open door of the bathroom, arms crossed, a cigarette she only occasionally bothered to drag from between the fingers of her left hand.

—That was the phrase, was it not? *He just cut him up a little.*

She looked from the floor.

—Yeah, that was it.

Jaime waved the latest in a long line of Malibu nips.

—*A little?* I just about did a *Silence of the Lambs* on him. Just about peeled him raw.

I looked again at Soledad.

She shook her head.

Based on the amount of blood I'd seen at her house, and how much less there was here, I was inclined to think he was full of it. But thinking isn't knowing. Is it?

So, not knowing which of them to believe, I went back to work.

I'd done as I saw Po Sin and Gabe do at the Malibu house, started at the top and worked my way down. Like cleaning a dirty window. There hadn't been anything on the ceiling, but along one wall next to the bed there was a nice spackling of blood that rose nearly to the top. I'd worked my way down it, spraying with a bottle full of Microban and sopping it up with paper towels that I dropped in the room's waste basket. To be disposed of later.

Jaime narrated as I worked.

—See, if he'd just come in here and conducted business in a responsible manner, I wouldn't have had to cut him. I mean, I understand that in this business contingencies sometimes arise without having been accounted for, but it's not the exclusive burden of the producer to absorb those costs. The deal starts going all *Waterworld,* I don't see where I should be on the hook for the overages. He got all *the situation has changed.* Shit like that. I told him, said, *Dude, I'm working this deal on a short schedule with, like, no budget at all. So maybe you should get out of my fucking face before I fucking cut your ass.* He didn't listen. All that blood up there, that's where he freaked out, started waving his arms around after I'd cut his hand. He'd stayed still he wouldn't have got blood on my new jeans and I would have left it at that. As it was, I had to stick him to make him sit down and shut up. Gave him a poke in the shoulder and he settled down. Wadded up those sheets and got them over the hole to stop the bleeding.

By that point in the conversation I'd shot about my hundredth look at Soledad, all of them saying pretty much the same thing: *What is the nature of his birth defect, and do you have the same one?*

Her looks in reply clearly indicating: *I know, I know, just please don't provoke him because I don't want to fetch any more ice for your swollen testicles.*

Still unsure if Jaime was a congenital moron or just your average drunk fucking idiot infected by a particularly nasty form of the Hollywood Virus, I was working my way down the wall, deliriously happy that the blood hadn't had time to seep through the wallpaper, as he drew his tale to a close.

—Asshole wanted to take the sheet with him. Fuckin' believe that? Told him, *No way, man, I'm on the hook for this room. Those sheets end up on my bill if they go missing. That's not an expense I'm gonna carry.* Asshole.

That detail bringing me up to where I was looking under the bed, finding nothing worse than more almonds.

Jaime pointed at the sheets.

—Way I figure it, some bleach'll get those spic an' span. 'Course, I'm not much when it comes to cleaning, doing laundry, whatever, but I knew Sol would be able to help.

He smiled at his sister.

—She's always good for lending a hand. Any wonder I got pissed when she told me some asshole'd been messing with her today of all days? Then she's gonna call that asshole to help us out over here? I mean, what the fuck, right?

He pointed at her.

—Above-line expenditures kill a production, Sol.

She looked at the long ash on the end of her cigarette, tipped it and watched it fall.

—I'm just trying to help, Jaime. I can leave at any time.

—Aw, don't be like that. Get all bitch on me.

—A bloody hotel room's not the same as when you dropped the cookie jar. Something happens to that guy you cut, you want this room to be *more* than spic and span.

—Nothin's gonna happen to him. He was fine. I just didn't want to pay for, you know, room damages and shit.

She stared at the tiny coal at the end of her nearly dead smoke.

—Fine. Whatever you need. Taken care of. No problem.

—Shit, Sol. C'mon.

I got to my feet.

—Well, I don't think the room's gonna pass any kind of close scrutiny by a team of crack experts with ultraviolet lamps, but it's as clean as I can make it.

And it was. Walls and furniture gleaming in the lamplight. The only signs remaining to tell that the carpet had been bloodied were patches where the original color showed brighter from my scrubbing. The offending bedding stuffed in the wastebasket with the paper towels.

A job well done.

A potentially very criminal job, well done.

Details, details, details.

Jaime lurched up from his chair, scattering the litter of tiny bottles at his feet, and toed the wastebasket.

—So all you gotta do is wash those out an' you can get the fuck out of here.

I peeled the rubber gloves from my hand and dropped them on top of the stained sheets.

—Jaime, my man, I don't know how to tell you this, and I don't much want to, but I'm afraid you're going to have to eat the deposit on the sheets.

He watched me as I packed the cleaning gear back into the carrier.

—Fuck is that supposed to mean?

I wedged a pack of disposable paint scrapers into the carrier.

—It means that shit is not coming out.

—Little bleach. Fuck do you know?

I pointed at the sheets.

—I had a girlfriend once, had the heaviest periods you ever saw. Dated the girl for over a year, and I threw away enough sheets in that year to know a lost cause when I see one. Those are dead soldiers.

Soledad came over.

—Can you get rid of them for us?

I nodded.

—Yeah, I can get rid of them. I can do that.

She nodded.

—Thanks.

I bent to pick up the wastebasket and Jaime slapped my hand away.

—Fuckin' way, man. Sheets stay here.

I looked at the clock. Almost four. My eyes ached. My head and my mouth throbbed. I don't want to talk about how I felt below the waist. Suffice to say, I was really looking forward to lying down.

I picked up the carrier.

—OK by me, the sheets stay here.

I started for the door and heard his knife snap open behind me.

—Fuckin' freeze, asshole. No one leaves till these sheets are clean and this location is wrapped.

I turned and looked at him, swaying drunk, knife in hand.

I set the carrier on the dresser, between the TV and the lamp.

—Do you have a gun?

—What?

I looked at Soledad.

—Does he have a gun?

She tossed the stub of her smoke through the bathroom door in the direction of the tub.

—No.

Jaime twirled the knife, almost lost his grip on it, recovered, settled into a credible kung fu stance that I was pretty sure I recognized from Chev's copy of *Game of Death*.

—Don't need a gun.

I picked up the lamp, knocked the shade from it, yanked the plug from the wall, turned it upside down and showed him the pointed corners of the heavy wood base.

—And I have a lamp. If you take one more step toward me with that knife, I will hit you as hard as I can with this lamp. If you die, I will clean up the mess and leave. If you don't die, you can clean up your own blood. Asshole.

He looked at his sister.

—Sol?

She went to the closet and got a jacket and pulled it on.

—Don't look at me, Jaime.

He jabbed the knife at the air.

—Dude's threatening your brother. Gonna let that happen?

She walked to the wastebasket.

—Still willing to get rid of this stuff?

I hefted the lamp.

—Yeah. Sure.

She picked up the wastebasket.

—Can I come with?

—Sure.

She came to my side of the room and picked up the cleaning carrier.

—Let's go.

I followed her to the door, eyes on Jaime, the lamp held out.

—It won't cost much, they're crap sheets.

He dropped his arms to his sides, knife dangling from his fingers.

—Fuck do you know? Didn't even clean up the almonds, asshole. Fucking don't call me, I'll call you, fucker.

And I backed from the room, pausing to set the lamp inside the door before I closed it and ran for the van, taking the carrier from Soledad, she taking my hand, running along with me. Laughing.

ONLY A SMALL EARTHQUAKE

—How'd you get out here?

—Taxi.

   I took my eyes from the road.

—You took a taxi from Malibu to Carson?

   She kept her eyes closed.

—Yeah. They say when you've had a loss in the family, a sudden and un-expected loss, they say driving is a bad idea.

—Why's that?

—Because you're distracted, I guess. I mean, I don't know by what. Un-less they mean the memory of finding your dad with his head blown all over the room.

   She opened her eyes, shook her head, pinched her cheek.

—I think I'm going to have to learn not to be so flippant about that. I'm not handling it as well as I thought I could.

—So the taxi was probably a good call.

—Probably. Of course, the driver no doubt assumed I was coming down here for a late-night hookup with some rough trade I'd been chatting with online. But I'll live with the dim opinion of my cabby this once.

—We should all be so well adjusted.

   She waved a hand.

—Well, *well adjusted,* let's not get carried away.

   I smiled.

—Yeah, especially as your brother seems to have the market cornered on that particular quality.

—He's really just my half brother.

—Yeah, same mom, I got that.

   She stopped inspecting the glories advertised on the massive illumi-nated signs looming over the 405 North mega car lots of Torrance, and looked at me.

—How'd you get that?

   I hit my blinker and changed lanes to get out from behind a Pinto stuffed with the amassed possessions of its owner; boxes and bags heaped from the floorboards to the headliner and smashed against the windows, leaving just enough space for the driver, one of the rolling homeless of L.A. I glanced at him, talking endlessly to himself, as we passed.

I looked back at the road ahead.

—He kept saying *your dad*. I just assumed that meant you had different dads is all.

She looked back at the signs.

—Oooh, Detective Web at work. Did you suss out any more family secrets?

—Just that the black sheep of the family back there is also a fucking moron.

—Hardly a secret, that one.

—Yeah, he does rather wear it on his sleeve.

She began going through the pockets of her jacket, searching.

—He's actually kind of OK. Or he was, anyway. When we were kids. Just spoiled mostly. And starved for attention.

—Interesting combination.

She came up with a hair bungee from her pockets and began to pull her hair into a ponytail.

—Well, my mom is an interesting woman with strange abilities. Especially when it comes to screwing with her kids' heads.

I adjusted the shoulder strap of my seatbelt where it snugged too tight across my neck.

—Yeah, moms are tricky that way.

She got her hair where she wanted it, a couple wild curls poking loose, and settled back into her seat.

—Our mom is a little more than tricky. Her special talent with Jaime was to give him anything and everything he asked for. This being the easiest way she knew to keep him occupied, and keep her from having to actually deal with him as, I don't know, a human being. Jaime's response was to ask for more and more extravagant toys, trips, parties, whatever he thought would force her to deal with him, I guess.

—How'd that work out for him?

—Well, I didn't witness much of it, not wanting to be around her myself, but the way I put it together, the more he asked for, the more she worked to make the money to see he got it, the more he got, the more he asked for, and the more she worked . . . and so on.

—Kind of a perpetual motion machine of familial alienation, then?

She slid her eyes at me.

—That was clever.

I rubbed my eyes.

—Yeah, clever, that's me, always doing clever stuff. That's why I'm in this van at the moment with a load of someone else's bloody sheets and all.

She went in her pockets again and came out with a pair of big black plastic film star sunglasses.

—I said it was clever, not smart.

—True.

She took off her regular narrow black-framed glasses and slid the sunglasses on.

—Anyway, Mom just worked and worked to get Jaime what he wanted, which meant she was never around to look at him, which is what *she* wanted. Until he turned eighteen.

—Then what?

—She kicked him out. Of course. If behavioral scientists had designed a scenario meant to create an adult utterly unequipped to provide for themselves and emotionally cope with the world, they could not have done a better job than my mom did with Jaime. And, to make it more interesting, when she set him loose, she did it in Hollywood.

The lights of a jumbo jet cruised over the freeway on approach to LAX. Inglewood sprawled low and wild to the east, endless stucco blocks of small houses with barred windows and dead lawns.

—It's a tough little town, ain't it.

She shrugged.

—It's designed to fuck the weak is all.

—And how'd you avoid the mommy treatment?

She leaned forward and adjusted the heater.

—Dad divorced her when I was three. Seeing as she didn't want to have the responsibilities of actually raising kids, it wasn't much of a challenge for him to get custody. And by then I'd already started loathing her pretty well. I mean, Dad didn't have to run her down at all to make me not want to see her. Not that he would have done that. Still, holidays, occasional weekends, he'd pack me up and drive me over to the valley. It sucked, but it got better when I was five and she had Jaime. He was cute. And fun.

—Till he grew up and turned into a prick.

—Like I said, he had help.

—We all get help, that doesn't mean we all end up cutting guys up in motel rooms after a drug deal turns sour.

She fingered her sunglasses lower on her nose and gave me a look over the tops of the lenses.

—My, how very hard-boiled of you.

—I'm just saying.

She pushed the sunglasses back into place.

—I know what you're saying. And you're mostly right. He's definitely defective. But he's my brother. So I. You know.

—Sure.

—Anyway, it wasn't a drug deal.

—No? Stocks then? Commodities futures?

—I don't know. I mean, he does deal some stuff. Weed and ecstasy mostly. Works craft services and deals to the P.A.s and the extras. That knife, he was on set for a John Woo movie, one of the prop guys traded the knife for a few hits of X. He loves that knife. Anyway, whatever he's up to, it's not drugs. Jaime always gets into something crazy. Usually it's something having to do with movies. I don't think so this time. But movies is what it usually is. He's going to get the rights to some Hungarian sci-fi movie. He's going to manage the movie career of a Balinese pop star who's the Madonna of Indonesia. He's going to negotiate U.S. distribution for a Canadian production company that specializes in remaking Paraguayan classics. That kind of thing. Movies. He got it from my mom.

I slid into the interchange lane for the 10 West, thinking about L.L. and the movie game, and what it does to people.

She pointed at the sign for the 10.

—Where are you going?

—Take the 10 out to the PCH and up to Malibu.

She sat up and reached toward the wheel.

—No, no, don't, just. Just go.

She grabbed the wheel and shoved it to the left, sending us veering in front of a barreling SUV.

I slapped her hand.

—Hey! Hey!

The SUV cut around us, horn sounding.

She took her hand from the wheel as the exit to the 10 slipped away behind us.

—Sorry.

She put her face in her hands.

—Sorry.

She took it out and looked at me.

—I don't want to go west right now. I don't want to go home. I want. Oh fuck.

Tears were leaking out from under the lenses of the sunglasses.

—Shit, Web. Shit. My dad.

I nodded.

—Yeah, no problem. *Shit.* I get it.

I stayed with the 405, looking ahead to where it would climb through the Santa Monicas and meet the 101 on the other side.

—I got a place to go.

She pushed her fingers up under her sunglasses and wiped her eyes.

—Thanks.

I drove, thinking about families. Not my favorite pastime, but one I seem incapable of avoiding. I glanced at her from time to time, black hair pulled back, light olive skin flushed, muscles of her long neck taut as she bent to lean her head against the window, the sky lightening beyond her above the rim of the San Gabriels. And all that shit.

I thought to distract her from her sadness, strike a chord of shared experience. You know, cheer a girl up.

—So. Your mom's in the biz? So's my dad. Or he was. Screenwriter. What's your mom do?

She rolled her head around, pointed the big lenses at me, rolled back against the glass.

—She was a porn star. So I guess we both have parents who were whores.

I drove some more. Choosing wisely, I think, not to talk anymore.

—I suppose it was naïve of me to think you were going to take me to your place and tuck me into your bed while you slept protectively on the floor, wasn't it?

I watched her as she flipped through Po Sin's binder of before-and-after photos from various job sites, sunglasses still over her eyes.

—I thought this might be more romantic.

She froze on a picture of a shotgun suicide, turned the page to a picture of the same room after it had been cleaned.

—You could play that game with these, you know: *What's the difference between the pictures?*

She flipped back and forth between the two shots, the one featuring glossy pink bits that looked almost like strange candy, and the one of a scrupulously clean livingroom stripped of odd bits and pieces. Pointing to where a sofa cushion had been removed, the shade from a lamp, a square cut from the carpet, a blank spot on the wall where a piece of needlepoint used to be.

She closed the binder.

—Looking in his bedroom. No mattress. This lap blanket he used to cover his feet with when he sat up at night working in bed. He'd sit on top of the covers in a robe and drape it over his bare feet, you know. That's gone. And he always, always had a handkerchief folded on the nightstand. That's not there. Just things, they tell you someone's gone. And they're not coming back.

She put the binder back in its place on the office desk and spun around a couple times in Po Sin's chair.

—So, Web.

I sat on the bed.

—So, Soledad.

She put her feet down and stopped spinning.

—Do we have to do it this way?

—Which is to say?

She got up, took off her jacket, draped it over the chair, and walked over to the bed, where I sat scooted into the corner of the room, my back against the wall.

—Which is to say, do we have to tease this out with all kinds of *will we or won't we?*

She put a hand to the wall and lifted one foot and unlaced her sneaker and kicked it off.

—I hate that shit.

She did the same with the other shoe.

—I mean.

She reached under the skirt of her dress, the same black knit knee-length she'd been wearing at the Malibu house, and pushed her black leggings down, stepping first on one toe to pull her foot free, and then on the other, kicking the leggings away, her light blue panties nestled inside them.

—I mean, can't we just fuck?

She took hold of the waist of her dress and peeled it over her head and dropped it, standing flat-chested and braless, naked except for her sun-glasses.

—Fuck and get it over with?

I could see part of a Quonset hut out the window behind her, a bit of sky turning blue, old-growth palm trees arching up from the streets, brown rocket trails detonating into green tufts. It was chilly in the office. Goose pimples on her stomach.

I quickly sorted and discarded several responses, none of them delicate enough for this circumstance; a wounded and emotionally vulnerable young woman naked and throwing herself at me in my place of employ.

Finally knowing what to say.

—So romance isn't dead after all?

She smiled, put her knees on the edge of the bed, edged close to me, reached out and poked the wound on my forehead.

—Don't look a gift horse in the mouth, Web.

I winced.

—I'm not looking at your mouth.

She took hold of my hoodie and pulled it over my head, not bothering to unzip it.

—Wise man.

I watched her hands as they undid the buttons down the front of my shirt.

—I don't know when Po Sin will be here.

She took me by the collar of my T and pulled me forward and pushed the Mobil shirt down my arms.

—I don't care.

I lifted my arms and let her pull the T off.

—And, you know, all joking aside, my balls still really hurt.

She tossed the T over her shoulder and it landed on top of her dress.

—I'll be gentle.

She reached for my belt.

So.

She wanted to fuck. And get it over with. Who was I to say no?

A very little later, while she was on top of me, not being gentle at all, the earth moved. It was only a small earthquake, but it made us both laugh.

And, finally, I reached up and took the sunglasses off her face, and I could see her eyes, so very red from all the crying.

And a little later after that, she had them back on.

—He hated my smoking.

I held the lit cigarette for her as she pulled her leggings up.

—He smoked like a chimney when I was a kid.

She picked up the Mobil shirt from the floor and put it on and took the smoke from me.

—Thanks.

She put it in her mouth and started buttoning the shirt.

—But he stopped and was one of those classic ex-smokers. A pain in the ass.

She found one of her shoes and sat back on the edge of the bed.

—I mean, I don't even smoke that much. And when I smoke at the house I only do it on the deck or in my room.

She put her right foot in the shoe and started lacing it up.

—Anyway, I was there, this was during a Christmas break when I was in college, a few years back, four or five. Before I graduated and didn't know what the hell to do with a degree in art history and moved back home.

She bent and looked for the other shoe.

—There it is.

She pulled it from beneath the bed and put it on.

—So I was at home, on break, and we'd stayed up together watching *It's a Wonderful Life* or something, and I'd been smoking a lot because we were having some Christmas cheer together. I was standing with the door to the deck open, blowing smoke outside. After he went to bed, I stayed up to watch something else. *White Christmas*? I don't know. But I cheated and snuck a cigarette inside. Didn't finish it though.

She turned, facing me, left foot tucked under her right thigh.

—And I was a little loaded so I forgot to put the ashtray back out on the deck. And in the morning.

She leaned and snagged her jacket from the back of the chair and reached into an inside pocket and came out with a small journal.

—In the morning I came down and found this.

She opened the journal and flipped some pages and pulled out and un-folded a deeply creased sheet of notepaper.

She handed it to me.

FROM THE DESK OF WESTIN NYE

WESTLINE FREIGHT FORWARDING AND TRADE

When I was smoking (in the 1970s) I learned that when returning to a par-
tially smoked cigarette, you should put it to your lips (before lighting it) and
blow your breath out and through it—thus removing most of the foul-
tasting residue that you would otherwise be drawing into your mouth on
your first "drag" after lighting up.

With love,
your father

I handed it back, and found my T on the floor and pulled it on.

—Did you crawl into a closet and bang your head against the wall?

She stood and went to the door to the bathroom.

—No. I laughed. He didn't mean it to be funny. Which made it funnier. Which was kind of his style.

She fiddled with one of the buttons on the old blue gas station shirt that hung to tops of her thighs.

—I keep thinking there's a good laugh in his suicide somewhere. But I haven't found it yet.

She ducked into the bathroom, the taps ran, she came out with her cigarette doused and pitched it in the overflowing wastebasket by the desk.

—I think I need to go.

—OK. Let me get my shit together and I'll give you a ride.

I started looking in the blankets for my jeans and underwear.

She shook her head.

—No. I want to walk a little.

I found my BVDs and pulled them on, taking particular care as I snugged them into place.

—Pretty long walk to Malibu.

She looked out the window, balled her dress tightly and stuffed it into one of the large outer pockets of her jacket.

—I can catch the bus in Sherman Oaks and over the hills and out to Santa Monica. The coast bus from there. I'm not, as you may have noticed, in a hurry to be home.

I sat with my jeans in my lap.

—Sure, but the bus sucks.

She shrugged.

—I like the bus. I like to watch the sides of the road.

I looked at the floor, trying to keep a lid on something that didn't seem to want to cooperate at that moment of exhaustion and postcoital confusion.

—I don't like buses.

—Don't like riding them?

That was a tricky question.

—No. I mean, yeah. I don't like riding them. But I also just kind of don't like them.

—Have you always felt this hostility toward public transportation?

—Not public transportation. I'm fine with light rail or trams. Subways. Just buses I don't like.

—Forever?

I thought about that. But I didn't need to, really, I knew it wasn't forever.

—Um, no, no, not forever. I used to ride them quite a bit.

—When you were a kid?

—No. I mean, yeah, but.

Words just kept occurring to me, kept finding ways to put themselves together. While I was trying to corral one bunch, another slipped out. These were the next ones.

—Yeah, come to think of it, it is kind of a new thing. Not liking buses. Hating them, really.

She took a step over.

—Web, you're killing me. Are you serious? Are you trying to cheer me up? Because I hate that. If you're making this up to cheer me up I will be so fucking pissed at you.

Again, I tried to get things under control, knowing where this conversation ended. Not wanting to go there. Ever again.

But things, they have a way of going out of your control sometimes. Have you noticed that?

And I kept talking.

—Yeah. Hell yeah. I mean, no. I mean, really, I can't stand the things. Make me crazy.

—Why?

She folded her arms.

—I want to know why. You better not just be trying to get me to hang around longer.

I laughed.

—Well, they're loud and they smell. They get in the way. And they're really kind of ugly.

She smiled.

I took this as encouragement and kept talking, something that's rarely gone well for me in my life.

—And they're haunted.

She raised her eyebrows.

I raised a hand.

—No, no. Really. This is so strange. I don't know. Just this thing. Kind of started. Something happened and I started not liking them.

She laughed. Sort of.

—Because they're haunted?

I rubbed the spot between my eyes and squinted.

—Yeah, OK. Um, let me think.

—You're lying. You're so trying to sucker me.

—No, I'm not.

—You totally are. You're trying to think of something funny to say. You are fucking with me and you are so busted.

I laughed again.

—No. It's just that it's complicated and I sometimes, I don't know, forget exactly how.

I looked up at the sky outside the window.

A piece of it snapped off and dropped and hit me on the head.

And it was all there again, the whole thing, back in my head, one picture, entire. No longer broken into the little fragments I liked to keep it scattered in. Fragments hidden on ghost buses cruising L.A. Freighters of lost things. But not of me.

I looked at Soledad, who'd just helped me to put it all together again.

And I thought, *How kind of her.*

—No, I got it! Yeah, huh, it's funny. You know. Because, it's not like I forgot. It's more like I think about it all the time. So I kind of forget it's there. Like white noise?

She tilted her head.

—Web?

—Yeah, funny thing. Totally fucked up, but funny in a distinctly *not* ha-ha way.

—Web. Hey.

—Weird how I had to think really hard to remember the . . . details? Details. Yeah.

—Are you OK?

—Yeah, I'm fine. So I was on this bus. I was teaching. I was a teacher before. Did I tell you that? I was. My dad always wanted me to be a teacher. Well, not always, but that's a long story. So I was a teacher. And I was on a bus. With my class. Fifth grade. Ten- and eleven-year-olds. Great age for kids, I think. Because they're really coming into their own as people, but the hormones haven't gone entirely berserk yet. They're mostly still kids. So my class and two other classes a little younger are on this bus. It's a field trip. Remember those?

—Sure.

—Yeah. This was cool. Did you grow up in L.A.? Cuz when you grow up in L.A., when I was a kid anyway, you always, sooner or later, you always go up to the Griffith Observatory. The planetarium. But it had been closed for renovations for like a year. Then it reopened. So we were going. I'd had to twist arms to make it happen. Field trips are a major production these days. So we were going. And we're riding in the bus. Lalalala. Kids talking, yelling, texting to the kid in the seat next to them. Kids in the back of the bus shoving each other and playing with toys they're not supposed to have because they start fights over them. I'm walking the aisle, talking to kids. Talking to this kid Tameka. Cute girl. She's pissed at one of her friends over this hat she's been wearing that no one else had, but now her friend is wearing the same hat and she doesn't understand how her friend could bite off her style like that. And we were talking about that. So then. Um. Crap. What happened then? Oh, yeah, man, how could I forget this part? So then, yeah, there's like a noise, like, like, like when you dent a soda can and pop it back out. But louder. There's a couple sounds like that. And someone screamed for the driver to stop. Crap, who was that? Oh, oh yeah, it was me. So I screamed for her to stop. And she did. And the kids. Some ran for the door. But I told them to get on the floor. Under their seats. And most of them did. Then I thought, *Crap, we should get out of here.* Or did I yell it? Anyway, I yelled at the driver to drive away. But she was on the floor, too. Aaaaand. There were sirens. And a helicopter. And it happened really fast. But pretty soon there were cops and they came on the bus and got the kids off. And they tried to get me off. But, you know, I really didn't want to leave Tameka behind? So they had to kind of, pry me loose from her. Embarrassing, kind of. And then, well, that was kind of it. Except that there was a real mess in there, in the bus. Man, I had stuff all over me. Don't know how I got those clothes clean. No, that's right, Chev threw them out. And, what happened was there was some kind of thing, some thing on the street between some guys who had a beef with each other, never found out about what. So, bullets were exchanged. Obviously some hit the bus. So. That's what hit Tameka. That's why it was such a mess in there. Aaaaanyway, that's why I guess I don't like buses. Funny, right? That I'd forget something like that? So thanks, you know, for pushing the point, really digging into me and getting me to stir all that up. Because, you know, I clearly haven't been doing enough to keep people at arm's distance and it's a good reminder to me to tell you to get the fuck out of here.

—Web? Web, are you OK?

I looked at her from under the bed where I'd crawled and curled into a ball.

—GETTHEFUCKOUT!

And she did. And I felt tired. So I went to sleep.

TO KEEP HIM FROM CRUSHING MY SPINE

—Motherfucker!

I opened my eyes and looked up at the extremely pissed off giant standing over me holding one edge of the bed off the ground and threatening to stomp on my head.

—Motherfucker, are you high?

I shook my head, looked around the sun-filled office.

—No. What? No. I don't even do drugs.

He hefted the bed.

—Get the hell out of there before I drop this thing.

I scrambled out and stood in my T and underwear, jeans clutched in my hands.

—Um.

Po Sin dropped the bed.

—Jesus, Web, what the hell?

I slid one leg into my jeans.

—No, I'm fine, I was just sleeping. I sleep a lot.

He shook his head.

—You sleep *a lot*? You sleep like the fucking dead, is what you do. I was yelling, running around yelling your name for five minutes. Saw you under the bed, I freaked out. *Oh, shit, Web's fucked up.* Almost had a heart attack. And I don't mean that figuratively.

He squinted at me.

—You sure you're not high?

I buttoned my fly and looked at him.

—Man, I smoked grass *once* when I was eleven and got so paranoid I thought the air was trying to kill me. Only time I ever got high. I hate drugs. I never do drugs.

He licked his lips.

—OK. Fine. Then help me with something here.

He walked to the outer door and swung it open and pointed at the empty parking spot out back.

—Help me and tell me where the fuck my van is.

I took a step toward the door.

—I. I. I.

He nodded.

—Yeah, and when you figure out the answer to that one, you can tell me this.

He unballed one huge fist and showed me the pair of blue panties in his palm.

—Who the fuck do these belong to and why are they in my office?

The thing about getting beat up twice, spending big chunks of time cleaning up other people's blood, seeing your dad for the first time in two years, getting in a fight with your best friend, and having sex with someone you think you might really like a lot and then totally going psycho on her, all in a twenty-four-hour period, is that it's likely to affect your judgment. And if your judgment is pretty much for shit to start with, that may result in some spectacularly lame lies.

I'm not saying it's cool or anything.

I'm just saying that when I proceeded to tell Po Sin exactly what had happened that night, the fact that I left out the part where I drove to Carson to clean a bloody motel room and then brought one of his clients back to his office and had sex with her, just didn't seem relevant. I mean, nothing happened to the office while I was away, man. So why bother him with the information that I'd, you know, gone and used his equipment to sterilize a crime scene? And the van was clearly stolen while I was *in* the office asleep. That would have happened even if I'd spent the whole night here. And as for telling him the girl who'd come over to keep me company on a long lonely night was Soledad, well, that just would have required I tell him the rest of the story. And I just explained why that didn't matter.

So I streamlined things to make it easier for everyone involved.

But I digress.

—Stop lying to me, Web.

—I? What? Lying to you? I would never.

He took his face from his hands.

—Before you say anything else and really fuck up our relationship, let me tell you something about modern technology.

—Uh. OK.

He leaned back in his chair.

—Modern technology is an amazing thing. It allows us to do amazing things. Go to the moon. Cure disease. Watch TV. It also allows us to communicate over vast distances.

He reaches for the phone.

—And check our messages remotely.

He pressed a button on the phone.

Um, hi, this is, uh, this is Soledad Nye. The woman in Malibu. You cleaned my dad's mess? I mean, oh fuck, that was horrible. You cleaned the house. Anyway. I was hoping I could get in touch with one of your employees. Web. I wanted to talk to him about . . . anyway. My number, well, he should call me on my cell. The number. Hang on. Hello? Hello? Crap! Crap!
Uh, Web?
Yeah, yeah, it's me. Oh fucking crap! Jesus.
Are you OK?
Beeeeeeeeeeeeeeep.

—Motherfucker!

—Didn't we already cover that?

Po Sin stopped hammering his desk and faced me.

—What?

—Nothing.

He put his hands on his knees and rose from his chair.

—Are you certain of that?

—Yeah.

He took a step.

—Because I'm just about positive I just heard the guy, the guy who had a female client, I expressly told him to stay away from, over here when he was on watch last night and played fuck games on the job till he passed out *under the bed* and my van was stolen, I think I just heard that guy make something like a joke. Am I mistaken? Because if I am *not* mistaken, I would take it very poorly.

—I.

The phone rang, cutting off whatever verbal strategy I might have mustered to keep him from crushing my spine.

Po Sin raised a finger.

—Hold that thought.

I wondered if he meant whatever I'd been about to say, or the thought that he was about to crush my spine. This leading to the sudden worry that perhaps he could read minds. Sleep deprivation, etc, having clouded my reasoning a bit.

Po Sin picked up the phone.

—Clean Team. What?

He looked at me, slitted his eyes.

—No. He is not.

He hung up the phone and pointed at it.

—Do you know what this is *not* for?

—Um, I'm sorry, the structure of the question got me a little confused.

He raised a finger.

—We did just talk about what a bad fucking idea it would be for you to be making jokes at this moment, didn't we?

—Yeah, yeah we did.

—OK.

He pointed at the phone again.

—So, do you know what this is *not* for?

I shook my head, assuming this was one of those rhetorical things that would allow Po Sin to make a point and lead, soon after, to him chilling out a bit. I was right about part of that assumption.

He opened his mouth and a small hurricane wind blew out.

—It is not for your fucking personal use, motherfucker!

He made a fist, raised it high, brought it down slowly, and rested it on top of my head.

—It is *not* for desperate young women to call you on, looking for comfort in the middle of the night, and it is *not* for your buddies to be calling on during business hours asking if you're around. Understood?

I tried to nod under the weight of his hand.

—Yeah. Totally. No personal calls.

He took his hand from my head.

—OK. Now. I, I'm a man. As evidence, I have a wife and a couple kids. I know all about screwing and how great it is. I also understand that when a chick calls you in the middle of the night and asks if she can come over, only a fucking corpse says no.

—Or a gay guy.

He made the fist again.

—Web!

—Right. My bad.

He relaxed the fist. Sort of.

—Now I'm not saying you're off the hook. But, you know, I get it.

He brought up both hands, cupped my face in them, from crown to chin.

—As long as you were here, Web. As long as you were here when the van was stolen, I can understand. But if you guys were down the street messing around at the Stardust Lounge, or making a run for condoms or something, if you were not here as you were supposed to be, that is a very different matter. Yes? You do understand? You were here?

OK, this part here, I won't lie, this is bad. You might want to look away and not acknowledge the fact that I did what I did.

God knows I don't.

I brought up my hands and covered his.

—Po Sin, Yes. I understand. And I was here when the van was stolen.

True, every word. And, in an odd case of transmutation, also one of the worst lies of my life.

He took his hands from my face.

—OK. OK. Now. I need to, I need to start formulating a response to this act of aggression from Aftershock. You. You need to make yourself very fucking useful right now.

I looked around, saw a broom, grabbed it, looked at him.

He nodded.

—Yes. Start with that.

I started sweeping.

Gabe came to the open office door.

—Where's the van?

Po Sin brought his leg back and lashed it at the wastebasket and garbage exploded over the office and the tin basket hit the cinder-block wall and folded in half.

—Motherfucker! Motherfucking Morton looked us in the eyes and told us he'd agree to a cease-fire and then had one of his fucking peons come over here and rip us off! You were right! You were right on the fucking money, Gabe. That motherfucker cannot be trusted.

The garbage floated down to the floor.

Gabe watched it.

—Not like I'm happy about being right.

Po Sin stood in the middle of the trash.

—We'll have to do something about it.

—OK. Tonight?

Po Sin took off his glasses and rubbed his eyes.

—Lei has her yoga class tonight. I need to watch the kids.

Gabe nodded.

—OK, but better if we take care of it right away.

And he looked at me.

And Po Sin looked at me.

And I stopped sweeping trash.

—What?

Po Sin slipped his glasses back on.

—Got any plans? A pressing date with your new girl, maybe?

I bent and picked up the wastebasket and looked at the shape it had been twisted into when Po Sin booted it. It occurred to me that it was probably in better shape than my prospects of ever seeing Soledad again after my epic spazmatic display.

—No, I don't think that's gonna be a regular thing.

—All free, then? Not intending on another sleep marathon?

—No. I guess not.

He spread his arms.

—Then it's no problem?

—Um, no? I mean, what?

—You can help Gabe out tonight.

—I can? Sure. I. To do?

Gabe tugged an earlobe.

—Nothing big. Just business communications.

I shook my head.

—I don't know, man. That sounds. I don't know.

Po Sin turned and looked out the open door and turned back and looked at me.

—Ahem.

I looked at the empty parking spot out there where his van wasn't parked and decided I should shut up and do as I was asked to do.

Gabe observed the silence for a moment, nodded his head.

—OK. So I'll pick you up tonight.

He turned to leave, turned back.

—Wear gloves.

And leave he did.

Po Sin walked through the door into the shop.

—Time to get your hands dirty, Web.

—Got a hug for Daddy?

Po Sin stuck out his index finger.

—Just a little one?

The twelve-year-old boy looked out from under his long bangs, raised a hand, extended his pinkie, and touched it to the tip of his father's finger.

Po Sin smiled.

—I love you.

The boy withdrew his finger and walked to a corner of the room and sat on the floor and wedged himself tight into the angle of the walls and put his backpack in his lap and squeezed it to his chest.

Po Sin pushed himself from his squat and looked at his wife in the doorway.

—What's the matter?

Lei came into the office, ruffling her spiky black hair.

—He lost a piece from his Bat Cave.

—Oh, Christ. At school? Please tell me it was at school.

She shook her head.

—Nope.

—Aw, shit.

She raised her hands.

—And I've already done what I can do about it.

—OK.

—You can take your best shot.

—OK.

—I'm just praying I can find some kind of mellow in yoga class and not fall asleep on my mat as soon as I get there.

—OK. OK.

She took a deep breath, exhaled.

—Sorry. Long one.

She looked at him and smiled.

—How about you, everything OK?

Po Sin scratched his moustache, waved a hand in the air over his head.

—Nothing's blowing up.

She pointed out the open door.

—Where's the van?

He glanced through the shop door at me where I was bleaching the slop sink, looked back at his wife.

—Gabe's out doing some pickups.

She looked where he had glanced, saw me, raised her eyebrows at Po Sin.

He pointed at me.

—Sorry. That's Web. Remember?

Her forehead creased, uncreased.

—Web. Yes, of course, I'm sorry.

She came through the door into the shop, hand held out.

—Nice to finally meet you.

I dropped my sponge in the sink and started to reach for her hand with one of mine, pulled up and stripped the thick rubber glove off.

—Hi. Nice to. Po Sin's said a lot about. Hi.

She took my sweaty hand; hers tiny and strong and cool.

—So he finally got you in here.

—Uh, yeah.

She kept my hand firmly in hers, looking up at me, smiling.

—He's been talking about it forever. Saying how he thinks you should be working.

Po Sin came to the door.

—Lei.

She waved her free hand over her shoulder.

—Shut up, Grandfather Elephant.

She touched the jade necklace that hung down over a loose orange cotton blouse.

—He'd just as soon no one knew he cares about anything, but he does. Of course.

—Lei!

—Ignore his bluster. He thinks I'm not minding my own business. How have you been? Are you feeling better? You're working here, you must be feeling better. Not spending all your time slacking at your friend's tattoo shop. Good, that's good for you.

—Jesus, Lei.

She tugged on my hand, pulled me a step closer, put a hand to her mouth for a stage whisper.

—I'm embarrassing him. Being overly personal with someone I've just met. He hates it.

—He has work to do, Lei.

Still holding my hand, she turned.

—*You* have work to do.

She tilted her head toward their son tucked in the corner, clutching his bag.

He slapped the back of his neck.

—I know, I know. Where is she?

—She's out in the car.

He started for the door.

—I'll get her. Just let Web do his work, OK? I don't pay him enough to get grilled by you.

He stepped out the door.

—Xing. Xing, over here. Now. Now. No, I will not carry you. Now, I said. No, you are perfectly capable of walking on your own two feet. Now. Now! Damn it.

He walked out of sight.

Lei turned back to me.

—I'm not a Hindu, Web, but I swear I must have done something in a previous life to deserve my daughter.

She nodded her head.

—I know, I know, it's my own fault, our own fault. She's ours after all. She didn't just appear out of thin air. We made love, we made a baby. One baby wasn't enough. We had to go back to the well for more. So we got what we deserved. And with all Yong's problems, beautiful boy that he is, she doesn't get all the attention she maybe deserves.

She leaned close.

—What she deserves is a good whack on the ass from time to time, but Po Sin won't allow it.

She leaned back.

—Of course, I'd be terrified to try it myself. Have you ever seen *Demon Seed*?

I nodded.

—Sure.

She tapped the tip of her nose.

—That's our Xing.

—But I *didn't* take it.

We both looked as Po Sin ducked through the door, Xing on his shoulders.

—Honey, don't lie.

—But I'm *not* lying.

He took her from his shoulders and stood her on his desk and looked her in the eyes.

—Xing, my little lovely apricot, no one likes a liar.

She stomped.

—But I'm *not* lying.

He put a finger to his lips.

—Shh.

—But I'm *nooot!*

He shook the finger at her.

—Nu-uh. No more. Listen to me. Listen.

—*Buuut.*

He snapped his fingers, a meaty slap of flesh.

—Shht. Now!

She stopped talking and looked down at her feet in their pink and white sneakers.

Po Sin pointed at her brother.

—Does Yong ever lose his Legos, Xing?

She bit her lip, not looking up.

Po Sin put a finger under her chin and tilted her face to his.

—I asked a question.

She blew out her cheeks.

—You *told* me to be *quiet* and *listen.*

—And now I want you to answer. Does he ever lose his Legos?

—I don't *know.*

—Yes you do. You know he doesn't. Sometimes people take them at school. But he never loses them. Because after your mom and me and his loving sister, the most important thing in the world for Yong is his Legos. Isn't that right?

—I don't *know.*

Po Sin straightened, folded his arms, shook his head.

—Xing, I will never take you to the American Girl store ever again if you don't stop lying.

Her eyes went big. She looked at him, found him unyielding; looked at her mom, found her utterly fed the fuck up. Her eyes darted from side to side, surveying the room, found no escape. She made little fists, pounded them against her thighs twice.

—But I *didn't* steal it! I just *borrowed* it!

Po Sin held out his hand.

She frowned, squatted, unlaced her left shoe, dug a finger inside and came out with a little knobbed bit of black plastic.

She put it in her father's hand.

—It's just a *little* piece. He has *hundreds* of them.

Po Sin folded the piece in his hand.

—And they're all equally precious to him. Just like the two of you are equally precious to us. We wouldn't want to lose either of you, no matter how much we love the other one.

—But he has so *many.*

—That doesn't matter, honey.

He turned and walked to his son.

—That doesn't matter at all.

He squatted and opened his hand in front of Yong's face. Yong looked at the piece, started to reach for it, stopped. Po Sin nodded, set the piece on the floor. Yong snatched it up, opened a zipper on the side of his backpack, dropped the piece inside, and zipped it back up.

Po Sin held out his index finger again.

—Now can I have a real hug?

Yong nodded, wrapped his little hand around Po Sin's finger, squeezed, and let go.

Po Sin looked over his shoulder at us.

—There, all better.

—Today was a bad day.

I walked with Lei to her car.

—Usually he's more interactive. But when something gets out of sequence, or lost, he gets untracked, his mind, and he can't focus on anything else. Emotions don't make much sense to him, so he has to concentrate very hard to read signs he's been taught to recognize. When he can't, he gets confused and scared. He withdraws. And touch is difficult. He doesn't like too much contact. Random contact. It's hard to explain. He loves being sandwiched. We have these pads at home we can put him between and apply pressure over his whole body, and somehow that comforts him, makes it easier to think. But generally, he needs a task to focus. The Legos.

She opened the driver's door of her tiny yellow Scion.

—Those kits? The impossibly difficult ones? Cities, trains, huge airliners. He opens the box, glances at the instructions, and builds them without ever making a mistake. You can take thousands of pieces, mix them all up, pull out one and show it to him, and he'll know exactly what kit it's from, where it goes, even what page it's on in the instructions, and its code number. The other kids know he's different, but they're young enough to think it's cool that he knows so much about Legos.

She shaded her eyes from the sun to look up at my face, smiling.

—They come to him with all their Lego dilemmas. He's like their shaman. Treasured for his oddness. For now, anyway.

A big sigh.

—We'll see in a couple of years how they deal with him.

—Um, Lei.

—Yes?

—Speaking of touch, could I have my hand back.

She looked at the hand she'd not released since she first took hold of it, laughed, let it go.

—Sorry. Sorry. Poor Yong hates to be touched, and his mother is so touchy-feely. I have to struggle not to hold his hand or rub his neck. And then it gets bottled up sometimes, next thing I know I'm stroking the cheek of someone I met five minutes ago.

She raised and dropped her shoulders and climbed into the car.

—I've invaded the personal space of every checkout person at our Ralph's. The tellers at the bank, they're lucky they have those Plexiglas shields to hide behind or I'd be hugging them every time I go in.

I pushed the door closed and she rolled down the window.

—Nice to meet you, Web. Glad we finally did. When I didn't see you last year, at the memorial, I was disappointed. I'd wanted to thank you. I was going to track you down, but then Po Sin said he ran into you at your friend's shop. I figured it was a matter of time before he got you over for dinner or something. And then time kept passing. I stopped thinking about it as much. I guess I got lazy about finding you and telling you how grateful we were of you sitting with Xing. Taking her off the bus. Her teacher told us she wouldn't get out from under her seat for him or any of the police. And I know how. You must have been very. Upset is a lame word. But. So to go back on the bus and help get her off and sit with her and help settle her. That was special. It meant a lot when we heard about it.

She reached out the window and grabbed my hand and squeezed.

—So there. I said it without crying, and you didn't even run away.

She let me go.

—Hope I didn't freak you out too much, Web.

I showed her the hand she'd held.

—Nothing a bar of Ivory won't cure.

She laughed.

—Takes more than that to get me off.

She put the car in reverse, started to roll.

—Hey, keep an eye on Po Sin for me. Don't let him eat crap. If he has a stroke and dies on me I'll be stuck alone with Xing, and I just know she'll kill me in my sleep one night.

She pulled into traffic and drove away.

I went to the door and stood there and watched Po Sin on the floor, taking turns with Xing, handing Lego pieces one by one to Yong, who assembled them.

I came into the room.

—I like your wife.

Po Sin rested a hand on his daughter's knee, handed a Lego to his son, never taking his eyes from them.

—Yeah, me too.

Xing looked over at me.

—You were Tameka's teacher, weren't you?

I stood there. Po Sin turned his head. Yong built his monstrous, hidden cave.

I nodded.

—Yeah, I was.

She touched her head.

—She had a cool hat.

I nodded.

—Yeah, she did.

She smiled and went back to helping Yong.

I walked into the shop, pulled on my gloves, and started scrubbing.

AQUISITIONS

—Do you have any other clothes?

I looked down at the T and blue jeans and sneakers I'd been wearing for over twenty-four hours.

—My dinner jacket is at the cleaner's just now. But if you don't think it would be gauche, I could wear my morning coat.

Gabe's expression remained immobile. Except maybe his eyes rolled around and around behind his shades without me knowing it.

—Nothing else to wear.

He extended his arm, shooting his wrist free of his jacket cuff, and looked at his watch.

—OK.

He steered us east on Burbank Boulevard.

—Po Sin lock up?

I pointed back in the direction of the shop.

—What tipped you off? I mean, besides the fact he left me sitting outside waiting for you after he took the kids home? What the fuck, I can't be trusted now?

Gabe drove, reserving comment. Reserving just about any indication that he was alive, as I was already learning, being a big specialty of his.

I picked up the slack.

—Really, man, I'm not trying to get off the hook for the van or anything, but I was supposed to watch the *shop*. I succeeded in that. Now, when Po Sin has to take the kids for dinner and you're late, I have to wait on the sidewalk? That, frankly, is bullshit.

Gabe took a left onto Lankershim.

—You tell Po Sin all this?

I looked out the window.

—Well. No.

He pulled to the curb at a Goodwill and killed the engine.

—That was probably a good idea.

He climbed out and walked around the car and stopped on the sidewalk and looked back at me.

—You coming?

I got out and closed the door.

—I didn't realize I was required.

He pushed through the glass doors into the shop.

—Certainly required if you want anything to fit.

—Here, hold out your wrist.

I held out my wrist and Gabe flipped open the knife blade on his Leatherman and cut the tag from the sleeve of my jacket.

I fiddled with the stiff collar of the white button-down that was chafing my neck.

—You know, when you said you needed help with *business communications*, I assumed that was like code for doing something illegal. I didn't realize I needed to actually dress in business attire.

He slipped the Leatherman away and started the Cruiser.

—You have that other bag?

I pointed at the two bags in the footwell, one containing my sneakers, stinking jeans and T and socks, the other holding the odds and ends he'd bought at the Goodwill.

—Yeah.

I clicked the heels of the worn loafers that were the only black shoes in the shop that fit me.

—Hey, are these technically work clothes? Can I write these off? I mean, with what I make, a twenty-five-dollar suit and six-dollar shoes are major deductions.

We drove down a long boulevard of beige stucco apartment buildings and strip malls, the mission school architectural palette of Los Angeles as it had blossomed in all its late twentieth-century glory.

Gabe shook his head.

—I wouldn't know how to file a tax return.

The ride west on the 101, and then south on the 405, was undertaken to the accompanying squawk of the police-band radio mounted under the dash, calling out numbered codes and responses that Gabe kept one ear cocked for. I was reminded of listening to a ball game with certain avid appreciators who have moved on from rooting for one team or the other, and became highly tuned appreciators of the game and its nuances. Gabe hemmed, grunted, clucked his tongue and, once, snorted in reaction to the story the radio was telling him.

As the 405 cut past the Veteran's Administration Healthcare Center, I pointed at the radio.

—Anything good?

He leaned forward, turned the volume up slightly, and tsked at whatever the cops were currently getting up to.

I nodded.

—Just tell me when someone wins.

And I closed my eyes.

—We're here.

I opened my eyes on a residential neighborhood of fake Tudors and Georgians and haciendas with large front yards crawling with bougainvillea, gardenia bushes, and lemon trees in the midst of huge lawns and thick ficus sculpted into hedge. I looked around for a street sign and found one up at the corner. Butterfield and Manning.

I rubbed sleep from my eyes.

—West side, huh? No wonder I had to dress up.

Gabe looked at the house we were parked in front of, a large stucco job done up adobe Pueblo style. Lots of terra-cotta tiles jutting over the eaves, long cone chimney, large wooden gate mounted in an arch in the garden wall.

He took a notebook from inside his jacket and flipped it open and looked at the pencil marks on the page and checked them against the address numbers painted on the curb. Satisfied he'd not become suddenly dyslexic, he put the notebook away and looked me over.

—Do up that top button and cinch that tie.

I dabbed some sweat on my forehead.

—Can't I do this business-casual? Kind of hot to be wearing this shit in the first place.

He waited.

I did up the top button and cinched the tie.

—Better?

He nodded.

—Let's go.

I got out of the car and looked for a bell or something.

—Web.

I looked back at Gabe, standing at the rear of the Cruiser with the window rolled down and the gate dropped. He reached in and pulled the gurney halfway out.

—Give me a hand with this.

Again I found myself in a dead man's bedroom while someone else did the paperwork elsewhere.

—Do you like this one?

I looked at the purple suit the old woman had draped over the corpse on the bed.

—It's a nice color.

She fingered the material.

—Yes, it is. He liked to be seen, Wally.

Whatever Wally once liked, it didn't matter now. And being seen wasn't something he was going to be doing much more of. Judging by the suit, he'd been built on a scale that might have had him approaching Po Sin's rarefied air, but the withered thing lost in the bedclothes could be swaddled in just the vest.

The woman sat on the edge of the bed, the suit overflowing her lap.

—Such a nice suit. Will they cut the back out of it to get him in?

I looked down the hall and longed for Gabe to get the fuck back in there.

—I'm not certain, ma'am. I think so. But I can't. I'm new to the job.

She took the corpse's hand in hers.

—Really? And do you like it so far?

I ran my eyes over the bedpan and oxygen tank and wheelchair and rows of pill bottles, all the other accoutrements of a long and miserable death that littered the room.

—It's OK.

—Must be sobering work for such a young man. Not very exciting.

I considered the last forty-eight hours of my life.

—Ma'am, there is never a dull moment.

She looked at the dead man again.

—Well, I suppose it must be very different. Each time. Wally is the second husband I've outlived. We were only married fifteen years. My first, we were married thirty. Cancer got him, too.

She arranged the suit over him again, resting her hand on his chest.
—Fucking cancer.

—Thanks for this, Gabe.
He pointed at the catch near my hand.
—Squeeze there.
I squeezed and the gurney's legs collapsed and we lowered the impossibly weightless corpse.
—No, seriously, thanks for this. The fair warning and all is what I particularly appreciate.
—Lift.
We lifted and slid the gurney into the back of the Cruiser and Gabe leaned in and flipped the levers that locked the wheels in place.
I loosened my tie.
—If it wasn't for that, I'd have walked into that situation totally unprepared for what I was going to be dealing with. Never would have been ready to chat with a grieving widow and help her to pick out a burial suit for her second dead husband. So thanks. I would have truly been out of my depth without your aid and assistance.
He swung the gate up and the black-tinted window rolled closed.
—Let's go.
I walked around and got in.
—Sure, let's go. But only if we can do this again right now. That was such a walk in the park, I can't wait to repeat it.
He put the key in the ignition.
I clapped both hands to my cheeks.
—Such a lovely, life-affirming experience, Mr. Gabe. That just put everything into perspective. That just made me realize how sweet my life is and how I need to live it to its fullest before it slips away.
He turned the ignition.
—Glad to hear all that, Web. Glad I could help.
I dropped my hands and settled into my seat, becoming aware that sarcasm and irony had no place in whatever laconic universe Gabe lived in.
—So what now, drop him at Woodlawn or someplace?
He put the car in gear.
—Just a quick errand first.

He looked at me.

—Don't worry, we don't have to bury him ourselves.

He pulled from the curb.

I looked over my shoulder at the body under the sheet.

—Wouldn't have surprised me at this point.

—Isn't Woodlawn west?

By way of answer Gabe continued east on Olympic.

—Please tell me we're not picking up another body.

He gestured at the back of the station wagon.

—There's only room for one.

I continued rolling up my sleeves.

—Thank God, I thought I was gonna have to put my jacket on again.

Just past the 3 Day Suit Broker he took a right on Federal, cruised slow, and pulled to the curb beyond Lasky Coachworks. I looked out at the auto shops and A-American Self Storage.

—Nice spot. Looking to get lucky?

He unbuckled his seatbelt and turned and pulled a red fuel bottle from one of the camping gear milk crates behind his seat.

—Hand me that jug we bought.

I picked up one of the bags from the Goodwill and pulled out the little clay moonshine jug with a cartoon of a drunken hillbilly stenciled on the side.

—Gloves. Gloves.

I looked at the black leather gloves Gabe was slipping onto his hands.

—Didn't I tell you to bring gloves?

—There's a dead body in the vehicle.

Gabe finished filling the jug with camp fuel and handed me the red bottle.

—Hold that between your legs.

I placed the bottle between my thighs, the fumes strong in my face.

—A dead body, Gabe. And I'm virtually certain you're preparing to do something extremely illegal. Wouldn't it be best if whatever that is were done in the absence of a corpse?

He held out a hand.

—Get that glider out.

I took the Styrofoam glider from the Goodwill bag.

—Yes, let's play with this. Let's play with this and talk about the sudden attack of crazy you are suffering from.

—Break it up into pieces. Little ones. No, smaller. Small enough to fit in the jug. Good.

He took the pieces I handed him and dropped them down the neck of the jug.

—Now the cork.

I handed him the cork and watched as he worked it into the jug, using the heel of his palm to pound it snug, flush to the lip.

I dropped the mauled remains of the glider back in the bag.

—OK, so we're not going to toss the glider around. But. Fuck. Fuck, Gabe. What the fuck are we doing here?

—That baggie of junk jewelry in there.

I dug it out.

He shook his head.

—No, dump out the jewelry, just give me the bag. And that bandanna, stuff it down into the fuel bottle.

I used my index finger to stuff the Bon Jovi bandanna he'd bought into the fuel bottle.

—This is fucked up, man.

—Now pull it out, carefully, and put it in here.

He held the baggie open right next to the fuel bottle. I pulled the bandanna free, and dropped it in the baggie, a little fuel dribbling my thighs.

—Now seal that bottle and put it away and tear off a strip of duct tape from that roll.

I screwed the cap back onto the bottle, put it in its milk crate, found the silver roll of tape and tore off a strip and handed it to him and watched as he used the tape to attach the sealed baggie to the side of the jug.

—Hold this.

He offered me the bomb.

I measured the distance I had traveled down this road I was on. I tried really fucking hard to figure out how I got from sprawling on the couch in Chev's tattoo parlor to the moment when a stoic ex-gangbanger corpse fetcher was asking me to take possession of his jumbo Molotov cocktail. I measured and weighed the consequences of my actions in the next few minutes.

Sort of.

—Fuck it. Give me that thing.

I held it while Gabe spilled rubbing alcohol from his first-aid kit onto a rag and carefully wiped down the jug, shifting my grip so he could get every surface.

Done with the fingerprint wipe, he nodded and patted his pockets.

—Don't suppose you have a light?

I brightened significantly.

—What? Hell no! I don't smoke! Wow, too bad, guess that means we have to delay the big firebombing.

He reached into one of the milk crates, took out a bag of disposable lighters, and allowed the corner of his mouth to tip slightly upward.

—I was just joking. Here, let me have that thing.

I let him have the thing, delighted to have discovered just what kind of scenario brought out the prankster in him.

I watched as he got out of the car and walked to a weathered brick building that I had taken for one of the garages, but saw now by its sign was not.

—Oh, oh fuck. Gabe, shit no.

But he was well beyond hearing my little gasps of dismay, and flicked the lighter and held the flame to the edge of the baggie, patiently waiting till it caught fire and ignited the fuel-soaked bandanna within. Pocketing the lighter, he raised the jug high and brought it down, throwing it at an angle under the van at the curb.

The jug shattered, spilling flaming jelly over the asphalt under the van, fire tickling the undercarriage and licking up the sides. Gabe walked back to the Cruiser, silhouetted by the flames, and climbed in.

He looked at the small inferno, looked at me, the fire in the lenses of his sunglasses.

—Well, that should make it clear to them where we stand.

He started the car and pulled easily from the curb, rolling slowly by the burning van as the front door of Aftershock Trauma Cleaning slammed open and a wiry bald man just barely five feet tall, brandishing a broom handle, ran out followed by Dingbang and several other Aftershockers.

The wiry guy made straight for the Cruiser, the broom handle cocked over his shoulder. Behind him, Dingbang was fumbling with a set of keys, trying to find one to open the driver's door on the van, dancing side to side to avoid the thrashing flames.

Gabe stuck a hand under his seat.

—Stupid sons of bitches.

The wiry guy was coming at my window, mouth moving, spittle flying, curses lost in the roar of the flames. My window rolled down as he reached the car, the broom handle bouncing off the chrome trim instead of shattering the glass.

—*Fuckinguslesslyingshitdogeatingfuckwadambushingdicksuckers!*

He started to bring the handle back up.

I twisted around, trying to squirm between the seats to join the dead body in the back of the station wagon.

Gabe shoved me back down in my seat, leaned across me, and stuck the gun in his hand out the window.

—Drop that shit and back up out the way, Morton.

Morton pulled up, dropped the broom handle and backed up out the way.

—*Fuckingniggerfuckingshitdogfuckingniggernigger.*

Gabe pointed the gun at the van where Dingbang was still trying to get the door open while the flames grew higher.

—Cover your ears, Web.

I covered my ears and jerked and screamed each of the three times Gabe pulled the trigger. My screams were somewhat louder than those of the men scattering on the street, away from the van where all three bullets had dimpled the hood next to Dingbang, sending him first to the ground and then crawling behind a dumpster at the curb.

Only Morton kept his place, pointing at Gabe, mouth tight shut now. Shaping the finger of his other hand into a pistol, he pointed it at his own head, and pulled the trigger.

Gabe shifted the aim of his gun, centered the bead on Morton's chest.

—Not wise, Morton, threatening a man with a pistol in his hand.

Morton seemed to make a similar assessment of the situation and dropped both hands to his sides. But was, I can only assume, the kind of man who can't leave well enough alone.

—Fuck you, nigger.

Gabe nodded.

—That's enough of that.

I covered my ears again, and the windows of the Aftershock shop exploded one after another while I did the flinch and scream thing again.

He settled back into his seat, tucked the gun between his thighs, put the car in gear, and drove slowly past where Morton had thrown himself on the street, screaming newly invented obscenities that I couldn't hear for the sharp ringing in my ears.

Of course, I did hear it when the van's gas tank blew and a fireball climbed up the sky, but we were some ways down the street by then.

Gabe observed the detonation in the rearview and, nodding his head, raised his voice over the ringing in his own ears.

—Stupid crackers, I'd have let them, they'd have climbed in that thing and tried to drive it off the fire, got their asses blown to hell.

I turned from staring out the back window as he took us round the corner onto Santa Monica Boulevard.

—You're a paragon of charity and compassion, Gabe. A real model to the rest of us when faced with the opportunity to think of our fellow man's well-being before our own.

He took the gun from between his legs and put it back under his seat.

—Good of you to say so, Web.

He straightened his tie.

—Now let's go drop that stiff.

One of the keys on the big ring in Gabe's glove box got us into Woodlawn and we rolled the gurney down an empty tile corridor, one wheel balky and loud.

Gabe stopped at a steel door.

—Hold up.

He took the ring off his belt, sorted keys, and unlocked the door.

—OK.

He pushed the door open and we rolled into the morgue.

I held up.

—Wow.

Gabe looked at the butterflied corpse on the table in the middle of the room.

—Yeah, it's a sight. Come on.

He guided the gurney to the back of the prep room and jerked the handle on the door of a walk-in.

—Park it here. OK. Got the legs, by the heels there. And lift.

We swung the body onto an empty rack at the side of the walk-in.

I looked at the dead in their rows.

—Lotta dead people, man.

Gabe took a look.

—Yeah. And the world isn't running out of raw supplies to make more.

We walked back down the corridor, the jittery wheel squeaking.

Gabe pulled up and tapped it with the toe of his shiny black shoe.

—Got to take that off and straighten it out tonight. No one wants their dead rolling out of their home on a gurney sounds like a shopping cart with a bum wheel.

Outside he locked up behind us.

I pointed at the keys.

—So you work for Woodlawn?

—No. Work for a company that does accommodations all over. Night shift I handle, never know if someone will be around to let you in.

He pointed at the Cruiser and we took the gurney over.

—Funeral homes contract with the service. Give us keys so we have access. Got keys to pretty much every home from the Valley down to Long Beach.

We dropped the gurney down to its wheels, lifted it into the back of the station wagon and swung the door shut.

I rested my ass on the gleaming chrome bumper.

—So, Gabe, tell me, how's one go about getting the job as the grim specter of death?

Gabe took a clean white handkerchief from his breast pocket, blotted his upper lip, tucked the handkerchief away and pointed at the car.

—Let's go.

I circled to the passenger door and got in.

—That's OK. I understand you're the reticent type. I just thought that since we were accessories in a few felonies together that you might warm up a little and share a couple biographical details. For the sake of conversation.

He pulled his seatbelt across the shoulder and buckled it into place.

—I make an observation here, Web?

I buckled my own belt.

—Sure, but don't go crazy. You've already spoke more in the last fifteen minutes than I thought was possible. Don't want you to sprain your tongue or anything.

He nodded.

—No danger. No danger.

—Good. Well, as long as you're careful, what is it you've observed?

He licked the pad of his thumb and rubbed a spot on the inside of the windshield.

—Some looks. A few silences.

I nodded.

—Wow, man. Fascinating stuff.

He looked at the speck he'd rubbed onto his thumb.

—It is. In its own way.

—Uh-huh. Well. Thanks, Gabe. That was enlightening. Thanks for the observations.

He took out the handkerchief again and wiped his thumb on it.

—The way you and Po Sin talk about some things. Don't talk about others. The way I know Po Sin, and the way he is around you, that suggests things. About you, I mean.

—Deeper and deeper, Gabe. Deeper and deeper.

He tucked the handkerchief away.

—Way I know Po Sin, how little he keeps from me, lets me know that whatever it is you two talk about where you're not talking about anything, that it's pretty personal to you.

I scratched at a spot on my new old slacks.

He turned his lenses on me.

—A person, he's got a past. Everyone dragging one behind them. You want to know how I ended up driving dead people around? Cleaning up after them? Well, that's my past, ain't it?

I nodded.

—Yeah. I get it.

He shook his head.

—No. You don't. See, point here isn't *mind your own goddamn business.* Point is, Web, you want to know how it is I can be comfortable with the dead?

He looked out the windshield.

—You might first ask how *you're* so comfortable with the dead.

He fired the engine.

—What's that they say about familiarity that I read somewhere?

—Breeds contempt?

He checked his mirrors, began to back down the drive.

—Way I read that, just means you're around something enough, you get used to it.

We bounced down into the street and he dropped the gearshift into drive and pointed us east.

—Me and Po Sin, there's just shit we have reason to have gotten used to when we were younger. That's all.

SKEWED

Chev's Apache wasn't out front.

Whether that was good or bad, I couldn't say. Letting another day go past before I could do some serious ass-kissing, well, some serious sarcastic ass-kissing anyway, might be what the doctor ordered. Or it could be one step closer to him being done with my shit and throwing my possessions out the window for me to claim from the street.

From the alley, a sudden burst of dialogue.

—You fucking bitch, you fucked him, didn't you?

—Fuck you.

—You fucking cock tease bitch.

—Fuck you.

—You had his cock in your cunt, didn't you?

—Fuck you.

Going up the stairs, I considered the virtues of being homeless and friendless. The first of these being that no one would offer me a job that would turn into a crime spree.

I unlocked the apartment door, found I was just a little disappointed not to see Dot inside waiting to irritate me, walked into the dark livingroom, got tripped by someone hiding behind the door and went face-first into the carpet.

The someone lurking behind the door put his foot in my back and shoved me deeper into the carpet.

—Where's our fucking can?

My hands flailed and hit something solid and heavy and I grabbed it.

—It's down the hall.

The foot shoved harder.

—What? What the fuck? Are you fucking? Is that a joke?

Of course it wasn't a joke, I was telling the absolute truth. The can, or bathroom if you will, was indeed down the hall. I wasn't sure why this person was referring to it as *our* can, or why finding it required battering me, but it was there. Perhaps I was a bit confused. That, along with, you know, my general exhaustion, emotional chaos, and fedupness with being fucked around got the better of my good manners as a host and the next thing I knew I was twisting and swinging the huge old phone my hand had found and listening to it make the kind of heavy thunk against a man's shin that only genuine craftsmanship can produce. This, followed by a faint ringing as the bell inside was jangled by the blow. A tone, oddly, in perfect harmony with the ringing still sounding in my ears from the shots Gabe had fired.

The guy, with what I can only assume was a genuinely desperate bladder condition, hopped off me and dropped into the Barcalounger that Chev had bought at the Melrose Trading Post, and clutched his shin.

—Fuck! Ow! Fuck!

I pushed myself off the floor and went to the wall and turned on the light and looked at him, a guy for whom the terms *wiry* and *pockmarked* had been invented. He may also have been the inspiration for *gap toothed, scraggly haired* and *waxen. White trash,* I assume, goes without saying. But if one needs to have the point emphasized, I can draw attention to the oversize Dale Earnhardt, Senior, memorial-motif tank top he was wearing.

I blinked and looked at his bandaged shoulder and hand.

—I don't know you.

—You know *me,* son?

I turned, looked at the guy on the couch who had just spoken. He was tall and lean and wore well-used cowboy boots, jeans, Levi jacket, and a face that was just slightly more weathered than his clothes. Oh, and the gun in his work-gloved hand was really fucking big.

I figured answering him was a good thing to do.

—I'm gonna say no and hope it's the right answer.

The guy with the bandages picked up the phone and hit me in the back of the neck with it.

—Want our fucking can.

He may have said more nonsensical shit, but I was way too knocked out to hear it.

—Guy, wake up, come on, get it together.

I got it together. No, that's a lie. I woke up, but I did not get it together. Not even a little bit. What I did was come to and discover a wrenching pain at the back of my neck, my hands tied behind my back, and the dude with the bandaged hand shoving a cellphone against my ear.

—Someone wants to talk to you, asshole. Wake up and listen.

The phone was ringing. It stopped, the line clicked, and one of those robot voices started talking.

Hello, you have reached 209-673-9003. Please leave a message.

I looked at the guy.

—What should I say?

—What? Say? Just answer the question.

—I. What question? It's voice mail.

—What? Jesus fucking.

He held the phone to his own ear.

—Sonofabitch.

Fingers snapped.

We both looked at the cowboy on the couch with the gun.

—Just dial it again, Talbot.

Talbot disconnected and started to dial.

—Fucker doesn't have any sense.

He listened to the phone ring, nodded at the cowboy.

—Here we go. Hello. It's me. Yeah. Well why the hell didn't you pick up? So take it off vibrate and turn on the damn ringer. No, do it later. OK. She there? Fuck you, I know she's not going anywhere. I meant is she next to you. So put her on.

He stuck the phone against my ear.

I cleared my throat.

—Uh, hello?

—Web?

—Yeeeah?

—Is that you?

—Yeah.

—What the hell are they doing with you?

—I.

I looked at Talbot.

—She wants to know what the hell you're doing with me.

—She? Damn it.

He took the phone from my ear and spoke into it.

—Bitch, just tell him what you were told to say. Jesus.

He put the phone at my ear again.

—Fucking people.

The voice on the phone spoke again, still a little blurred by my ringing ears.

—Web?

—Yeah?

—I think I've been kidnapped.

I swallowed.

—Soledad?

—They want their container, Web. They say to get it for them fast or they'll do something to me.

—Wait. Hang on. I.

I looked at the Talbot.

—What container?

He slapped me.

—The can, fucker. Listen to the girl.

I listened.

—Go ahead.

—They want their container. They'll give you a number to call when you have it. They want it by tomorrow night.

—OK, OK, I can . . .

My brain did a few doughnuts in the mud while I tried to figure out what words should come next. What exactly *could* I do? Could I call the *cops?* Could I *rescue* her? Could I crawl under the wheels of a speeding vehicle and let myself be *crushed* if it meant having some peace?

And wait just a fucking second, my brain screeched to a halt and declaimed, *are you totally being set up or is it just me?*

I shook my head, almost laughed, was too pissed to actually do it.

—You're totally setting me up, aren't you, Soledad?

—I? Web?

—This whole deal has been one long setup. Like, that shit with your brother, all this. Even fucking me. It's all a setup. I'm so being used here. You have been totally working me.

Silence on the line as she struggled to find something to say to squirm her way loose from my accusation.

Silence broken as she found the words.

—Web, you are such an asshole.

And she hung up.

Talbot poked me in the neck.

—Stop fucking around with her, she's not setting you up. Just listen to the bitch.

I looked up at him.

—She hung up on me.

He looked at the phone screen.

—Jesus.

He started to dial again.

—Man, you are one asshole. Girl calls and needs your help, been snatched, and you make like she's in on it. Way to trust people, man.

He put the phone to his ear.

—Fuck, going straight to voice mail. Bet he's calling me back now.

He looked at the cowboy.

—Should I hang up and let him call or keep dialing?

The cowboy rose from the couch.

—Put the phone away.

Talbot put the phone away.

The cowboy scratched the whiskers on his neck and walked over until his boot heels were inches from my face.

—She tell you what we want?

I looked up the length of his denim legs, past the scratched longhorn belt buckle to his leathered face.

—The can?

He tucked the gun into the belt at the small of his back.

—Yeah, that's it.

He squatted, held up a finger.

—She tell you what we'd do?

—Something bad?

—Yeah. Something pretty bad.

He looked at Talbot.

—Go take a look out that window and see what's to be seen.

Talbot limped to the kitchen window and looked out.

—Nothing. Just the stairs and part of the parking lot and the street.

—Keep looking. Been here awful long without no one else coming home.

He rested a hand on the phone I clobbered Talbot with, and with which Talbot returned the favor.

—Old phone.

—Yeah.

—Must have hurt.

—A lot.

—Uh-huh.

He hefted the phone.

—Talbot's been spoiling a bit to put a hurt on someone. Since he got him-self cut.

Talbot turned from the window.

—That wasn't my fault.

—Just keep your eyes out there.

Talbot looked back out.

—Not my fault.

The cowboy rested the phone on his knee.

—Was his fault. Fella like your girl's brother, he shouldn't be no trouble for no one. Talbot, he just isn't the kind who can admit he screwed up and let someone get the better of him.

He stood, took three steps, heels loud on the linoleum, and pounded the phone into Talbot's face as he turned. And pounded it again as he went down. And again when he was on the floor. And again.

He hunkered next to the bloody rag-dolled man and stuck a gloved fin-ger deep under his jaw alongside his throat. Apparently not liking what he detected, he raised the phone and brought it down once more.

For luck, I suppose.

This time, when he checked under Talbot's jaw, he felt the stillness in the man's pulse that he was looking for, and he dropped the phone on Tal-bot's dead body.

He stood and looked at me.

—You took that pretty well. Figured you for the screaming and crying type.

I shook my head.

—No, not me, I've seen that kind of thing before.

He nodded his head, went to the sink, looked in the cupboard under-neath, and came out with a plastic garbage bag.

—Yeah, guess you would have, with your job and all.

I rested my head on the carpet and watched as he shook out the bag and fitted it over Talbot's crushed head.

He came over to me.

—And it looks like that training's going to come in handy for you.

He grabbed one end of the knot that tied my hands and gave it a tug and it came apart.

—You best get cleaning.

He took the rope to the corpse and used it to tie the bag around its neck.

—And then go get our can, and call.

He tossed Talbot's cellphone onto the carpet.

—Just call the last number he called on there.

He took the corpse under its arms, pushed up with his legs, let it flop over his shoulder and stood.

—I'll take care of this bit here.

He walked to the door, easy under the weight of the dead.

He opened the door.

—Go get my can. I want them damn almonds. Alright?

I stared at Talbot's blood in my kitchen.

The cowboy tapped a heel on the floor.

—Said *alright?*

I looked away from the mess.

—Yeah. Alright.

He touched the brim of his hat.

—Good then. And, oh yeah, I got your boss's van. You can have that back too, when you bring the can. Case you need any other motivation.

And he went out the door, corpse on his shoulder, apparently prepared for any questions such a thing might raise.

That or just quick on the draw.

Almonds.

As I cleaned yet another crime scene, I thought about almonds.

Stripped to my underwear, a pair of sneakers, and rubber gloves I took down the white pillowcases I had hung over the kitchen windows to keep the morning sunlight from pouring in when I used to get up early and have my coffee before going off to teach kids how to read and write and add and subtract. And I thought about fucking nuts.

In all their guises.

Starting with myself.

Dropping the pillowcases into the bathtub after rinsing them out and dousing them in about a half gallon of bleach, I considered just how crazy I actually was. Not a question I'd been apt to embrace for the last year, but one that seemed appropriate to the moment.

I brought my desk lamp and a clip light from Chev's bedroom into the kitchen and plugged them in. The improved lighting gave me a better idea of what I was dealing with. Studying the remains of a man's face spattered about the area where I prepared my meals, or opened my to-go containers anyway, and finding that I didn't really have any emotional reaction to speak of, gave me a better idea of just how out of normal mental alignment I'd gotten.

I looked down at my nearly naked, blood-scrubbing self.

—Skewed.

I pulled a strip of paper towels off the roll I'd gotten from under the sink and started wiping the little card table under the window.

—Your mentality, Webster Fillmore Goodhue, has become seriously fucking skewed.

I cleaned, wondering if the fact that it had taken witnessing a man deliberately murdered in front of me to shake this realization loose was a bad thing, or a really really *really* bad thing. There seeming to be no other options available.

The table clean, I carried it to the edge of the linoleum kitchen and set it safely across the carpet border of the livingroom. Along that edge, I spotted a rim of dark wet spots on the dirty carpet. I soaked a hand towel in cold water and blotted the spots before they could set. I worked some dish soap into the carpet fibers and left it to be finished later.

The worst of the mess was puddled below the window. Talbot had, quite fortunately it seemed, looked down after the first blow, sending most of the blood that had poured from his ruptured nose to the floor, rather than hosing the walls with it. Of course the cowboy had swung the phone in an uppercut on the second blow. Not so good. That meant the ceiling had a nice spray pattern on it. But the last three blows were all placed squarely once Talbot was on the floor on his back.

I looked up.

—Ceiling first.

I got the stepladder from the hall closet and started spraying and wiping, moving from side to side as my body crossed the beams of the lights and cast shadows over the blood, trying to see clearly.

When the worst was done, when I'd scooped the partially congealed blood from the floor and scrubbed the walls and mopped and wiped and wiped some more, and taken four ruined sponges and the shredded remains of two paper towel rolls and three old Ts I'd had to use as rags, and the mop head, and stuffed it all in the cleaning bucket and carried it downstairs and locked it in the trunk of my crapped-out 510 in the driveway, I poured the remains of a bottle of hydrogen peroxide into the empty window-cleaner spray bottle and misted the carpet and floor and walls. The carpet foamed in a couple spots, but it wasn't anything visible to the naked eye, so I let it go. Back up on the ladder, I sprayed the ceiling, searching for any last remains, and caught a glimpse of myself reflected in the dark window.

All but naked, on a stepladder, cleaning dead man's blood from my kitchen ceiling, I stopped and addressed the young man I saw there.

—Is it possible, my friend, that your coping mechanisms have been over-compensating for the shit that happened on that bus?

The young man in the window responded.

—What shit are you speaking of?

I continued the dialogue.

—That shit where a little girl from your class was hit by a stray bullet and died in your arms and you were covered in her blood.

He shrugged.

—Oh. That.

I put my hands on my hips.

—See, that's what I'm talking about, that nonchalance about the whole thing, and also just kind of being a dick to everyone, that's not the way people react to traumatic situations.

He was unimpressed.

—It's not? You know of another reaction? You've experienced another re-action? Man, as far as you know, this is totally normal. This may be the most normal thing you've ever done in your life.

I jabbed my finger at him.

—Fuck you! That's fucked up. I'm trying to really talk about this for a change and you're being all.

—What? I'm being all what?

I froze, looked at my reflection for a long and deeply disturbing minute. I shook my head.

—Man, I am not even having this conversation with you right now.

And I climbed off the ladder and laid myself spread eagle on the floor and stared at the flawlessly clean ceiling, and I think I may have cried for the first time in a year, but I'm not entirely sure because a huge mass of sleep loomed and got its arms round my middle and dragged down and I was gone.

Mumbling as my eye slammed shut.

—Fucking almonds.

—I appreciate you cleaning up, you know.

I opened my eyes and found the daylight the pillowcases were meant to keep at bay was shooting me in the face.

—But it's not really going to change anything.

I looked at Chev, sitting on the edge of his lounger, rubbing his eyes.

I pushed myself up on my elbows.

—I'm sorry about the money, man.

He flopped back in the chair and let out all the air in his lungs.

—See, that's the point right there.

I shaded my eyes from the sun.

—I didn't even know he gave it to me, Chev.

He shook his head.

—Fuck the money. That is not the point. You missing the point is the point. I get the money thing, I get you going to see him. He's your dad. I understand that more than you do. Jesus, man, I saw him like six months ago.

I sat up.

—What?

—When you didn't stop acting all fucked up after a few months, I went and saw L.L.

—Chev.

—I didn't know what to do, you know? Thea was like, *He'll heal in time.* People I talked to, the grief counselor at the hospital, they all said you needed to confront what had happened, talk about it in a supportive envi-ronment. Well, I knew sure as fuck that wasn't gonna happen. I read these books on Post-Traumatic Stress Disorder, they described you pretty smack-on. I mean.

He laughed.

—Dude, you could be the poster boy for PTSD.

He untwisted the sleeve of his black T, where he'd tucked his pack of smokes.

—But knowing what the situation was, that didn't help me to figure out how to help.

I was still wearing the cleaning gloves. I pulled them off.

—I didn't know you were doing all that.

—I know you *didn't*. You didn't have a clue.

He lit his cigarette and blew smoke.

—Web, it wasn't just me, it was everyone you know. At first, anyway. We were all running around trying to figure out how to get your shit together. The guys from the tattoo shop, teachers from the school, Po Sin, some other parents from over there. But you were so, man, acting like such a dick. People just got tired. They didn't know how to deal and got frustrated. It was tiring, man. Jesus, it *is* tiring.

He looked around for an ashtray, couldn't find one, flicked on the carpet.

—So. I went and saw L.L.

—Man. I.

He held up a hand.

—No. Don't. Now is not the time. I mean. I went over to Chez Jay, took a look at him, man, I started to cry. And. You know, not because I was pissed. It was, man, it was so fucking good to see him, you know.

He clenched his teeth.

—And that hurt like a son of a bitch. Let me tell you it did. Talk about feeling guilty. Anyway. He turned around, saw me. Know what he said?

I nodded.

—The wrong thing.

He took a long drag.

—You got that right. Said, *Ah, Chev, come to see me after all these years. What's gone amiss, son, lost the strength of your convictions?*

I closed my eyes, tried to imagine he was mistaken about what my father had said, knew he was not.

I opened my eyes.

—Did you hit him?

Smoke drifted from his nostrils.

—No. I walked out. Because right there, man, in that moment, I ceased to care anymore.

He leaned forward, elbows on knees.

—The man had finally, after the, after the accident, after the shit he told us, he had finally, in that moment when something could have been done, he had finally gone too far. Man, I didn't even know there was road left to travel on that route, but he found it and drove it and that was the end of the line for me. I didn't hit him. I did not want to hit him. I just wanted gone. I walked out.

—Good.

He nodded.

—Yeah. Good. But here's the thing, man, the point.

He looked at the floor, shook his head, looked back up at me.

—Like fucking father, Web, like fucking son.

I opened my mouth.

He closed it.

—No. Wait. Listen.

I listened.

—He wasn't *always* like that. He was always a son of a bitch, always talked shit, but he wasn't always *mean*. That didn't really start till after the accident. He didn't really start forcing everyone out of his life until after the accident.

He scratched his shoulder.

—If that rings any bells.

He got up.

—So it's not about the money. Or about you seeing L.L. If my dad were still around, no matter if he'd turned out to be the biggest bastard ever, I'd want to check on him every now and then. It's not even about you hurting my new girl's feelings so bad that she doesn't want to come here and I had to go to her place and sneak in and out of her bedroom because her folks would freak out if they knew her new boyfriend was a twenty-nine-year-old rocker with a tattoo parlor.

He walked to the hallway, stopped.

—It's about you not trying to get better. It's about everyone else trying so hard that they wear themselves out and can't try anymore, and you just letting them beat themselves against you while you act like nothing fucking happened. Acting like you're no different. Like you haven't changed at all.

He turned from me.

—Web, it's about *me* getting tired, man. It's about, I, man, it's about I feel like I'm on that same road I was on with L.L., about thinking we're almost out of blacktop. And you just keeping the pedal to the metal, and not even trying to put on the brakes.

He put a hand on top of his head.

—And I hate that feeling, man.

He walked into his bedroom.

—I hate it.

And he closed the door.

Me, I sat on the kitchen floor and thought about how it was a good thing I'd cleaned up as well as I did. Because if Chev had known a man was killed in his apartment last night, the shit would really have hit the fan.

Then I got up, cleaned myself up a little, put on some clothes, got the keys to the Apache from Chev's jacket, and went out to go talk to a man about why the girl I'd fallen for, and, you know, already thoroughly alienated, had been kidnapped.

THE WORLD WITHOUT ME

—Cut you bad, cut you like Rambo cuts a redneck.

—Yeah, sure, I know. To avoid that, I'll stay over here.

—Cut you like I cut that other motherfucker.

I sat on the stripped mattress.

—Yeah, about him, you may find that it's in your best interest not to brag overmuch about how you cut him.

Jaime emptied his nip bottle of Malibu and added the empty to the vast array of them heaped at his feet. To judge by the population density around his chair, and by the paths worn through them between the chair and the door and the bathroom, he'd apparently done little since I last saw him other than drink Malibu, void his bladder to make room for more, and stumble to the liquor store on the corner for fresh supplies. He'd most certainly not had the maid in during any of his sojourns out.

He felt in the plastic bag in his lap, found it lacking, turned it inside out, found it still lacking, and dropped it on the floor.

—Well how the fuck 'bout that. Ain't that a bitch?

He pawed in his pockets and found the twenty I'd just given him in order to persuade him to let me into the room.

—Need to go hit the store. Back in a sec.

He stood with the great care and instability of the tragically inebriated. I watched him take a step and place his foot squarely on a couple empty bottles that rolled from beneath him, and let gravity take it from there.

—Ow! Fuck! That hurts.

I got off the bed and walked over and held out a hand.

—C'mon.

He took my hand and I pulled him halfway up and let go and watched Newtonian physics at work again.

—Ow! Fuck!

—Sorry. My bad.

I stuck out my hand. He took it. I pulled and let go.

With anticipated results.

—Ow!

—Whoops.

I stuck out my hand. He eyed it. And decided, I imagine, that based on a model of the universe drawn from the Hollywood catalogue, no one could be so cruel as to intentionally abuse a poor drunk in such a manner.

I proved him wrong.

—Ow!

I held out my hand.

He slapped at it. Missed.

—Fuck you. Fuckin'.

He got to all fours, crawled to his chair and climbed back aboard, where he knew he'd be safe.

—Cut you bad, motherfucker.

I bent over and picked up the knife that had fallen from his back pocket.

—You might want this.

I tossed it on his lap.

He looked at it.

—Right. Thanks.

He picked up the plastic bag from the floor and stuck his hand inside.

—How the fuck 'bout that.

He dropped the empty bag.

—Fuckin' tragedy that is.

He pushed himself up, the knife falling to the floor.

—Gonna go hit the store.

I put a finger in his chest and pushed and he dropped back in the chair.

—Jaime, that guy you cut. Talbot.

—Yeah, weakass Talbot, cut him bad.

—What did you steal from Talbot and his friend?

He squinted.

—Fuck you talking 'bout? Didn't steal shit. 'M a producer. I facilitate the vision of the talent. Bring it together with the money.

I kicked some bottles aside and picked up something from the floor and held between my thumb and forefinger and showed it to him.

—What about this?

He looked at it, looked hard.

—Fuckin' almond.

—Right the first time. What can you tell me about it?

He grinned, winked.

—'Sa nut.

I nodded.

—Yeah. Dead on. But a little outside the point. What I'm getting at here, Jaime, is why would someone kidnap your sister and, just out of pique as far as I can gather, kill Talbot over some nuts?

—I didn't kill Talbot. Jus' cut his ass up.

—Sure, cut him bad. Cut him like he was a Turkish prisoner in *Midnight Express*. But his buddy or boss or whatever, the guy who looks like Sam Elliot without the moustache, he killed him.

His eyes flicked back and forth a couple times, looking for connections between things that seemed impossible to unite.

—Killed him? Harris killed Talbot?

—Is Harris a tall cowboy with a big gun?

—Yeah.

—Then I'm going to go out on a limb and say that yes, he is the one who killed Talbot.

He rubbed his mouth with the back of his hand.

—Damn. That's. Damn. That's fucked up.

—Yeah. Especially when you take into account that he beat him to death with my telephone.

His face scrunched, he opened and closed his mouth a few times, he stuck out his tongue.

I recognized certain signs I'd seen many times in college, and took a big step back as he bent over the side of the chair and heaved a half gallon of Malibu rum onto the floor.

I edged from the puddle.

—Think it's bad to think about, you should have seen it.

He shook his head.

—No, no, man, ain't that bothers me. Just.

He spat.

—It's just that Harris is Talbot's uncle that's so fucked up.

He flopped back in the chair, wiped pinkish vomit from his chin, and threw up in his lap.

I went for towels, assuming we'd have to shoot this again.

—Almonds, Jaime.

He swallowed the last of the water from the glass I'd gotten for him, and held out the empty.

—They stole 'em.

I took the glass and passed him a damp towel. The only towel left in the room that wasn't draped over the huge pool of rum puke.

—Stole what?

—Almonds, asshole. That's what you're asking, right?

I sat back on the bed, at as safe a distance from the stink of his vomit as I could manage. I'd contemplated cleaning it up, but decided I'd reached my limits on cleaning other people's messes for the day. In theory, after all, I was here to clean my own mess. Or exert some kind of influence over my own life. Or some shit like that. I thought it best to keep that in mind.

So, by focusing relentlessly on the idea that I *may* have been responsible for the grinding inertia that was carrying me away from anyone and anything I'd ever cared about, I was able to reverse my usual view of things, which made it appear as though I were standing still, resolutely my own man, unchangeable, inured and immune to the blows of life, while the rest of the world went on without me, unable to support the idea that it could not live up to my standards.

But it wasn't easy to maintain that focus, especially when I was having to fight off a series of fantasies wherein I was capable in matters of fisticuffs and gave Jaime the proper thrashing he so clearly deserved.

I coughed into my hand.

—Yes, allowing that I am indeed an asshole, it is what I was asking. I'm sure, now that you've had a moment to clear your head, and, you know, up-chuck on yourself, that you'll understand how I might be confused about the notion of *almond thieves.*

He rubbed the towel over his bared teeth, scrubbing away a film of bile.

—Asshole, they stole like a can of them.

—Sure, I got that part. See, Harris, before he murdered his nephew, was very clear that he wanted his *can* back. So I'd managed to put together can and almonds and come up with can full of almonds, but I'm still not connecting that to kidnapping and killing. I'm dim on matters of criminal enterprise. You seem to have this kind of behavior all locked up. Care to enlighten me as to how a can of almonds is worth all the bother?

He stared.

—You are such a huge asshole. You always talk like that?

—Mostly it's only when I'm stressed. Or when I'm not so subtly making fun of someone I think is an idiot. In this case, I'm engaged in both endeavors.

—Asshole.

—Yeah, takes one to know one.

—See, *that* I get.

—Almonds. Can. I mean, are there diamonds hidden below the almonds or something?

He threw the towel on the floor, got up and pulled off his pukey shirt.

—Asshole, a *can* is a cargo container.

—You buy any almonds lately?

—No.

—Well you should. They're like full of good cholesterol.

I watched as he dug clean socks from his backpack.

—Did I mention they kidnapped your sister?

He sat on the bed and pulled the socks on.

—See, because they're so high in HDL, people are crazy for almonds right now. Put them out on the crafts table and the talent eats them by the handful. Can of almonds is like eight bucks. Like a regular size can, I mean.

He rose and tucked the tails of his clean Ed Hardy shirt into his equally clean Ed Hardy jeans, both garments covered in commodified Ed Hardy tattoo tigers.

—Cali produces so many fucking almonds, like a billion fucking pounds a year or something, business is booming. It's like we export nothing but airplanes and produce. And movies, man.

He ran his fingers through his hair, still damp from the shower he'd taken.

—All these places, China, Spain, Portugal, India, they love fucking almonds. Buy like seventy million pounds of California almonds a year. But with increased U.S. demand, they have to pay a higher premium.

He took a bottle of some kind of hair product from his bag, sprayed into his hand, and began shaping his hair into a wedge.

—Know what almonds wholesale for on the open market? Fucking guess.

I shrugged.

—No idea.

He looked in the mirror, tweaked the angle of the fauxhawk.

—Right, you have no idea. Who's the fucking genius now, asshole?

—You, you, you're the fucking supergenius.

—Right, I am. Deal with numbers, that's what I do.

He turned from the mirror.

—Six dollars a pound, man. Know how many pounds of almonds load into a shipping container? A marine container, I mean, a forty-footer.

—No clue.

—Fucking right no clue. So let me clue you in, asshole. Forty-four fucking thousand pounds. Want some help with the math?

I didn't need help with the math. I could do the math. And suddenly, it became very clear why Harris was willing to kidnap Soledad. Less clear about why he'd be so willing to kill his own nephew. But I figured that was a family matter more than anything else, and you just never knew what kind of history was involved there.

Jaime was nodding and smiling.

—Two hundred and twenty thousand dollars, asshole. That's how much that truck full of almonds is worth. And as expediter on this deal, I'm in for ten percent. Twenty-two thousand.

I rubbed my nose.

—That what they offered?

—Huh?

—Ten percent, that what they offered?

—Huh? No. They. Wait. They offered the twenty-two. Said that was ten percent of the total haul.

—But. Never mind.

He came toward me.

—Never mind what, asshole?

I stood up.

—It's just that six times forty-four thousand is two hundred sixty-four thousand.

He stood there.

I filled in the gap in his misunderstanding.

—Ten percent of that is twenty-six thousand and four hundred American greenbacks. But you go ahead and crunch the numbers and see what you come up with.

—What? The fuck you. Oh! Oh! Those assholes, I am gonna cut their asses. No, man, I am gonna sue their asses!

His hand went to the pocket where his knife could usually be found, didn't find it there.

I pointed at the towel-covered mess on the floor.

—Last I saw it, it was there.

He stared at the lump under the towel.

—Shit. I loved that knife.

—Nice ride. Could be a movie car. Make some extra ducats renting it out.

—It's my roommate's.

—Yeah, he lets you borrow it? Must be pretty cool, let you borrow a ride like this.

I unlocked the door.

—Yeah, he's cool.

I climbed in.

—But he doesn't let me borrow his truck.

Jamie got in and ran a hand over the custom leather bench seat Chev had put in.

—Snaking the roomie's ride, huh, asshole?

I started her up.

Granted, yes, I had taken Chev's prized truck without permission. Granted this could be interpreted as *snaking*. But I was playing a perspective game with myself here.

Like, which would be worse?

A) Explaining to Chev all the fucked up shit that was taking place? In which case he would feel obliged to become involved, and perhaps put himself at risk. In which case he might get hurt. In which case my already questionable mental stability might come crashing all around me.

Or

B) Taking his truck and risking that he'd be utterly and finally through with me and amputate himself from me in the same manner he had amputated himself from L.L.? In which case my already questionable mental stability might come crashing all around me.

OK, same net result. But option B had the wonderful advantage of being the one in which there was no actual risk to anyone except me and the asshole riding in the truck with me.

And Soledad.

But that wasn't my fault.

And least I was pretty damn sure it wasn't. Then again, by driving her away after we'd had sex, I sent her outside into the arms of the guys who kidnapped her. Let's just say that blame on the last one was difficult to assign accurately. So I was going to dodge it as long as humanly possible.

Jaime pointed at the liquor store.

—Just pull in over there.

I shook my head.

—No.

—What? Why not?

—Because you just got sober enough to communicate. Plus, you've displayed your puking expertise and I don't want to see you going for a perfect score in my friend's truck.

He folded his arms.

—This is my production, man, you want to go indie on it, be my guest. But I don't get a pick-me-up, you're gonna get fuckall from me in the way of help getting my sister back.

I punched him.

Now, I don't want to mislead, it wasn't like it was a bone-crunching roundhouse that would have made the Duke proud, but I do want it recorded that I finally lost my cool and did punch the fucker. Well, *hit* might be a better word. OK, more accurately, it was kind of a slap.

But I slapped him hella hard, man.

He touched his shoulder where I'd slapped him.

—What the fuck was that?

I slapped him again.

He raised a hand.

—Dude.

I slapped him again.

He slapped me back.

—Cool it, asshole.

Then I kind of lost my cool for real and turned on the seat so my back was against the door and brought up my feet and started kicking him.

He opened his door and jumped out.

—Asshole, what the fuck?

I came out of the truck after him.

—She's your sister, fucker.

He ran around to the other side of the Apache, trying to keep it between us.

—So what?

I ran after him and we circled the truck.

—So you are the biggest dick ever and you got involved in some stupid shit with some real criminals and now she's kidnapped and you're acting like it doesn't matter.

He stopped running, turned to face me.

—Asshole, what are you talking about?

I ran up to him, stopped, fist cocked to throw my first real punch since junior high.

—I'm talking about taking some fucking responsibility for your actions, asshole.

Irony noted.

He had his own fist primed and ready to fly.

—Asshole, *taking responsibility*? I mean, it's not like she wasn't involved in this shit from the beginning.

I lowered my fist.

He smiled.

—Oh, she didn't tell you that one?

I shook my head.

He nodded.

—Asshole.

And he punched me. A real punch. A roundhouse the Duke would have been proud of.

—What you get for hitting me.

—I slapped you.

—You kicked me.

—Not hard.

—So what? Still you started it.

He finished off the half pint of Malibu he'd gone across the street for while I collected myself from the ground after he punched me and reopened, yet again, the cut on my forehead.

—I seem to be developing this brand-new talent for getting my ass kicked.

He tossed the empty bottle on the ground, shattering it over a parking space.

—That a new talent? Way you got it mastered, I figured you to be an old hand.

—Fuck off and tell me where the almonds are.

—Harris is from way up north. Paradise or one of those hick redneck mountain towns like that. Ozarks of the West, man. Guys come down from those hills, they mostly got like three teeth, a wandering eye, cleft palate, and third-degree syphilis. Straight out of *Deliverance*. Soooooeeeyyy. They get as far as L.A., you'll see them standing outside the corner 7-Eleven bumming change so they can buy a taco-dog. Losers.

Jaime punctuated his last comment by taking his finger from his nostril and flicking a hard-won booger out the window. I chalked that up to good breeding. Having assumed he'd pop it in his mouth for a snack.

—Harris and his clan, they're mostly hijackers.

I looked from the rearview, where I was eyeballing the latest in a long line of cars with their noses shoved up the rear of the slow-rolling Apache, as we switched from the 405 North to the 110 South to San Pedro.

—Hijackers? What, like, *Release twenty of my fellow believers or I'll crash this plane into the Sears Tower?*

He went digging for another nose nugget.

—No, asshole, like, *get out of the cab of this fucking truck and give me the manifest or I'll shove this gauge up your ass and blow your torso open.* Trucks. They hijack trucks. Boost farm equipment. Tractors. Irrigation pipe. Fertilizer. Do some rustling now and then from what Talbot said.

—Rustling? No way.

—Way. Not like herds or anything. Just when they get a shot at a couple studs, they boost 'em.

He grinned, flicked more snot.

—There's a real market for quality bull jizz. Thought about going into that market. My own brand. Jaime's Horny Homegrown.

He pumped his fist in front of his crotch.

—Jizz like mine, probably get a bull pregnant as easy as a chick.

—Cow.

—Huh?

—You don't get bulls pregnant. You get cows pregnant. I mean, if you have a thing for fucking bulls you should just come out in the open with it. Kind of thing was frowned on at one time, but people are far more open and accepting now.

—Fuck you, asshole. I'm not gay.

I stuck my hand out the window and flipped off the driver of an overdeveloped Italian sports car as he blasted past us, leaning on his horn.

—I wasn't suggesting you were gay. I was suggesting that you liked to fuck bulls. The two are not in the least related.

—Bulls have dicks.

I looked at him.

—Are we having this conversation?

He stuck his finger in my face.

—Bulls have dicks. If I like to fuck bulls, I'm gay.

I turned back to the road.

—Have it your own way.

He leaned into the seat.

—Just saying, I am not gay.

—Like I said, as you wish. Anyone asks, I got the information. *Jaime? No, he's not gay. Just likes to fuck bulls.*

He popped out of the seat.

—Listen, asshole!

I jammed on the brakes and he flew into the steel dash. I floored the gas and he bounced back onto the seat, cracking his head against the rear cab window.

—Ow! Fuck! Shit! Ow!

I dropped back into my slow, steady, road rage inducing, pace.

—You OK there?

—Ow. Shit, my head, man.

—Yeah. Better chill. Maybe buckle up.

—You did that on fucking purpose.

I nodded.

—Yes, Jaime, I did. And I am, take note, *still* driving this thing. So you may want to do as I say and chill and buckle up. Because while I may hit like a little girl, I drive like a born and raised Los Angelino. Which means, you know, I think I'm the best driver in the universe, when in fact I probably shouldn't be allowed in a bumper car.

—Asshole.

He buckled up.

Crossing the PCH we hit Harbor City. The Harbor Park Golf Course, garden spot of Harbor City if the truth be told, rapidly turning traffic-poisoned brown along the freeway. And on our left, a sudden outbreak of cranes, a thicket of them marking the edge of the Port of Los Angeles.

—So before the aside about bovine human relations, you were talking about Harris?

He rubbed the back of his head.

—Yeah, try this kind of shit with him, he'll fuck you up. *Unforgiven* style.

I thought about my special perspective on the kinds of things Harris would do if he took a disliking to you.

—I don't doubt that. Where'd the almonds come from?

He settled back into the seat, careful of his tender shoulder.

—Harris gets tips from drivers sometimes. These two trucks, they were supposed to go out the Port of Oakland. But traffic from the central valley was all screwed up. The drivers had to turn around and park the trucks on the producer's property and leave them overnight. So one of the drivers, he called Harris. Told him two semis loaded with almonds were sitting there with nothing but a fence and a German shepherd for security. He's got some place in Stanislaus County where he can park the trucks once they're off the lot. The almonds have to be offloaded, repackaged in case the container gets opened, and put back aboard. Some third cousin by marriage or some shit has a place. He cultivates a couple acres of almonds himself. So his wetbacks do all the work for five cents, he labels the almonds like the rest of his crop, and they ship 'em out.

—You're half Mexican, yeah?

—What?

—Your mom is Mexican?

—Dude, don't talk about my moms.

—No, I mean.

—And she's American. I'm American. I'm of half-Mexican descent, but I'm full fucking American. Talk about wetbacks all I want. Give me that politically correct bullshit. I hate that shit.

—Yeah. Again, my bad.

—Right it is. Talk about my moms. Fuck you up. Shit.

The Harbor Freeway bent west at a smokestack with the words WEL-COME TO SAN PEDRO running down its length. More practical smokestacks and the storage tanks of a refinery covered a hillside, a Naval Fuel Depot or something. On our left, a vista of more towering gantry cranes, a tangle of steel rooted in piled cargo containers, Yong's Legos grown massive and scarred.

—So with all the wetbacks and other resources at their disposal, why do they need someone like you? I thought your game was film.

—Movies, asshole. My business is movies. Films are fag shit comes in from Europe or out of New York. Films don't make box office for shit unless they win the Oscar. Movies are all about the box. I make movies. But, you know, financing comes from all kinds of sources these days. The studio system, in case you missed the news, is totally dead. These days, we like to spread the risk. Get maybe a bank to pick up the bulk of the load. Bring in some private investors for bridge financing while the package takes shape. All that shit. I expedite relationships that help create financing opportunities for my movie projects.

—So Harris wants to get into the industry?

—No, asshole. He wants to pay me to help him ship his almonds overseas, and then I can redirect those funds into these online filmmakers I have a relationship with. These guys, they had a top-ten most-viewed clip on YouTube for over a week. Fucking sensation. They shot this thing about a dog eating its own shit, it was hysterical. Made it for nothing. I'm gonna take my cut of the almonds deal, funnel it into my production company, and lock up these guys' creative output for the next ten years. I'm gonna pay these kids a couple grand and they're gonna make these videos of animals eating their own shit, and I'm gonna stream them over a dedicated website where people have to subscribe for the service.

—Wait, a website dedicated to shit-eating animals?

—No, asshole, dedicated to humorous clips. Shit-eating animals will be the initial draw, but I'll expand after we attract more capital. Kids are gonna make me rich. And I'm gonna own everything they do. Fuckers didn't know enough to negotiate points or anything.

I got a feeling about something. And I had to ask.

—Jaime. How old are these *kids*?

—I don't know, thirteen maybe. But they have talent. Raw. Think it's easy to get a dog to eat its own shit? Let alone a, I don't know, a parakeet?

—They got a parakeet to eat its own shit?

—Well, no, still working on that one. But they got mad footage of dogs eating their own shit. They mix Alpo into it. That's the secret.

Beyond the massed containers, the long humped spine of the Vincent Thomas Bridge stretched from the mainland across the water to Terminal Island.

—As much as I hate to admit it, Jaime.

—What?

—You'll probably get rich off shit-eating animals.

He grinned.

—Yeah, and that's just one aspect.

I took us past the turnoff to the bridge, heading toward San Pedro.

—Yeah. Imagine. So, I see where you have this thing all mapped out from an industry angle, but I'm still unclear on where the connection comes from. You know, Central Valley agro-hijackers meet shit-eating-animal entrepreneur.

—Heh, sounds like a pitch. Pretty good one, too.

Having spent my earliest formative years at L.L.'s feet, and at his always bent elbow, listening to various habitués of the movie-making community swap pitches, I couldn't really argue with him.

—Sure, when you're an Internet success, you can parlay it into a TV show.

—Feature, man.

—Sure. But it's light on plot details. Like how'd you and Harris hook up?

—Just ways and means. Contingencies and eventualities.

Up ahead, the freeway drifted to a stop at a traffic light at the top of Gaffey Street.

—Translation, man, I'm an asshole. Remember?

—Man, I remember. It was the wetbacks that did it. Warehouse up north got busted by La Migra. Took all the workers out. Only half the almonds had been turned around. Harris didn't want to have that shit sitting around while his cousin's cousin's cousin's whatever got a new crew together. He told him to keep the second load of almonds and the other truck instead of a cash payment for the services. They had an argument. Harris may or may not have fucked him up and took off with the loaded truck. But the third cousin, *he* was the connection for the freight for-warder up there. The guy who could contract a shipping line and get the load onto a terminal and through the Port of Oakland to the buyer on the other end. That meant he had to find an alternate shipping route.

—*Contingencies and eventualities.* He found you.

—What? Hells no. He found Soledad's dad.

At the stoplight, a caged pedestrian bridge crossed over the intersec-tion. Kids hang banners there sometimes. *Class of 2008 Rocks! Welcome Home Sgt. Alberto Juarez. Happy Birthday Tina!*

I stopped for the red light, looked at Jaime.

—Soledad's?

—Her pops, asshole.

—You hooked him up with Harris?

—What? No. You listen to anything? Told you I'm in movies. Old man Nye, he was a professional. Shipping and trade, man. Westline Freight Forwarding, man. That's what he did. You have something going overseas, Pacific Rim, you pay him a fee and he lines up shipping, all the paperwork, even find a buyer for some products. All that shit.

—But how's he? How'd they find him? I mean, why'd they go to a guy like that to smuggle almonds? Why'd they?

The light turned green. I didn't move.

—Why? Asshole, anyone with any savvy knows Westin Nye is the man to go to you got shit that needs to come clean through the Port of Long Beach. That's just smuggler's 101 in this state.

Drivers honked.

—So you worked for him?

—Fuck no. Asshole. I mean him, not you. I mean, he was OK, but he wouldn't let me work for him. No. I only got involved after he bit it.

He turned and flipped off the cars behind us, looked back at me.

—I mean, I never would have had this opportunity if Soledad hadn't asked me to step in after her pops ate his own bullet.

I looked at the road, took my foot from the brake and drove under the banners. The biggest one in red paint, *Jenny, I promise I'll never do it again!*

OTHER THINGS BLOWN

Down Gaffy, under crisscrossing phone lines, between once decorative and now weedy palms, past a glut of gas stations and fast-food places and the Ono Hawaiian BBQ, just across from the Payless Supershine Carwash, but before the Club 111 at the Holiday Inn, Jaime pointed at the curb.

—Here.

And I parked us outside the one-stop shopping opportunity promised at the Bait-n-Liquor.

—Where's the can?

—Around. This is the first stop.

He opened the door and I grabbed his arm.

—I'm not waiting while you get stocked up on Malibu and go all shitfaced on me again.

He looked at my hand.

—Dude, I could just beat the hell out of you if I wanted to.

I didn't let go.

—Yeah. You could. So what?

He pulled his arm free.

—So come in. Fuck do I care. Just keep your mouth shut. Let a man conduct some business.

So I went in with him.

The shop was, as advertised, devoted to both bait and liquor. Although liquor seemed to have the upper hand.

Jaime raised his chin at the old salt central casting had sent up to play the proprietor.

—Homero.

Homero looked away from the screen of the laptop he was playing Free-Cell on, pushed up the brim of his fishing cap and took the pipe from between his teeth.

—Jaime.

He stuck out his hand. Jaime looked at it, took it.

Homero smiled.

—You come down to do some fishing, boy?

Jaime ducked his head.

—No, no, man. Just saying hey. Business, she calls as usual. No leisure.

Homero nodded, waved a fly from in front of his face.

—Sure, man. You want leisure, you got to grow old. No one young should be standing still. Sitting around with a fishing pole in your hand, that's for old men like me. You got to hustle up there, eh? Dog-eat-dog, that business, eh?

—You know it, man. And the more success, the harder you got to work. Everyone, they come for you.

—Gunning for the top dog. Yes, yes.

Homero smiled and nodded.

Jaime shifted from foot to foot.

—Homero, that stuff? You know?

The old man rubbed the stem of his pipe across his lips.

—Yes, yes.

—I need that now. It ready?

Homero tugged at the collar of his baggy V-neck T.

—Yes, yes.

He turned back to the laptop, closed his card game, opened a browser and typed in an address. From beneath the counter he uncoiled a cable and plugged it into the laptop. His index finger slipped across the touch pad as his thumb tapped left-right a few times, and a printer began to whir as the carriage zipped back and forth. The printer clicked twice and went silent and he reached under the counter and came out with a couple pieces of paper.

He held them up, both sheets dense with print, and pointed at a bar code.

—They're gonna have to scan this. Your driver gotta show his license, but this is what they're going to scan. OK?

He came from behind the counter and passed the papers to Jaime.

Jaime took them and folded them in half.

—That other thing?

Homero nodded and walked to a row of Styrofoam coolers sitting on up-ended milk crates down one wall of the shop.

He waved me aside.

—Make way, make way.

I scooted and he shuffled past, down the row of coolers to the last one.

He took the lid off and set it aside and looked back down the shop at Jaime.

—You talk to your mama?

Jaime was staring at the rum bottles behind the counter, he kept staring at them.

—Sure. All the time.

The old man stuck his hand into the cooler.

—Good. You're a good son.

He pulled his hand from the cooler, the tentacles of a small squid wrapped around his wrist, a plastic bag dripping water between his fingers.

—Your mama, she take care of you, then you take care of your mama. So many sons, they don't know that.

He peeled the squid free, looked at me.

—For the sharks. Gray smoothhound. Leopard.

He dropped the squid back inside the cooler.

—Maybe for guitarfish.

He put the lid back on the cooler and came back to the front of the store with the dripping bag.

I made way for him and he walked past, wiping one hand on his T.

—Or mackerel. A nice bloody piece of mackerel for rays and for sharks.

He circled back around the counter, untwisting the neck of the bag.

—Jaime, what did I teach you for croaker? When your mama left you with me? What did I teach you?

Jaime never stopped looking at the booze.

—Mussels. Bloodworms. Ghost shrimp. Live ghost shrimp for croaker.

Homero smiled, putting a hand inside the bag and coming out with a zippered vinyl bank envelope.

—Mussels are easiest. Dig them up.

He showed Jaime the envelope.

—But ghost shrimp are best.

Jaime reached for the envelope, the old man pulled it back.

—Still owe a hundred.

Jaime knuckled the corner of his mouth.

—Gave you a grand.

—Yes, yes. Paid the grand. That was for the paperwork.

He nodded at the cooler full of squid.

—For storage, it's another hundred.

Jaime looked at me.

—You got a C?

—What?

—You want this deal greenlighted or what? I need a hundred fucking dollars.

I went in my pocket for what was left of the cash Po Sin had paid me the last couple days, what I hadn't spent or given to Chev.

—I got seventy-nine and some change.

I walked over and dropped it on the counter. Jaime looked at it, looked at the old man.

The old man shrugged and handed Jaime the envelope.

—You owe me the rest.

He scooped the money from the counter.

—Don't forget, ghost shrimp for croaker.

Jaime headed for the door, I followed.

Homero opened his cash register to put the money inside.

—And tell your mama I said hi.

Jaime pushed out the door, mouth closed, waiting for me at the truck until I unlocked his door. He jerked it open and climbed in.

I walked around and got in and put the key in the ignition.

—Uncle or something?

He shook his head.

—Mom's first pimp.

He looked at me.

—Croaker is the worst fucking fish in the world. Rather eat shit.

He looked out the window at the old man waving from inside the shop.

—Rather eat shit like a fucking dog.

—What went wrong?

Jaime took his eyes from the water below us as I worked the Apache up the steep incline of the bridge, past the parti-colored bulk of a Swedish cruise ship moored on our right.

—Mean, *what went wrong?* Motherfucker turned her out. That's what went wrong. Not that I give a fuck. Bitch wanted to whore, that's her business. Not like she stuck with it anyway. Moms is talent. Adult films. Got a name.

Feeling, I will admit, more than a bit awkward, I clarified.

—No, I mean, what went wrong with the almond deal? Why'd you cut Talbot and all that?

He played with the zipper on the envelope.

—That shit. *What went wrong.* What went wrong with that shit was Soledad's dad went totally off script and started improvising. Killed himself. Fuck do you think went wrong?

—But you didn't get involved until he was already.

—Yeah. So? Still, motherfucker had been alive, it all would have worked out.

I kept my own counsel, unable to find a hole in his logic.

He provided enlightenment.

—Not my business, this shit. I'm a dream merchant, yeah? Commodities aren't my thing. I mean some X, sure, but not produce. Took me a bit of time because they needed someone on the other end.

—Like who?

—Like a buyer. Harris, he lost his buyer on the other end, the one his relative had him hooked up with. He came down here, it wasn't just that he needed to get the load shipped, he needed a new buyer. Soledad's pops supposed to have one all lined up.

—So?

—*So?* So whatever the buyer's name was ends up splattered all over the wall with the rest of the contents of Westin Nye's brain. Asshole. You, not him.

We crested the midpoint of the bridge and the Ports of Los Angeles and Long Beach rolled away below us, spiked with endless cranes, crossed with rail sidings, piled with containers. Industrial wasteland parceled and fenced and knitted together by wide roadways traveled by caravans of eighteen-wheelers, all of it reeking of oil and exhaust.

L.L. loved it down here. Wrote it into any number of unmade screenplays.

One of the great American metaphors, Web. The outer reach of manifest destiny, the point from which we ship the material instruments of our cultural dominance. The physical bookend to the work we do in Hollywood. Fuck, you could shoot an amazing chase scene here. Blow the shit out of The French Connection.

Other things could be blown the shit out of at the port. I remember drinking a milk shake in a diner between a truck wash and a strip club up on East Anaheim Street while L.L. had his pipes cleaned by one of the strippers who worked both long-hauler conveniences.

I put aside my reverie.

—So, no buyer. What else went wrong?

He looked back at San Pedro, over the bridge and across the water.

—I couldn't find a forwarder who would handle the load. Turned out I was gonna have to deal with people I didn't want to have to deal with. Homero. And he wanted that grand for the paperwork, up front. Seeing as all my liquid capital is tied up with the YouTube kids, I'm a little cash poor just now. So I had to move some X and that took time.

—You blew your end of the deal.

—I did not blow my end. Obstacles came up that I hadn't been able to avoid. Shit took longer than I thought. They wanted turnaround like yesterday. But from working in the industry, I'm geared toward things moving at a steady pace. I'm used to weighing the pros and cons of decisions when millions could be at stake. Someday. These guys, they want to sell shit and get paid right away.

—Strange how thieves might be in a hurry.

—Fucking cool it with the smartass, asshole. Here, over here.

—Here?

—Yeah.

We came off the 47 onto Ocean Boulevard, past the twin domes of the waste reclamation plant, a monstrous installation far too evocative of colossal and perfectly symmetrical breasts for Jaime not to comment.

He pointed.

—Looks like big tits.

I declined to respond.

—Big titties.

I changed the subject.

—So what happened when you couldn't do what they wanted when they wanted it?

He threw his hands up.

—Fucking Talbot gets all in my face. Starts talking about the delay means costs and how they're gonna have to come out of my ten percent. Bullshit.

—Yeah, total bullshit. And that was before you knew they weren't even paying the full ten percent.

—Fucking right! Shit. Telling me I was gonna have to cover their hotel and meals for the extra days. As if.

I took a moment to replay what he'd said. Decided I had to be wrong. Realized I probably wasn't. Thought I'd ask. Thought I'd rather not know for sure. And finally couldn't help myself.

—Um, they wanted you to cover their expenses?

—Believe that shit?

—For like a couple days, right?

—Fucking gall!

—They wanted you to cover their room and board for a couple days was what they wanted? Am I correct about that?

—Yeah, that's what I'm saying. You need it in some other brand of English?

—You cut Talbot and started this whole round of shit because?

—Because motherfucker was reneging on a business agreement. I mean, shit may fly in Butte County, but not in Hollywood.

I stared at the rear of the bobtail we were stuck behind.

—Jaime. You cut a man. His boss, his uncle got pissed. He got so pissed, he killed the man you cut.

—And?

I cranked the wheel over and took us off Ocean onto the access road to Terminal T and pulled to the side of the road.

—Dots not connecting, are they? Pointless for me to continue? Yes, I can see that's the case. I won't even bother with the part where they must have been watching your hotel room when I showed up. The part where they followed me and Soledad up to L.A. and snatched her and, by the by, stole my boss's van. Oh, and that, that bit of grand theft auto, for the record, that led to another van being firebombed and shots being fired into a place of business. But I will refrain from lining it up so you can see how all these events result from you not being willing to pick up someone's fucking per diem. Asshole.

He brushed his hand at me.

—Not my fault. People responsible for themselves. Nobody in this, nobody that didn't put themselves in it.

I raised my hand.

—I'd beg to differ. My ass is in this because I got dragged in by a psycho cowboy who told me to get his almonds or *something bad* would happen to someone I like.

He leaned close.

—No, you're in this because my sis called you in the middle of the night for a little help and you came running as fast as you could because you wanted to get in tight with her and tap that ass.

It would have been nice to tell him he was wrong. More to the point, it would have been nice if he had *been* wrong. But he wasn't.

I slumped back in the seat.

—OK. Fuck you. Fuck me. Fuck us all. We're all fucked. Now what?

He unzipped the bank envelope and took out a pistol and pointed it at me.

—Now we discuss terms. Points of gross and shit.

—They have your sister!

—Man, I don't care. I mean, I care. And I'm gonna get her back, but I don't want any misunderstanding, I'm getting my fucking ten percent.

—Wait, is that the real ten percent, or the fake ten percent you were too stupid to realize wasn't really ten percent because you are so fucking stupid?

—Man, did I show you this?

He picked up the gun from the dash again and showed it to me.

—That's all you've shown me for the last half hour.

He pointed it at me.

—So stop fucking around.

—You stop pointing that thing at me! I told you in the first place, I cannot think when you point that at me! I'm like a freak that way, all my brain juice runs out my ass when some moron who doesn't know his multiplication tables points a gun at me and might accidentally pull the trigger because he thinks it's his nose and he's trying to pick it!

—OK, OK, chill, chill!

He put the gun back on the dash.

—There, it's down. Chill.

I chilled. Or I tried to chill. My ability to chill being seriously hampered. My sense of proportion, already in sorry shape before I first walked into a cockroach-filled apartment and started hauling little plastic bags of shit out of it, was fucked beyond recognition.

And I was having some very creepy thoughts.

Like . . .

What if none of this is real? I mean, does it seem real to you, Web? Have you ever had experiences like this? Has anyone you know had experiences like this? Does this not seem rather more like a bad screenplay L.L. might have brushed up in the '80s than like real life? Are you, perhaps, going a little more loony than you first suspected? Or, wait, how about this? Maybe you're not going crazy, maybe, wait for it, maybe you're dead? Get it? Like, you got hit by one of the bullets on the bus? Like you died on the bus and all of this is like after-death experience, like your journey into the afterlife? Or maybe you're still alive, still on the bus? Like it all just happened, is happening, right now? What about that shit?

I shook my head.

—No. No way. Too weird.

Jaime shot me an eye.

—Say what?

—Nothing. I'm cool. I'm here. This is happening. I know this is happen-ing. I'm here. This is here and now. I'm here.

—Dude, are you?

—I'm fine. I'm cool. So. You were saying, ten percent?

He tilted his head.

—OKaaaaaay. So, Mr. Scary Asshole, what I'm saying is, I want it under-stood that if we bring them their can, with the almonds, I'm not sacrific-ing my ten percent. They're the ones pulling out of the deal. I took the time and expense of arranging a buyer for their property and all that shit. I'm not just walking away with nothing.

I finished taking the deep breaths that seemed to be doing very little to help calm me.

—Yes, but you will not be getting *nothing*. You will, in fact, be getting your sister.

—That wasn't the deal! I want my ten percent! And the *real* ten percent. Whatever you said that was.

—OK, fine. So how do we?

He picked up the gun.

—With this. Motherfuckers try to duck out without paying my due, I'm taking action. So you know how I roll. That's what I'm saying. Respect, gotta have it.

That bit of dialogue coming straight from *Boyz N the Hood* if I'm not mistaken.

I stared at the gun in his hand. I thought about how my brain might react to a sudden outbreak of gunfire. Another sudden outbreak of gun-fire, I mean. I thought about how my body might react to a sudden out-break of bullets hitting it. I thought about cops, and who would be screwed if I called them, and found I couldn't keep track of all the details. I thought about thinking about what I said next, but knew if I did I wouldn't be able to say what I said. If that makes sense. Which, of course, it does not.

—I'll cover it.

—Huh?

—The ten percent, I'll cover it.

—What? How?

—I can cover that. If they don't come through, and I kind of think we shouldn't even bring it up, I'll pay it.

He weighed the gun on his hand.

—Bullshit. You clean up after dead people. Where you gonna get twenty-two Gs?

I waited.

He shook his head.

—Twenty-six four! I mean twenty-six four! We're talking twenty-six four here.

—I can get it. I have savings and shit. I can cover it. I'll cover it. If they won't pay you, I will.

He looked me over, licked his lips.

—Know if you're fucking around what will happen, right?

—You'll cut me bad, is what I'm thinking.

—At the least.

—Yeah, at the least.

He nodded.

—OK. OK. Deal. We give them the can no matter what.

—After they give us Soledad.

—Yeah, right, whatever.

I pointed at the gun.

—And you leave that behind when we meet them.

—Fuck that.

—Fine, fuck it. Forget the deal then. Go shoot it out. Get all the respect you want. Shit wears well in the grave.

—Maaan.

He set the gun on the dash.

—Shit. Fucking sister. Fucking Soledad.

I thought about Soledad.

Man, I liked that girl. A lot. And man it sucked that I was right and she'd dragged me into this deal knowing there was a deal to be dragged into.

Shit. I'd really thought . . . I don't even know what. But hey, she could have all kinds of reasons for being involved deeper than she'd let on. She could just be trying to clean up a mess her dad left behind. Not like she was thinking clearly or anything. Girl's dad commits suicide, she's all screwed up and . . . oh. Oh shit.

Suicide.

Criminal enterprise.

Violent suicide.

Moneymoneymoneymoneymoney.

You see how long it takes me to put these things together? That's because I'm not as smart as I think I am. But you probably gathered that. Because you're probably not as stupid as I am. I know that because no one is as stupid as I am.

No one except maybe Jaime.

—What kind of gun is that?

He looked at it.

—Nine.

—Again?

—It's a nine-millimeter. Gun of choice for all.

—Where'd it come from? You get it off a set like the knife?

He raised an eyebrow.

—I got it from Soledad.

HINTERLANDS

—What are you staring at, asshole?

—Nothing.

That's what I said. What I was in fact staring at was the gun. The gun he'd gotten from Soledad. The nine-millimeter he'd gotten from Soledad.

I looked at him.

—I'm not staring at anything.

I started the Apache and turned us around.

—What now?

He took the papers he'd gotten from Homero and slipped them inside the envelope.

—Now we cruise over to Terminal F and check out the can.

I pulled to a stop at Ferry.

—Really?

He bapped my forehead with the documents.

—No, asshole, I'm jerking your chain because I want to spent more time in your company. Yes, *really.*

He held up the papers.

—That was what Homero was doing, getting the export order changed so we can get that can back.

—What about the buyer?

—What? Fuck him. Some Chink? Fuck does he know? Not like he's paid yet. Verbal agreement means shit. Hell, in my line, a *contract* barely means shit. Nothing is nothing till the cash is in your hand.

He fingered the papers.

—Think of it, maybe I should get him to front some of the money for the almonds.

I shook my head.

—No way, man. No more complications. I'm gonna pay you off. But that's it. No double dipping. No shenanigans.

—*Shenanigans?*

—Yeah, it means.

—I know what the fuck it means, I'm just trying to figure how someone born this side of a Lucky Charms commercial thinks it's OK to talk like that.

I pointed up and down the street.

—Just tell me which way to the can.

He pointed toward a smaller terminal, beyond a series of huge blue sheds connected by an enclosed conveyer belt through which petroleum coke was being moved to a container vessel.

—Over yonder, at the foot of that there rainbow we'll find me pot-o-gold.

I put the truck in gear. More than slightly delighted at the prospect that getting the truck was going to be considerably less trouble than I'd been afraid of.

Of such delights are dreams made.

Parked just under the 710, we watched the uniformed officers of Customs and Border Protection, plainclothes detectives from Immigration and Customs Enforcement a well-armed Anti-Terrorism Contraband Enforcement Team, and members of the Long Beach Harbor Patrol as they systematically and, I must say, quite efficiently impounded every last bit of cargo on Terminal F that had any association with Westline Freight Forwarding.

I pointed at a can.

—That one?

—No.

I pointed at another can.

—That one?

—No.

I pointed at another can.

—That one?

Jaime scooted further down in his seat as another CBP car rolled past us and through the gate.

—No, that's not our can. And why the fuck do you care at this point?

I shrugged.

—I don't know, I just thought it'd be nice to know where that pot-o-gold is.

He peeked over the edge of the window frame and pointed.

—That one. OK, asshole? Can we leave now? I mean, before someone comes over and asks what the hell we're doing here?

I waved a hand at the other cars parked on the edge of the road, the assortment of rubberneckers taking in the spectacle of our government's law enforcement community in the act of seizing control of the assets of what was, I gather, a rather extensive smuggling operation.

—So when you said that everyone knew Westin Nye was the man to talk to when you needed something shipped on the sly out of the Port of L.B., you really meant *everyone*.

One of the officers walked to the can Jaime had indicated to me. He inspected a seal, checked it against a clipboard in his hand, set the clipboard aside, and popped the seal.

Jaime dropped low again.

—Fuckfuckfuck.

The officer picked up his clipboard and looked from it to the stacked boxes inside.

I scratched my chin.

—So, what do you figure? They must have been onto Nye for a while. You think they had this planned, or did they decide to make a move after he killed himself?

—I don't fucking know, man. Can we just get the hell out of here? Can we just. Oh fuck!

He was looking at the envelope of documents in his lap.

—Fuck, I got to get rid of these.

He pulled the papers out and stuck them through the window.

I grabbed his wrist.

—Hang on, man.

—Hang on, my ass. I can't get caught with these.

I pointed at the officers and the plainclothes agents again.

—Dude, maybe throwing a sheaf of incriminating shipping documents out the window across the street from a huge smuggling bust is a bad call.

He pulled his hand back inside.

—OK, OK, but get us the fuck out of here.

I looked one last time at the scene, then put the Apache in gear and pulled into the road and turned around.

I hooked my thumb back at the load of almonds.

—By the way?

—Yeah?

—Once we gave them the paperwork and whatnot and they released the container?

—Yeah?

—Where were we going to get a truck, and do you know how to drive one?

He scooted lower in his seat.

—Just shut the fuck up.

—I'll take that as, *it never even occurred to you*.

—Harris has a truck and a driver.

—Yeah, but I just noticed he's not with us.

—Asshole, I know. I wanted to make sure they had the can out of the stacks and on a chassis and ready to roll. Far as Harris goes, all we needed to give him was these papers.

I paused at a stop sign.

—They would have gone for that?

He stared at the papers in his hand.

—Never gonna know now. Shit. Cost me a fucking G. Never gonna see that cash again.

I pointed us back at the 47.

—Jaime, not that I want to bother you with details at a time like this, but I think you're missing the point here.

He shook his head.

—No, man, I ain't forgot, I know this also means I'm out the twenty-two.

I didn't bother to make my point more clear. I mean, why bother? I was gonna force him to help me get his sister back no matter what, so why not let him wallow in his own misery for a while?

Someone screamed, more people screamed. I looked back at the terminal and saw a handful of small ragged men and women scattering from one of the cans, more of them popping from its top, the assorted officers of the law chasing them, brandishing arms and yelling commands. Something fell from the top of the fence along the road, got up and sprinted in front of us and I pounded the brake to keep from running over the fleeing Chinese boy in filthy clothes. A siren fired up and a LBHP vehicle took off after him.

Jaime shook his head.

—Fuckin' Chink wetbacks, man. Two weeks in a can and take their chances on the other side.

He pointed at the terminal where the CBP officers had the illegals down on the ground.

—Soledad's old man, he liked to have a finger in every pie, man.

—Cops? Why the fuck would you call the cops?

I fingered my knife and thought about sticking it in his ear. But it was plastic and would probably break before it went deep enough to hit his brain. And beside, even if I jammed it in there, I was uncertain it would do any real damage.

—No, you're right, Jamie, come to think of it, kidnapping is really more of a matter for the FBI.

—The FBI? Why would you want to call them?

I looked at my plastic fork, thought about jabbing him in the eye with it to get him to focus for a second. I settled for talking slowly instead.

—Jaime, I'm not saying I *want* to call the FBI. I'm saying I *will* call them if you don't help me.

He took another bite of the crappy diner burrito one should expect when one orders Mexican food at a place called Jim's Burgers.

—Fuck should I help you? You're threatening to call the cops on me.

—Other than the brotherly desire to help your sister?

I poked at my own burrito with the plastic fork.

—There's the added incentive that I'll still give you the money.

His ears jumped up a half inch and rotated slightly in my direction.

—Money?

—Help me with this, and I'll still give it to you.

He stuffed the last bite of greasy burrito in his mouth.

—Come on, man, there was never any question about me helping out. I mean, you want to give me the cash, I'll take it, but it's not like I was gonna let Soledad be fucked up or anything.

I nodded.

—Naturally. How could there be any question of that.

I got up from the table.

—I'm gonna make a call.

He wiped his mouth and got up.

—Take your time, I'm gonna get some of that action.

He headed for the aging Mortal Kombat machine at the back of the diner, and I headed for the door and out to the parking lot.

If not for the cranes on the skyline, the corner of Anaheim and North Henry Ford could be in any corroding stretch of the rustbelt. I stood in the middle of the lot and watched a driver pull his truck into one of the stalls at the wash and start hosing the road film off his Peterbilt. Another driver, done with the wash, ambled across the lot to Dreams, the obligatory strip club. I wondered if the same hooker that'd serviced L.L. still worked this spot. She'd be long in the tooth, but that wasn't much of an impairment in this locale. It would likely take a head-to-toe outer coat of leprosy to keep a working girl from scoring a date here at the northeastern rim of the Port.

And more than that to keep L.L. from giving her a try.

The hinterlands of the far western edge of the world, Web. I tell you, if I'd been on my toes, those years I wasted teaching I would have spent here learning something about myself. This is a place to test the limits of a man. His endurance and fortitude, his ability to stare into the abyss and have it stare back into him. Look at it, grotesque and magnificent! A paved waste of trade and industry. The end of the road for America, Web. The jumping point to other, older cultures. Inhale. Breathe deep. Smell that? Smell the sea air tainted by oil and gas fumes? That's what the world smelled like when life was first being formed. A place for new beginnings, son, a place to find out who you are. Here, pass me another of those Löwenbräus.

The edge of the world.

What better place to try and turn yourself around?

So I began trying to execute a U-turn at a very narrow part of the road, with oncoming traffic.

I took the phone Harris had given me from my pocket and dialed.

—Clean Team.

—Hey, Po Sin, it's me.

—Young Web. It seems like only yesterday you were falling asleep on the job and letting my van be stolen. Wait, it was only yesterday. My, how time does fly. What can I do for you today?

I scuffed at some gravel, looked around at one of the garden spots of my childhood in L.L.'s care, thought about the casual damage we inflict on each other by waking up and being ourselves.

—Po Sin.

—Still here.

—Po Sin. I left the office. I was back at the office when the van was stolen. But I lied about leaving.

Po Sin is a vast man, capable of vast silences. He put one on display for me. I waited for it to drift past, but didn't have the time.

—Po Sin?

—I'm here.

—I'm sorry, man. I'm sorry I didn't do my job.

There followed a sigh I thought might go on forever.

Eventually it ended.

—My kids, Web.

—Yeah.

—They need a lot of help. Yong, well, what can I say. That's going to be our whole lives, helping him. And Xing? It's impossible to give her the attention she deserves because of Yong. So she tries to get it other ways.

—I know.

—And they're expensive as hell. Kids always are. Care for Yong, therapy, the tutors, Jesus, you have no clue.

—Sure.

—Sure. Web. Thanks for the apology.

—I. Please don't thank me.

—Web. I said, *Thanks for the apology.* And now you say?

—You're welcome?

—Something like that. So, my kids are expensive and hard work. So, I don't have time for another one. Especially not one who costs me more money by fucking up. Understand?

—Yeah.

—Time to grow up, man. Yeah?

—Yeah. I seem to be hearing that from a lot of people lately.

—Could be there's a reason for that.

—Yeah.

—OK. Well, one way or another, we'll deal with the van. After the little errand you and Gabe did last night, I don't think I'll be talking Morton into returning it, but it was insured. In the end, it'll cost me some hassle and a little higher premium. And better to bring the shit with Morton to a head now than later. Not that any of that is meant to make you feel better, but that's about how it sizes up. That it? Got it all off your chest?

I looked around me, saw the horizon, the place where the ocean spilled over the sharp edge of a flat world, the sucking drain that flood would draw me into if I didn't get turned about soon.

And I cranked the wheel hard over.

—It's not just that I left the office. I left the office and got into some stupid shit. And that's why the van was stolen. Morton didn't steal it. Some other guys did. Some really dangerous guys. They have it.

No pause this time.

—Motherfucker!

—They have it and they have something else.

—Motherfucker!

—They have the girl.

—Motherfucker what?

—Po Sin, they have Soledad. And I want to help her. And.

—Motherfucker.

—And I need your help.

Which, when you think about it, wasn't the kind of request you'd expect would make him pause again, as opposed to continuing to say his favorite word when called upon to express how near he was to a stroke.

But it did.

And we had a conversation. And I promised to call again soon. And then I made another call, this one yet more pleasant. If you can imagine bliss.

—Hi, is Soledad there?

—What?

—Can I talk to Soledad, please?

—Who is this?

—It's the guy you sent to get your almonds.

—The what? Oh, right. Hey, Harris, it's the guy.

The phone on the other end was fumbled around.

—You got my can?

A tricky question given the circumstances, but I was prepared.

—We're ready to make the swap.

—Who's *we*?

—Me and Jaime.

—That jackass? Didn't say a word about that jackass bein' involved.

—No, you didn't, but you did tell me to get you your can and your almonds, and seeing as I had no clue what you were talking about, I thought it best I involve someone with some expertise on the subject.

—Hn. Funny.

I watched Jaime through the smeared window glass of Jim's, as his Mortal Kombat fighter pulled out the spine of its opponent.

—What's funny?

—Funny you didn't mouth off like that when you were in the same room with me.

—Well, I can explain that. See, you were in the same room with me, and you had a gun, that inspired me to pretty much keep my mouth shut. Now, in this case, I'm on a phone, so it's a slightly different situation and I'm feeling less inclined to worry about you shooting me if I say the wrong thing. Seeing as you can't and all.

—Hn. Yeah, mouthin' off. OK, well, you're right, can't do nothin' 'bout that over this phone. Not to *you* anyway. If you can follow that without it bein' spelled for you.

Having been a teacher, I didn't need it spelled for me.

—I understand.

—Good, 'cause without you here in person for me to take my aggression out on, I might need to settle for what's at hand.

—I said, *I understand.*

—Good. So, s'pose you want to talk to your girl.

—She's not really my girl.

—Not the picture she paints.

I stopped walking nervous circles around a garbage can.

—Really? Like, what did she say?

—You can ask when you get here with the almonds.

—You just said I could talk to my girl.

—No, I said, *s'pose you'd like to talk with your girl.* Way you do that is to get over here with my can. 'Sides, just said she's *not* your girl.

—I know what I said.

—So, what's to talk with her?

—Just tell me where to go.

He told me and I let my jaw drop the appropriate amount.

—You're fucking kidding me.

—Hell would I be kidding you?

I scooped my jaw up.

—No reason. Anyway, it's not you, it's just God playing fun with me.

—Boy.

—Yeah.

—Don't go making jokes about God with me. I don't have that kind of humor.

—No. I didn't think you did.

—And tell that jackass Jaime, he don't come up with what he owes us for the room here and our meals, this whole thing's gonna go up in his face.

And he hung up.

I closed the phone, looked back through the window at Jaime, still pumping his fist with every ripped limb, and walked down to the edge of the parking lot and looked west up Anaheim.

I looked back inside Jim's to make sure Jaime was well stocked with quarters, and then walked a couple blocks along Anaheim to Flint and took a left at the used-truck lot; a dirt yard fenced with corrugated steel and barbwire, filled with big rigs. Less than a block down from there, past a row of turquoise stucco bungalows, I found the Harbor Inn. I walked down the alley that ran along the north side and looked at a back wall dotted with little bathroom windows. I continued down the alley that wrapped around the whole building. No doors other than the emergency exit at the back. The Harbor Inn, a long two-story corridor of rooms, windows on the outer walls. I looked at the rear southeast corner, on the ground floor. I looked down another alley that ran away to the east, a passage of ridged cargo container steel, chopped from abandoned cans. I walked back to the street. Looked at the road-beaten rig with Yosemite Sam painted on the hood parked at the curb across the street between two campers. I nodded at the guy standing out front of the Inn with a Heineken in his one hand and a Tijuana Bible in the other.

The first thing I noticed about holding a gun for the first time in my life was that the damn thing was heavy. The second thing was that shaking it and just kind of handling it didn't make any noise like it does in the movies and on TV where you'd swear guns must be full of little tiny moving parts that click and rattle all the time. A real gun only makes noise when you do something to it. Like work the slide or snap the safety off, or pull the trigger. The last thing I realized about a gun was that holding one felt seriously fucking cool and dangerous at the same time. I didn't like that feeling.

I found a button on the side of the gun that was far enough from the trigger to make me feel reasonably secure nothing terrible would happen if I pushed it. I thumbed it in and the end of the clip popped out of the bottom of the grip. I pulled it free, finding more resistance than I expected, and set the gun on the seat. One by one I flicked the bullets from

the clip and into the palm of my other hand. Having seen what they do to a body, I didn't much want to touch them, but I did. Once the clip was empty I dribbled the shells into the breast pocket of my bowling shirt, and then slipped it back into the gun and pressed until I felt a firm click. I had the gun back in the glove box when I remembered something from one of L.L.'s screenplays. I took the gun out and looked at it. I made sure the little safety lever was firmly set to *o*, and, taking care to aim the damn thing out the open door of the Apache at the ground away from Jim's or the truck wash or Dreams, I pulled the slide back and watched the bullet Jaime had been stupid enough to keep chambered pop out and arc behind the seat and down into the hollow where Chev stored his tool bag.
—Shit.

I gentled the slide back into place and found that the hammer was cocked. I placed my thumb over it, and, for what I swore would be the only time in my life, I pulled the trigger of a gun. Nothing happened, of course. I mean, there was a snap and the hammer came loose and I lowered it into place, but the gun didn't go off by some weird alignment of having a hidden bullet and my thumb not being strong enough to hold the hammer back or anything like that. But until I put the thing back in the glove box, I kept expecting it to fire of its own will and send a round ricocheting over the parking lot and through a window and into someone else's life.

But that didn't happen. Which was a huge relief.

Next I made a final call to Po Sin and told him what he needed to know. Beyond that information, there seemed to be little excuse for conversation. Especially seeing as he was clearly still contemplating bailing on the whole deal.

I thought it best not to think about what that could mean. And succeeded in doing so. Not thinking about bad things being a gift of mine.

Finally, I got out of the truck and walked to the storm drain in the middle of the lot and dropped the bullets down between the grates to splash into the dirty soapy runoff from the truck wash.
—What's up?

I looked up at Jaime as he came from the diner.

I shrugged.
—Just killing time.

I started back to the truck.
—We should get going.

—Fine by me. Where's my gun?

I got in and knocked on the glove box.

—In there. But for fuck sake don't shoot anyone with it.

He took the gun out.

—*Shoot anyone?* It's a gun. That's what it's for. I mean, what am I supposed to use with Harris to make him give Soledad back so I can get the fucking money you owe me?

—We don't need a gun, we have a plan.

—Fucking plan? You never told me about a plan. A gun is better than a plan. A gun is a guarantee. What you *planning* to do when your *plan* doesn't work and you need something to persuade Harris to go along?

I took out the envelope with the shipping documents.

—I thought we'd use these.

He grabbed the envelope from me and stuck it in my face.

—Asshole, they seized the terminal. The law has the almonds.

I had a sudden flashback to the classroom. The effort it could take on some days to explain rudimentary principles of the English language to twelve-year-olds.

—Jaime, I know this is an abstract concept, but follow me here. Harris, *he doesn't know* the almonds were seized.

—Yeah, but.

—Jaime. He. Does. Not. Know. The. Almonds. Were. Seized.

He opened his mouth. Froze. Nodded.

—Yeeeaaah, man. *He doesn't know.* Yeah, that's good. Hey, asshole, that's really fucking good. Great twist, man, great twist.

He slapped the envelope on his thigh.

—Will it work, asshole? Will he take the papers instead of the can?

I stared at him.

—Um, wasn't this the way it was supposed to work in the first place?

—Well yeah, but I never knew if it'd *really work*. Think it will?

I thought about the options, couldn't come up with any in particular.

—Yeah, it'll work.

—Well it doesn't work, we got the gat as backup.

—You shouldn't need the gun. All you need to do is stay out of sight.

He gave me a squint.

—What's that *stay out of sight* shit?

—I'm sure you'll be shocked to discover that Harris doesn't like you.

—Fuck him anyway. Like I like his hick ass.

—Just so. That being the case, I'd rather not have two armed men who hate each other in the same room while I'm negotiating for Soledad's release.

—Man, I got a stake in this.

—Yeah, it's your project, I know. And your stake is guaranteed. What isn't guaranteed is that Harris will deal straight. So if things go off, I want some backup. Follow me?

He cocked an eyebrow and nodded slowly.

—Yeah, *backup,* I follow. I like that. Buddy cop action. *48 Hours.* That works, it sells. And that's it, that's all I got to do to get my pay?

I nodded.

—Yeah. Just stay out of sight, keep your eyes open, make sure no one backdoors me while I'm inside. And be ready in case I call for help.

He gave the gun a spin on his index finger.

—So we do need the gun.

—We don't need the gun. Just be ready in case I need help.

—Be ready with the gun.

—Jaime!

—Chill, chill, I'm just fuckin' with you. I'll be cool and keep my eyes open and I'll be ready. And that's all, right?

—That and be yourself.

He leaned back and tucked his hands behind his head.

—Bein' myself is what I do best. Star quality.

He pointed at the keys in my hand.

—So we rolling or what?

I pocketed the keys.

—Naw.

—What, we just gonna sit around here?

I got out and started down the street.

—Nope. We'll walk.

And we did, walked back to the Harbor Inn where the bad guys were holed up waiting for the showdown.

BENEATH A RAGING EYE

—Where's my girl?

—Where's my can?

I looked at Harris, and I reminded myself about his really big gun and the way he'd used my phone to kill someone. I took into careful account that more was at risk in this motel room than just my miserable existence, and I formulated a response that was calculated to bring calm to a fraught situation.

—Could you shut the fuck up for a second and tell me where my girl is?

I raised a finger.

—Not that I really think she's my girl, I know that was an asinine thing to say, just that I'm a little hyped up right now and some weird things are liable to come out of my mouth.

Harris came across the room and kicked me in the shin and I bent to grab it and he rapped me on the back of my head with the butt of that really big gun I was supposed to be remembering he had.

I curled on the carpet, one hand on the lump growing from my shin, one on the lump growing from the back of my head, white light pulsing at the edges of my vision with every beat of my heart.

Harris looked down at me.

—Had a conversation, didn't we, about you and that mouth and bein' in the same room?

I nodded and felt my brain flop around inside my skull.

He nodded back.

—Don't keep that conversation in mind, weird things are liable to come out of my gun.

His driver, appropriately dressed in Wrangler jeans, a sleeveless Raiders T, and a meshback trucker's cap with Yosemite Sam on the front, barking *Back Off!*, opened the door.

—It ain't out there. Ain't on the street, ain't up on Anaheim. No truck, no can. Just this pecker.

He shoved Jaime into the room.

Jamie stumbled in, tripped over my legs and went on his ass.

—Fuck off me, hick.

The driver flipped him off.

—Fuck you, pecker.

I got up on one elbow and looked at Jaime.

—I told you to stay out of sight.

He untangled his legs from mine.

—I was staying out of sight! I was way down at the corner staying out of sight. No one told me Mr. Big Ten Four over there was gonna come poking around.

Mr. Big Ten Four hitched up the waist of his jeans.

—Pecker was lurking, Harris.

I rubbed my head.

—He wasn't lurking, he was just keeping an eye out in case you guys tried to pull something.

Mr. Big Ten Four reached in his back pocket and came up with Jaime's pistol.

—Was too lurking, man. With this on 'im.

Harris scratched the thin stubble on the crown of his head, lightly put the toe of his boot in my side.

—Looks like we're not the ones trying to pull nothin'. Looks like we're the ones showed up with what we're supposed to have. That bein' the girl.

He pointed at me and Jaime.

—As opposed to some jackasses who didn't show up with what they were supposed to have. That bein' a load of almonds.

Mr. Big Ten Four waggled Jaime's gun.

—And they're lurking.

Harris nodded.

—Looks like you ain't got your shit together at all here. Looks like you're trying desperate measures with some kind of ambush.

I pointed at Jaime.

—He wasn't lurking. He wasn't setting up an ambush. He was staying out of the fucking way. I told him to wait out there so he wouldn't screw things up.

Jamie punched me in the shoulder.

—Fuck you say.

Harris shrugged.

—Just had your boy out there hangin' about with a piece on him?

I pushed off the floor, trying not to put too much weight on the leg he'd kicked.

—Listen, man, you were saddled with this piece of deadweight as an associate, would you want him anywhere near the room where business was being attended to?

Jaime got himself up.

—Fuck you talking about, *deadweight*? This is my project!

I looked at him, looked back at Harris.

—You know I had to explain to him how you guys were nicking him on the ten percent thing? Seriously. I had to tell him it was happening, and then I had to do the math for him.

—Fuck you, asshole, that's bullshit. He's lying.

Harris rubbed his knuckles across the line of his jaw and covered the bit of a smile that crossed his mouth.

—Yeah. That started more as a joke. Bet my nephew that jackass wouldn't know he was bein' taken'. Mostly in the way of fun, you understand. Didn't really expect him not to know his numbers.

Jaime raised his arms over his head.

—I knew that! I knew it was a bet! I was, man, I was playing you guys! Man, like, thinking, *These fools think they got it over me, but I'm funnin' them like they don't even know.* I pulled a double twist in you. Total *Usual Suspects.*

I shoved my hands deep in my pockets and shook my head.

—This is what I'm talking about. Who wants this around when you're trying to get things done? I figured having him outside and otherwise occupied was the way to go.

Harris nodded.

—Yeah, I can see that.

Jamie slapped the air.

—Hell with you! Hell with you!

Then Mr. Big Ten Four butted in.

—Harris.

—Yeah?

—Why's the pecker need a gun he's just supposed to be out of the way? How 'bout that, Mr. Smartypants?

I let the Mr. Smartypants comment slide. A major achievement for me.

—It's not loaded.

Everyone looked at the gun.

I shrugged.

—Check it, man. It's not loaded.

Mr. Big Ten Four popped the clip loose, like a man used to doing such things, and showed us all the absence of ammunition.

Everyone looked at me.

—Hey, who wants a mental defective like this to have a loaded weapon? I just let him hold it 'cause I know it would shut him up.

It wasn't that hard for Harris and Mr. Big Ten Four to get Jaime off me, and they didn't hurt him doing it, but I wouldn't have felt all that bad if they had.

—Asshole! You are such an asshole!

Harris shoved him down into the space between the wall and the bed.

—Just sit your ass there and shut the hell up, jackass. Fact is, you're lucky to have this guy lookin' out that you don't bite off more than you can chew. But you keep openin' your mouth to take a bite and I'm gonna smash all your teeth out. You hear me?

Jaime gave me a stare.

—Yeah, I hear you.

—Good.

Harris turned to me.

—So. Just remains a large detail to be settled.

He came over, close by.

—Like where's my can?

I shook my head.

—I don't have it.

Mr. Big Ten Four took off his hat and slapped his thigh.

—Cocksucker!

Harris pointed at something behind me.

—See what's over there?

I took a look and saw the room phone.

—Yeah. I see it.

—Want to tell me a little more?

I nodded.

—Yes, I do.

I took the envelope from the back of my jeans, unzipped it and pulled out the papers.

—It is signed sealed and delivered and waiting for someone to pick it up.

He took the papers from me, looked them over, spoke as he did so.

—A man of less faith than my own might suspect this was a setup.

He looked up from the papers.

—Any reason you didn't just bring the almonds right here?

—Other than we weren't able to get a truck and a driver? No.

—Could have hired a driver. They're all over the damn place here.

I looked at Jaime.

—Thanks again, rocket scientist.

He balled his fists, but broke with tradition and kept his mouth shut.

I looked back at Harris.

—This is what happens when you depend on the weak-minded for professional counsel.

—Sure, but what say you go out to one of the bars around here, hire yourself some out of work and in-need long-hauler, and go fetch that can for me? Just drive out there and hitch up and bring it back.

I rubbed my forehead.

—Man, I, man, just, OK, look, look, I would not know where to begin with that shit. I mean, this?

I held my arms out.

—Guns? Assholes like Jaime there? Guys like you two? Kidnappings? Things like what went down with Talbot in my kitchen? That's all well outside my experience. I'm not the kind of guy walks into a trucker bar and hires a driver to take a load of hot almonds off a dock.

—Seems you're improvising pretty well so far.

I clapped my hands three times.

—Well, thanks! I appreciate the vote of confidence. And I'm not saying I couldn't manage, I'm just saying that by the time I have that shit taken care of, that terminal could be locked down for the night. Yeah? Whereas, your boy here can zip over there right now and be in and out and we can all go the fuck home.

Harris gave it a little contemplation.

Mr. Big Ten Four on the other hand, who was turning out to be a bit sharper than the stereotype led me to expect, had more observations to offer.

—He's talking pretty goddamn fast, you ask me.

Harris dragged a thumbnail down one of those long creases in his cheek.

—Watch the Lord's name there.

—Sorry.

—But you are right, he's chattering a little fast. Little fast.

I wagged my head.

—*Talking a little fast?* Man, you are lucky you can put together a thing I'm saying. You're lucky I'm talking in a pitch audible to human ears. *Talking a little fast?* I'm not just talking a little fast, I'm simultaneously pissing and shitting my pants out of fear. I'm on the extreme edge of losing all cool and just falling apart. I have no fucking clue what I'm doing here and I am borderlining as we speak. I, man, I clean shit for a living! Before that, before a couple days ago, I slacked for a living. Before that, I was, man, I was, I was, I was a fucking elementary school teacher! I am out of my depth and beyond my ken! You think this is a setup? Man, this is nothing. This is me trying to dogpaddle. This is me trying to keep my head out of the water.

I dropped onto the bed, my arms hanging, my head down, I breathed.

—Man.

I looked up.

—This is me just trying to keep everyone alive. That's all I want here. I just want everyone, not just me and the girl, not just retard there, but all of us alive and well and waving each other off into the sunset. That's all. That's my plan. That's what I'm in this for.

Harris looked me over, cocked his head at Mr. Big Ten Four, scratched his earlobe with the big revolver that had never left his right hand since he cracked me with it, and gave an inclination to his head that might be considered a nod among the tersest of the world.

—OK, boy. OK.

He tucked the revolver into his belt.

—I think we have a deal on that part.

He passed the papers over to Mr. Big Ten Four.

—All we need to settle now.

He hooked his thumbs into his belt loops.

—Is our bill for this room and our meals the last few days.

Jaime brought his head up.

—Fuck that! Don't do it, asshole, don't you give in on that shit! I'll fucking kill you, you give in on expenses!

I held up a hand.

—Chill, Jaime.

I looked at Harris.

—Let me see the girl.

He shook his head.

—Said payment's due.

—And I heard you. And I'm saying let me see the girl. It's time.

He pursed his lips, let a little air out through his nose, and wiggled a finger at the bathroom door.

Mr. Big Ten Four grunted and walked over and knocked on the door.

—Come on out.

There was a rustle from inside. I waited, doing my best to keep the few bites of Jim's Burgers burrito down where they belonged. My brain painting pictures of how bad she was gonna look.

And the door opened.

And Soledad came out.

And she looked just fine.

Tired as hell. Tearstained. Wrinkled and wrung out and in need of several showers. But other than that, just fine.

—Hey, Web.

I got off the bed and went over to her. I reached out a hand. I unbuttoned the pocket of the Mobil shirt she'd put on after we slept together. And I pulled out the fold of hundreds L.L. had left for me between the pages of *Anna Karenina*.

I turned from her and walked to Harris and held out the money.

—This cover it?

He took the bills and counted them.

—And then some.

He hitched a shoulder at Mr. Big Ten Four.

—Call when you got 'er rollin' back here.

Mr. Big Ten Four went out of the room. Harris grabbed a seat next to the door. Jaime continued to give me stink eye. And, still being pretty sure Soledad had lied to me about something, and being pretty pissed about it as well, I did my best to ignore her.

Not looking at her, being the best way I knew to keep my brain from forcing me to remember what she looked like naked and how smooth and downy the skin was at the small of her back.

—I didn't even want to bring the tweaked-out little bugger along.

—Web.

—Mean, his mom hadn't been in my business about how he needed someone to reach out a hand and get him on his feet if he was ever gonna get free of that crap, it never would have crossed my mind to take him on the road and put him to work. My sister just kept up on me 'bout how the best thing for him would be to get out of town and away from all his tweaker friends, so I went 'gainst my better judgment and had him ride with my crew when we hit the road for the season.

—Web.

—Guess it didn't pan out the way his mom hoped.

Harris blew out his cheeks.

—Gonna have a hell of a time explaining that to her. Not so much he died, boy had *early grave* tattooed on his shoulder. Not just making conversation there, he actually had the words *early grave* tattooed on his shoulder. He asked for it, he got it. Still.

—Web.

—Still, it's gonna be a bitch explaining how he died. S'pose I'll say he got crushed under a train or something. Tell her we were taking a load off a boxcar on a sidin' and he tripped up and went under another as it was pulling out on the opposite tracks. Somethin' 'long those lines. Make it clear why there's no body to bring back.

—Web.

Harris shifted his weight forward and dropped the front legs of his tilted chair to the floor.

—Boy, that girl's talkin' to you. Been tryin' to get your attention the last hour. You want to maybe give her a glance so she'll stop interruptin' me while I try to figure some crap out?

I glanced at Soledad.

—What?

She shrugged.

—I just wanted to say thanks.

—What for?

She looked at the ceiling.

—For coming to get me, what else?

—You're welcome.

I looked at Harris.

—OK, we're done.

He looked at Soledad.

—All done?

She folded her arms.

—Sure, fine, let him pout.

He tilted back and lifted the edge of the curtain and peeked out the window.

—Glad you got that bit out of your systems. Now you can maybe please shut the hell up.

He dropped the curtain and gave me a look.

—While I pass the time along till I get to a point that's coming soon where I figure this is all BS and I decide I have to do something to make amends for bein' made to feel foolish and all.

He tapped the cellphone he'd set on the table at his elbow.

—This don't ring soon.

He pointed at the room phone.

—I may have to replay certain incidents from our recent past, Web.

He laced his fingers behind his head.

—Know you know what I'm sayin'.

He was right, I knew.

I raised my hand.

—Can I go to the bathroom?

—Uh-huh. Just leave the door open.

I went into the john and unzipped and stood in front of the toilet and didn't pee because I didn't really have to go.

—I don't hear anythin' in there.

I stuck my head out the door.

—That's 'cause I'm pee shy around girls. Can I run the tap?

He waved a hand.

—Whatever it takes.

I ducked back in and turned the taps on full and stood at the can for a second and looked out the open door and turned and eased the shower curtain aside and stepped into the tub and tugged the bathroom window and it didn't open. I stepped out of the tub, hit the flush lever, got back in the tub and gave the window a good yank and it ground open on rusted tracks. The rush of toilet water was fading from the pipes and I got out of the tub and pulled the curtain closed and stuck my hands under the running water in the sink and turned off the taps and looked around and couldn't find a towel. I went out, my hands dripping.

—No towels.

Harris inclined his head at a couple athletic bags near the door.

—Got 'em packed away already.

I sat back on the bed, discovering that I suddenly had to pee very badly.

Harris pointed at Soledad.

—You need to go?

She shook her head.

He pointed at Jaime.

—You?

He furrowed his brow.

—Uh.

—Ain't something most people have to think about, jackass.

Jaime shook his head.

—No, no, I don't have to go.

—OK, well, from here on out, everyone's holding it.

Harris settled and put his hand back behind his head.

—Talbot. Know what you need to know 'bout that boy? Other than his teeth were gray from snorting crank and his hair was fallin' out and his skin was yellow and his nose was collapsin' in on itself? What else you need to know about Talbot was his car. Boy had this car, eighty-eight or eighty-nine Toyota or Honda or one of them other Jap cars all look the same. Had that car awhile. Know how long? Ten years. Had that car ten years. Know how he got it? Stole it. Boosted it off the street in Humbolt. Went there to score some grass and came back with some college kid's car. Used to brag on that car all the time. *Stole this car ten years ago and I'm still drivin' it. You believe that shit? Ten years in the same hot car and I ain't been busted. Bet I drive this car twenty years before they bust me for it. Cops so fuckin' stupid, had me pulled over twice since I stole it and they ain't busted me for the hot car I'm in.*

He shook his head.

—Said that. Said, *Bet I drive this car twenty years before they bust me for it.* Never occurred to him to maybe unload the damn thing *before* they arrested him. He just figured you steal a car, you drive it till you get caught. Whoever drives his longest wins. 'Course, six of those ten years he bragged about he was inside for dealin'. That was before his habit got so bad he couldn't be trusted by no one to deal. Anyhow, that's about all you need to know about Talbot. Boy was an albatross the whole season.

—Web.

—Some farmer's leavin' a stack of irrigation pipe at the same southwest corner of a citrus orchard for a week, we hear about it from one of his wetbacks and send Talbot with a couple hands to pick it up. He comes back with a truckload of PVC. Ask him, *Where's the pipe,* he points at the plastic in the truck. That he don't even know the points of the compass to find the right corner is one thing.

—Web.

—But that he can't tell between PVC and steel is another.

—Web.

The legs of his chair came down.

—Boy, will you acknowledge the girl, for peace sake?

I rubbed my shin where he'd kicked me.

—I don't want to talk to her.

She clapped her hands to her head.

—Why? What the hell did I do?

I pulled up my pant leg and looked at the big purple lump.

—She knows what she did.

—No, I don't, I really don't!

I looked at Harris.

—She so knows what she did.

She got up.

—What I did? What *I* did? What I did was *like* you! What I did was need someone to hold me.

She came across the room at me.

—What I did was fuck you and have you freak out in the morning and I walked outside when you told me to get away from you and got kidnapped by the Oakridge Boys!

Harris leaned forward in his seat.

—Settle down now.

—You fucked asshole?

We looked at Jaime, still wedged between the bed and the wall, but newly roused from the nap he'd been taking.

She stuck a finger in my face.

—Yes, I did. And it was nice. And I needed it. And I thought he was cool and safe. But he's acting like every asshole I've ever fucked, by turning into a dick now that he's gotten some.

Harris knocked on the table.

—Said *settle down.*

Jaime flipped me off.

—Knew you were an asshole.

I raised my hands.

—Hey, hey, I tried to talk you out of it.

—Oh yeah, you tried so hard!

I got off the bed.

—I did! I did! I knew it was screwed up and I tried, but you were all over me.

—All over you! OK, sure, I was all over you. But I. Shit. I. Oh, Web.

—Settle down!

Harris grabbed her by the hair and swung her around and slapped her and shoved her face down onto the carpet. Jaime started to push up from between the bed and wall and Harris planted his heel in the back of Soledad's neck and Jaime dropped back to the floor.

I didn't move.

Not being used to violence happening around me until recently, I didn't have a chance to move. But that didn't make Harris any more reluctant about planting the barrel of his revolver under my chin.

The barrel of a gun, it's cold to the touch.

I felt a vibration down that cold steel barrel as he cocked the hammer and the cylinder rotated and a live round slid into alignment with my brain. He pushed up and brought my eyes to his.

—Do you know why you are alive?

Well, there are questions and there are questions, yes? Sometimes you get asked the same question you've been asking yourself for a year. So you have the answer right there at your fingertips.

As did I.

—Man, I do not. I really don't.

He chucked my chin with the barrel.

—You are alive to clean up the mess after I kill these two. Because you have screwed me over.

A radio switched on and Waylon Jennings started singing "Lonesome, On'ry and Mean."

Harris let a few bars play.

—Come with me.

He backed toward the table, the gun still under my chin, and I came along with him, hoping he wouldn't trip. He reached back for his cell-phone, felt for it, opened it and the song stopped playing.

—Hello?

Behind his sealed lips, Harris ran his tongue over his teeth.

—And?

He listened for a bit, nodded a little.

—See you then.

He took the phone away, snapped it shut.

—Hn.

The cold barrel came away from my skin.

—Back up.

I did.

He pointed at the bed.

I sat.

He nodded.

—Well, can was there, ready to roll. And he is rollin'. Which, I have to say, that is an interesting turn of events.

He started to bring the gun back up.

—Not that it really changes much for you all.

The door swung open and Mr. Big Ten Four crashed through and stumbled into the wall next to the bathroom door and left a bloodstain when his battered face slapped against it. Harris twisted, the barrel of the gun rotating away from us and toward his partner.

—What the hell?

Mr. Big Ten Four slid down the wall, streaking blood, one arm out, pointing toward the door. Harris continued to swivel, bringing the gun around, looking for the threat.

But by the time he got there and faced the door, Po Sin was inside it, the pistol that had looked so big in Gabe's hand the night before looking like a toy in his own.

—Motherfucker.

Harris didn't move.

Po Sin took another step inside.

—Motherfucker, don't point that gun at me.

Harris didn't move.

Po Sin put out a hand and shoved the door closed.

—Motherfucker, I am a tempting target, but do not point that gun at me.

Harris didn't move.

And then Harris took Po Sin's advice and did not point the gun at him. Instead, he twisted 'round and pointed it at Soledad on the floor.

—Anyone does any damn thing and I'm gonna do the obvious.

Po Sin's lower lip swallowed his upper.

—Motherfucker.

Here's the thing about witnessing something truly awful.

It sucks.

Here's the thing about witnessing a small child being shot in the side of her face and having most of the rest of her face smeared on your clothes and covering her body with yours because some part of your brain has registered the fact that she has been hit by a bullet and you suddenly find out that you are more than willing to have the next bullet hit and kill you if it means that she'll not be harmed any further.

The thing about that is that it hurts when the next bullet doesn't come.

You end up thinking about it a lot. When you're not thinking about that second bullet, the one you knew might come, and therefore could do something about, you are actually, in point of fact, still thinking about it. You don't really think about anything else.

Some of your brain, in order to keep you focused on things it needs you to do, like breathing and eating and such, builds little façades to place over the surface of the world. Perfectly detailed overlays that mimic the world you lived in before you had little girl face on your clothes. Illusions as painstakingly crafted as the relic Old West street fronts on studio back lots. Scrims of normalcy that keep you walking and talking and breathing and eating.

And because that's what you perceive, the hyper reality you inhabit, it's the behavior of everyone around you that seems out of sync.

I'm OK, man. What the hell is everyone else's problem? Why is everyone acting so weird?

But some other part of your brain knows it's a fake. And knows, as well, who is responsible for the fake. And knows that you can't keep existing in a fake world propped on wobbly jack-stands in front of the real.

Sooner or later a stiff wind will come and blow it down on top of you.

That part of the brain sends out messages, bits of code meant to remind you of what's behind the sets. Scrawled missives.

Don't get comfortable. This all has to come down someday. Don't open that door, there's nothing behind it!

The gap between those two parts of the brain is dark and deep. Narrow, but wide enough by some inches to fall into and be lost.

But you're not thinking about any of that. The two worlds you're walking in are just background to one thing, one thought carved into endless variation.

Where is that second bullet?

And when is it going to hit me?

And make me useful again?

Always you're looking, whether you know it or not, for that opportunity, that chance to do it over again. A dream that will never come true. A shot at taking the bullet.

And saving the innocent girl.

Or a girl not so innocent.

I looked at the gun pointing at Soledad.

Heartbeat.

And I got off the bed.

Heartbeat.

And I laid my body over hers.

Heartbeat.

—Boy.

I looked up at Harris.

He centered the gun on my back.

—This thing is plenty big to go through the both of you.

—Web.

Soledad had twisted her face out of her armpit.

I tried to smile at her, but expect I grimaced.

—Hey.

—Web, did you just pee on me?

—Yeah.

—Thought you were pee shy in front of girls.

—I kind of got terrified out of it.

Harris snapped his fingers.

—You, Chinaman, put that weapon on the floor before I shoot these two with one bullet.

Po Sin put the weapon on the floor.

—And kick it on over.

Po Sin kicked it over.

—And sit your big ass down.

Po Sin sat his big ass down.

—OK. For the moment, we're all gonna stay pretty much like this till my boy over there comes to. Then we'll figure out how this all sorts.

He squatted and reached for the pistol near his feet and Gabe came out of the bathroom with the sap I'd seen in his glove box and smashed Harris' gun hand and the revolver dropped and hit the floor and Harris kept reaching for the pistol at his feet and Gabe kicked it clear and brought his knee up into Harris' face and Po Sin was up and moving and Gabe put the sap across Harris' knee and the cowboy went down and Gabe dropped and sat on his chest and took the sap and shoved it into Harris' mouth till it had to be at the back of his throat and Po Sin came over and looked down at me and Soledad.

—Get up.

We got up.

Harris gagged. Gabe took out the sap and forced Harris' head to the side and waited for the vomiting to subside before putting it back in.

Po Sin watched for a second then turned back to us.

—That the brother?

I looked at Jaime's feet sticking out from under the bed where he'd crawled to hide.

—Yeah.

He bent and grabbed an ankle and dragged Jaime squirming into the light.

—Get up.

Jaime stood, one big bundle of flinching muscles.

—Uh, hey, uh.

Po Sin pointed at Harris and Gabe.

—See that?

Jaime nodded.

—Sure.

Po Sin shook his head.

—No you don't.

Jaime nodded.

—No, no I don't. I do not.

Po Sin looked the room over.

—Anything in here belong to any of you three? A hat? Keys? Phone? Check your pockets, make sure you have everything you came in with.

Jaime pawed his pockets.

—I got everything, sir, I have all my stuff.

Po Sin looked at me and Soledad.

—You two?

We nodded.

He pointed at the door.

—OK, get out.

Harris jerked and tried to knee Gabe in the back and Po Sin took a pillow from the bed and tossed it to Gabe and Gabe muffled Harris' face and Po Sin stepped on the cowboy's ruined gun hand and there was a noise from behind the pillow.

Jaime bolted for the door. I pushed Soledad ahead of me, detouring to unzip one of the duffels and pull out a thin Harbor Inn bath towel. Jaime and Soledad went out. I closed the door to a crack and stood just inside.

—Po Sin.

He looked up.

—Yeah.

—What are you gonna?

—We're gonna find out where my van is. I don't think it will take long. But you probably don't want to watch.

—And that's?

—What?

—That's all, just find out where?

Po Sin crossed the room.

—Go home, Web. Nothing's gonna happen here.

He opened the door and pushed me out.

I stuck my foot in the door.

—Hey, man, just, you know. Not too much. I mean. I called for help, but.

—That's right, you called for help. Help came. Now we're just gonna clean things up a little.

And he closed the door in my face, cutting off my view as one of Harris' hands flailed and knocked Gabe's sunglasses from his face to reveal that single inked tear, dark beneath a raging eye.

WHAT SHE THOUGHT OF THAT

—I mean, is this how you think partners behave, asshole?

I flicked the blinker and shifted onto the exit ramp.

—We're not partners.

Jaime folded his arms a little tighter.

—Apparently fucking not. Partners let each other in on the plan. Partners have some trust between them. You think I could get anything done in the industry if I did business the way you do, just giving people half the information and not even telling them the details of what happens in the third act? I could not.

I came off the ramp and took a right.

—Seeing as you're a complete fuckup, Jaime, I thought it best not to tell you that what I really needed you to do was to get found sneaking around so they'd think they caught us messing with them and not be worrying about us trying to pull something else. Seeing as you have an obvious gift for doing the absolutely wrong thing, I figured that if I told you you needed to get caught doing something suspicious, you'd probably end up in the greatest hiding place known to man. If I'd told you to let yourself get caught, you'd probably still be hiding in some damn storm drain or something.

—Well no shit! What asshole lets himself get caught?

I pulled into the parking lot and stopped.

—How relieved I am to know I was correct.

He looked around.

—What's this?

—Your motel.

He didn't move.

—I thought we might go grab a drink or something. You know, wrap party. Kind of review the events and see how the numbers add up.

Soledad opened the door and got out.

—Come on, Jaime.

—Yeah, but.

He looked from me to her and back.

—Well, let's all go get something to eat first? Yeah?

She tugged his sleeve.

—Come on, little brother.

—Shiiit.

He got out.

—Hey, hey, asshole, so how 'bout my cash? My ten percent.

I rubbed my forehead.

—I don't have it.

—Well. What? That's not cool. I got a hotel bill to pay here. I got to pay for those sheets. Expenses eating my capital.

He pointed at Soledad.

—She got anymore in that shirt?

I looked at her.

—No. That's all there was.

—Man, you owe. None of this would have worked out without me. You owe. That cash is to pay my talent. This was my project!

I adjusted the Harbor Inn bath towel I'd wrapped around myself when I stripped off my pee-soaked jeans and drawers and dropped them in the bed of the Apache.

—I know what I owe, Jaime. I'll pay it. Now please, fuck off.

He flapped his arms.

—Yeah, fuck yourself, asshole. Just you better come up with my dough.

He started for the motel.

—C'mon, sis, get my stuff from my room and grab my ride. We can skip the bill. I put it on your dad's credit card anyway. And he won't mind. I can crash in Malibu tonight, yeah?

I looked at Soledad.

—You want to ride with him?

She looked at her brother's retreating back.

—No.

—Should I bother asking if you want to ride with me?

She wiped at a clot of eye snot.

—Yeah.

—So you want to ride with me, or what?

—Yeah.

—Get in.

She got in and slammed the door and Jaime turned and watched as I rolled toward the exit.

—Oh, oh yeah, go on, you two, go have fun. Fuckin' ditchers! Get rid of me and go do your thing!

He walked behind the truck and we drove slow across the lot.

—Just better get me that cash, asshole! You don't, know what happens!

I pulled out, Jaime at our heels.

—Cut you, asshole! Fucking cut you!

We drove.

She fiddled with the chrome knob on Chev's antique truck radio, watching the little red line scan the frequencies, stopping when she found a woman's voice singing something slow and very sad in Spanish.

She looked through the windshield at the sign announcing the 405 and 110 interchange.

—You gonna take me home?

I stayed lined up for the 405 North.

—Someplace you'd rather be?

She pulled her feet up on the seat and hugged her knees.

—You take me to your home?

I jerked the wheel over, skidding onto the shoulder fifty yards from the split in the freeways. The truck stalled out, headlights spotted on a spider-web of graffiti covering the tall cinder-block wall edging the freeway, traffic barreling past, Spanish song playing on the old speakers.

We looked at each other.

Eyes on mine, she put her head on her knees and started to sing along with the radio. I looked away and stretched my arm behind the seat and felt around and came out with a nine-millimeter bullet like the one that killed her father. I showed it to her.

—Know it?

She stopped singing.

—It's a bullet.

I set it carefully on the dash, business end pointing at the sky.

—Yeah. In somewhat more detail, it's a bullet from the nine-millimeter pistol you gave your brother.

She unfolded her legs.

—What?

—Don't *what* me. Don't. Just. Just tell me that's not a bullet from your gun. Tell me you were never involved with Harris and Talbot and that other hick. Tell me you didn't drag me into all this shit to make it end like this.

—End like?

I banged the dash and the bullet jumped and fell into the footwell.

—Like this! Like it's all cleaned up! Like those guys are out of the picture and you don't have to worry about them. Like! Jesus! Like. You know.

I spread my arms.

—*This.*

I dropped my arms.

She bent and picked up the bullet and rolled it between her fingers.

—Web.

She held up the bullet.

—This isn't from my gun.

She set it on the dash.

I stared at the bullet.

—Well. Good.

She dragged fingers through her hair.

—But if you got that bullet from Jaime, it's from one of my dad's guns. And I did drag you into things. And I was involved with Harris and those guys.

I slapped my forehead.

—Awww, man! I knew it.

—Listen.

—This is fucked.

—Listen, goddamn it!

I listened.

She stared out at the spray-painted wall and I listened.

—Web, my dad, he was, he was great. A great dad. But he was a dirty businessman. No, that's not true. He was a criminal. A smuggler. And I knew. For a long time. And not just almonds. Other things.

An eighteen-wheeler washed past, its wind rocking the Apache on its shocks.

She watched it disappear down the ramp.

—People. Human trafficking.

She went through her clothes.

—I'm out of cigarettes.

She opened the ashtray and found the longest butt she could. She fitted it to her lips and blew through it, then lit it, and the cab filled with smoke.

—Chinese. These people, poor as hell. Poor as. We don't have a frame of

reference. They just want a new life. Or something. Freedom. Or something. I don't know. They get locked inside a cargo container. Forty, fifty
people. Two weeks on the ocean. A chem toilet. Packaged food. Bottled
water. Sometimes, their container gets loaded out of sequence.

She cracked a window and some of the smoke drifted free.

—The people who set this up, they try to arrange it so these cans get
loaded onto the ships last, at the top of the stacks. In the air. Sometimes
something happens. A can gets mixed up, ends up loading in the hold instead of the deck, buried under dozens of other cans. The heat. No air.

She dropped a spent match out the window crack.

—One time that happened with a can my dad had helped to set up. They
all died. Forty.

She looked at me.

—And I found out about that. When he started getting sick, I began taking care of some of the business for him, and I found out about that.

She looked away from me.

—But I didn't. You know, I never did anything. About that. Except I had to
talk to him. I. Jesus. It was. He was my dad and he'd been involved in this
awful thing and I never. I mean, how was that possible? How did he live?
Right? I couldn't begin to fathom how he could get up and go to work and,
and he was still smuggling. After that. Like. So. And I thought, *Maybe I'm
wrong. I have to be wrong. He couldn't have done that. He couldn't have
been responsible for those people and let them die and hid it and never had it
show.* Because he didn't, you know? Let it show. In himself. I could look at
the dates, after I put it together, see when it happened, remember that I
was fifteen, remember how there was never a change in how he behaved
at home, around me. So I had to be wrong. Because people can't be like
that.

She took a drag.

—So I asked him.

She exhaled through the crack, into the air outside.

—I asked him, I asked him if it was true.

She watched the cigarette burn for a while, got tired of watching.

—And he told me it was. He told me he didn't do it anymore. That he'd
stopped after that. But it had happened. Those people, they come over,
they promise to work for someone, pay off the fifty thousand dollars it
costs to get here. They become slaves. They go from these miserable lives,

to worse. And some die horribly. But he said, he promised, that he didn't do it *anymore*. Like that made it better.

A crease formed between her eyes.

—And I told him what I thought of that.

She stuck her thumbnail in the crease and pressed till the flesh around it turned white.

—That night he killed himself.

She pressed harder.

—Which could have been his plan all along. Or not. His note didn't specify.

She looked at the butt in her hand, frowned, rolled the window down a little more and tossed it out.

—He was wrong about that whole blowing through the filter thing. Doesn't make it any better at all.

She looked at me.

—So where to now?

I started the truck.

I could have told her about her dad's continued interest in human trafficking. I could have told her what else he might have been thinking about when he wrote that note. But I didn't much see the point. She was going to know soon enough that he'd broken that promise. And I didn't feel like being the guy to tell her.

So instead I headed up the 110 toward home.

—I was getting these calls, these guys I knew my dad had a deal going with. He'd gotten involved with these truckers or something. It was a quick thing, I guess. Cash. A lot of it. And Dad, he liked the fast action, so he took it on. And now they called and I told them he was dead and they started freaking out. Threatening to go to the cops and. I don't know. I should have realized they wouldn't do that, but I was. Confused. I didn't. The cops. They would have dug into everything once they found out Dad was involved in that. I mean, these days, post 9/11, any kind of smuggling and I figured they'd dig up his whole life. I didn't want people to know. What had happened before. I didn't want them to know I had known. And that I'd confronted him. And what happened after. I.

She jammed the heels of her hands against her eyes and pressed.

I took the interchange to the 10 West, the traffic loop circling, a lone apartment building jutting high enough from its center for me to be able to see into an uncovered window on the top floor, a glimpse of a woman in front of a vanity mirror, rubbing away the day's makeup.

Soledad uncovered her eyes, looked around.

—Where are we?

I pointed north.

—I need to make a stop.

—Jaime stole the gun.

She was staring out the window at the gated faces of the businesses along Fairfax.

—I mean, I assume he did. He knew my dad had two. A set of them. Those pistols. They were fancy or something. Dad knew Jaime liked that kind of shit and showed them to him once. After I called and asked if he could help with the truckers and their fucking almonds and he came over, he must have stolen it from Dad's desk. The one the cops hadn't taken. The one Dad hadn't used.

We passed the Silent Movie Theater just before Melrose. *Her Grave Mistake* on the marquee.

Soledad read it and turned and smiled at me.

—Now *that's* funny.

—I was with him at the motel. When I called you to clean up after Talbot. I didn't take a cab down there. I went with him to meet the guys to make sure Jaime didn't completely screw things up. I mean, by then I was a little more clearheaded. Fuck. If it had just been a matter of sending the almonds on their way, I could have done that. If it had been legal, I could have done that. But I didn't know what to do with a load like that. What precautions to take. And Jaime, he's the only, you know, shifty character I know.

She blew her nose into an already damp Kleenex.

—Except for my dad, I mean.

We crossed Sunset, climbed toward Hollywood Boulevard.

—And he screwed it up. I kept telling him to settle down, we'd pay for the stupid motel room and the food and whatever. But he'd been drinking. And he has to have things exactly his way. It's like he gets a picture of how it should all work, and if it doesn't work that way he freaks out. More baggage from our mom.

I took a left onto Hollywood.

—I met her first pimp.

She looked at me.

—Homero?

I stopped at the light.

—The bait dealer.

She nodded.

—Yeah. He and my dad did business sometimes. He *introduced* Dad to our mom. He's a scumbag. And there's a good chance he's Jaime's dad. Still.

She rapped the side of her head against the window.

—If I'd been thinking, I would have called *him* about the almonds.

The light turned green. I veered right and merged into northbound traffic again.

—Jaime did. It didn't seem to help.

She chewed a nail.

—Not much Jaime does ever seems to help. And he needs so much help himself. He needs something for himself. To make him, I don't know, to give him some kind of reason. Not that that's an excuse. The way he treated you that night. Web. I didn't mean to. I wasn't trying to cause trouble when I called. But that mess in the room. It would have caused problems. I was still thinking about police. And what they'd find. I wasn't thinking about. About anything. Except not wanting people to know.

I touched one of the many knots I'd collected on my scalp that last few days.

—Thinking clearly doesn't seem to have been anyone's specialty this week.

She nodded, pointed at the twisting road climbing ahead of us.

—What's in Laurel Canyon?

I took us around one of the hairpins and slid into the left-turn lane for Kirkwood.

—An old man.

· · ·

We were parked, the Apache pulled half onto the sidewalk to keep narrow Weepah Way open to two-way traffic.

—So, was the story as bad as you thought?

I looked at her, looked out at the sky. Here above the Los Angeles Basin floor, a sheet of stars visible.

—No, not quite.

She leaned forward to join me looking out the windshield and up at the stars.

—*Not quite.* You must have had some pretty fucked-up ideas about what happened.

I tapped the glass, pointing at a constellation.

—Know what that is?

—No. You?

—That's Corvus. The Crow.

—Never heard of it. I thought there were only twelve constellations. Like the zodiac.

—No. There are lots more.

—Where'd you learn?

—My dad.

I leaned back and looked at her.

—So on the subject of not thinking clearly, I thought Harris and those guys maybe killed your dad. I thought maybe you knew about it. I thought maybe you made a deal to take care of the almonds for them if they did it for you. Killed your dad for you.

I pulled the towel over my leg where it had fallen to the side.

—Still want to go home with me?

She kept looking at the stars.

—Well, I'm not really in much of a position to criticize you for thinking bad things about me right now, am I?

I put that in my top ten of *Most Loaded Questions Ever* and ignored it.

She ignored me ignoring it, and moved on.

—You promise to teach me a few more constellations?

—Sure.

She shrugged.

—Then I still want to go home with you.

I put my hand on the door.

—Soledad.

—Hm?

—The reason we didn't have the truck, the almonds, why we had to get all tricky and, you know, all that crazy shit. That was because Customs was seizing all your dad's property. So, stuff is probably gonna. You know.

She put her hand to the glass.

—Yeah. I know. Jaime told me outside the inn.

She tapped the glass.

—Is that one?

I looked.

—No. But.

I took her finger and traced a circle on the glass.

—All those, those are Vela. The Sails.

—Huh.

I got out.

—I'll be back in a few minutes.

She didn't look.

—OK.

I swung the door back and forth a little, the hinge creaking.

—Soledad, I thought maybe you had killed him yourself. Killed your dad.

She drew her finger around the circle I'd traced.

—You were close enough on that one.

I closed the door and went up to see L.L.

THE ABSENT PHOTO

The house smelled like mold and whiskey.

Piled books squeezed the entryway, leaving just clearance enough to open the door and scrape through. Bindings and pages swollen and dotted with rot from the damp canyon air, the stacks teetered and listed, propped up by more books. Shelves lined the walls. Shelves that were little more than more stacks of books broken by the occasional strata of a pine plank used to create stability. The fireplace, long out of use, vomited books. The couch rested on a pedestal of them. Looking into the kitchen, I could see that the doors had been removed from the cabinets to allow more room for the spines of oversized editions to jut out. If I opened the fridge, I had little doubt I'd have found paperbacks wedged into the crisper, first editions of Mailer growing ice crystals in the freezer. The only thing to challenge the rule of books were the empty bottles lining window ledges, mounded in the sink, overflowing from liquor store delivery cartons.

I picked my way through the heaps, noticing, above the books' high watermark on the walls, the occasional slightly less dingy patch of paint where L.L. had once hung posters from his halcyon years. *Five Easy Pieces* signed by Jack. An original lobby card from *The Thin Man*. An Alfred Hitchcock silhouette, also signed. A photo of himself and Mom, when the novelty of Hollywood could still hold her wandering attention, flanked by Francis Ford and Eleanor Coppola at the *Apocalypse Now* opening night after-party.

But over the mantel, on the wall that had been entirely rebuilt following the fire, there was no mark to show where there had once been a picture taken by Mom: L.L. reclining on a lounge chair, a wineglass in one hand, pen in the other, marking up a script propped on his knees, a sleeping baby in his lap. And beyond him, mugging and holding his own child over his head like a trophy, Chev's dad, a cigarette between his lips, sideburns to his jawline, his wife beside him in a purple Mexican housedress, brushing long gold hair.

I walked past the absent photo and out onto the deck where it had been taken.

Ringed with wood vegetable crates filled with more waterlogged books, by the light of several candles pressed into a mass of melted wax that flowed over a rusting tin-top table and dripped to the planks below, L.L. dozed with an open copy of *Tom Jones* on his stomach.

—L.L.

He lurched, came awake with a phlegmy cough.

—Nguh. Hm.

He took his glasses off and rubbed his eyes without turning.

—Money's in the jar, Raj. Leave it anywhere.

He put the glasses back on and started to crane his head around, the book slipping from his belly and onto the deck.

—Could you maybe take out a few of the empties for me?

He saw me. Cleared his throat. Looked at the book he'd dropped.

—I'd make a cliché comment about the prodigal, but it wouldn't really apply, would it?

He reached for the book, missed it, and his shoulder jostled the table, sending the candle flames jittering and the various glasses and empty bottles clinking.

I bent and picked up the book and held it out to him.

—Here.

He took it.

—Thank you.

He found his place and scanned the page.

—Thought you were the delivery boy.

—Late for deliveries.

He looked at his watch.

—Suppose it is.

I nudged a box of full bottles by the table.

—Looks like he was here earlier.

L.L. pulled his glasses low on his nose and looked at me over the rims.

—Is that someone I know casting judgments about? Is that, wait, allow me to cup my ear.

He cupped his hand to his ear and angled his head at me.

—Is that perhaps the voice of my absent wife speaking to me through her son?

He removed his hand.

—A prodigious bit of ventriloquism for her to accomplish from her far northern climes. Perhaps, if I speak distinctly, I can send a message back to her via the same medium.

He put his hand to the side of his mouth.

—Althea, dear bitch, get out of the boy's head, he's sufficiently fucked up now, we need neither of us endure in the effort.

He wiped his brow.

—There. With luck that will transmit to her and she will desist in dispensing her opinions about how I live my life, through my own flesh and blood. However misbegotten said flesh and blood may be.

He took a full bottle of Seagram's from the carton and held it to the light.

—Drink?

I shook my head.

—No thanks.

He shrugged, picked up a glass, sloshed the dregs at its bottom over the edge of the deck into the toyon, chaparral, coast oak and walnut growing up from the hillside, and poured himself a double.

—I'll have one for the both of us.

I moved some books from another chair and took a seat.

—Was there any doubt?

He saluted me with the glass.

—In your mind? Apparently none.

He downed the whiskey.

—But I generally don't drink alone.

I looked back into the dark house, the moonlight glinting off all the empty bottles.

—Been having a lot of company, have you?

He swung his arm in an arc, indicating his massed library.

—My oldest friends. My enduring companions. Those that stand by me.

I picked at the wax on the table.

—And experiencing the delights of Renaissance technology, as well, I see.

He topped off his glass, sipped this time.

—The electric bills. They send them, God knows they're here somewhere, I just never quite find the time to deal with them.

I looked up at the sky, remembered that same sky projected inside the Griffith Observatory planetarium, how the stars would swim and race down the horizon as the view shifted, season by season, between the hemispheres. L.L. providing commentary, whispering in my ear.

—You could always get someone to take care of that shit for you.

—I have an ex-wife, my boy, I don't need another.

—I was thinking more in the way of an assistant. Or a business manager. Didn't you used to have one?

He opened his book, turned a page, ignored the implication that he might once have been in the kind of business that would require a manager.

—L.L.

—Yes, I attend.

—Has it ever occurred to you, all these books, the alcohol, open flames?

He turned a page.

—Has it ever occurred to you, mother's son that you are, to mind your own business?

I snapped a stalactite of wax from the edge of the table.

—L.L.

—Web.

—I don't want you to die.

He pressed the back of his hand to the corner of his mouth and closed his book.

—I'm choked up, filled with emotion. Imagine, my son not *wanting* me to die. How many fathers can say the same?

—Shut the fuck up, Dad.

He turned his head, looked at me through the candlelight, and waited.

I threw the spear of wax over the rail.

—I don't want you to die. I don't mean just that I don't actively *wish* that you would die, I mean that I don't want you to die *at all*. I don't want you to trip and fall over that rail one night and break your neck. I don't want you to pass out on your back and vomit and choke to death. I don't want one of these candles to tip into a puddle of 101 and ignite a copy of *Madame Bovary* and incinerate you.

He touched his throat.

—I loathe *Bovary*. Wouldn't be caught dead with a copy in the house.

I stretched my arm and slapped the side of his head.

He looked at me through skewed glasses.

—You have my attention.

I stood up.

—You're a fucker, L.L. The champion fucker of the world. I'm never gonna take the crown from you. I concede, you have the throne all to yourself.

I showed my middle finger to him.

—But fucker that you are, that doesn't mean you can get rid of me, you pathetic misanthropic shit. I mean, I'm not saying you don't grow old after about the first five minutes I'm with you, but I can fucking take it. God knows I've had the practice. So.

I hooked a thumb at the house.

—I'll be here next week with a truck to start hauling away some of this shit and to get the lights turned on. And. Whatever.

He straightened his glasses.

—What's the matter, Web?

—Fuck you.

He stood up.

—What happened? What's been happening? What's this about?

I put a hand on his chest as he approached me.

—L.L., all this is about is how I don't want to get a call one day from someone, and find out your corpse has been rotting up here for five weeks and I have to come and smell it and see the stain where you melted into the carpet. I don't want to clean up after you when you're dead.

He nodded.

—Well, I didn't want to clean up after you when you were a baby. So I guess that's fair.

I nodded.

—King Fucker, L.L., that's you.

He dropped back into his chair.

—You hold your own, Web, you hold your own just fine.

—I have skills.

He turned his back, put his feet on the lower rail of the deck and picked up his book.

—Make the most of them.

I stood there.

—I'll be back next week with the truck.

He tugged a stained handkerchief from his pocket and waved it in the air.

—As you wish.

I went to the door.

—I found the money in *Karenina*.

—Did you read the book?

—Man, I know all I need to know about unhappy families.

He wiped his nose with the handkerchief and returned it to his pocket.

—I guess you would.

I scratched my head.

—But I could use some more money.

He opened his book.

—Yes, I saw that you are wearing a towel in lieu of actual pants. One suspects you might need the odd dollar or two. As I said earlier, it's in the jar.

—I need a lot. For a fuckup I know. Someone pathetic enough to need help from someone like me.

He picked up his glass and toasted the sky.

—Help yourself. If you need more than what's there, let me know.

I started into the house.

L.L. called after.

—Delightful to see you, Web. Nothing like a visit from the fruit of the old loins to make a man feel his mortality creeping up from behind. Ah, all this gloriously morbid talk. Just what a lion in winter requires on a chill evening. Thanks and thanks again. We must do it again soonest.

I listened to him as I negotiated the books and bottles in the kitchen and found the rooster-shaped cookie jar from my childhood and took off the lid and began sorting through the wads of bills stuffed inside.

Sparing a look at L.L. as I headed out the front door, the book back on his stomach, head dropped forward, shoulders rising and falling, King Fucker of the world at rest.

The light was on in our apartment when I parked the Apache in its spot.

I stared up at the light.

—What night is it?

Soledad had to think about that one.

—Sunday?

—Crap.

I opened the truck door and looked around the cab.

—It look pretty clean in here?

She looked at the seats.

—Looks really clean to me.

—Sure, to you and me it looks really clean, but to the guy who restored this thing from the axles up, it doesn't take much.

She brushed some ashes from the seat.

—Better?

I got out.

—Come on.

I jingled my keys and fiddled with the knob before going in. But I didn't need to give him any warning, he knew the sound of the Apache from a block away.

I opened up.

He looked from the TV screen showing a paused frame of *Spetters*, put a finger to his lips and pointed at Dot, curled sleeping on the couch with her head in his lap.

I nodded and came in and closed the door softly, and Soledad rapped on it and Dot lifted her head.

—Mfuh?

I opened the door.

Soledad tapped my forehead.

—Forget something?

—Sorry.

I held the door open and she came in.

—That's Chev. That's his friend Dot.

Dot rubbed her face all over and looked at Soledad.

—Whasas?

I closed the door again.

—Hey, Dot. Hey. This is Soledad. She's. This is Soledad.

Soledad pointed at the hall.

—Bathroom?

—Uh, yeah. Straight back.

She went down the hall.

Dot watched her go, looked back at me.

—She know what a dick you are?

I nodded.

—Most definitely.

She put her head back in Chev's lap.

—Must've been the steam room look that got her.

I pulled the towel tighter around my waist.

—Yeah, she digs the bathhouse scene.

I bounced the truck keys on my palm and Chev held his hand up and I tossed them to him and he caught them.

He looked at the keys.

—You put gas in her?

—Yeah. Stopped at the corner.

—It's too expensive there.

—I didn't remember before.

He let the keys dangle from his index finger and studied them.

—She give you any problems?

—No. No problems.

Soledad came out from the bathroom and stood at the mouth of the hall and pointed at the two bedroom doors.

—I'm tired.

I pointed at mine.

—That one.

She yawned, covered her mouth.

—OK.

She took her hand away and peeked around the corner.

—Hey, Chev, Dot, nice to meet you. Hope I get to talk later.

She waved at me

—Don't stay up too long.

And went into my bedroom.

Dot pulled a thin blanket from the back of the couch and put it around her bare legs.

—She seems nice.

I walked over to my bookcase.

—She is.

I took a book from the case.

—Say, Dot.

—Mhun?

—I'm sorry I was such a gargantuan dick the other day.

She closed her eyes.

—Chev says sorry don't mean shit.

I looked at Chev.

—He's right about that.

She found one of Chev's hands and tugged his arm around her shoulders.

—Then fuck your apology, just try to be nicer to me.

—OK. I'll try.

Chev pointed at the TV.

—You're in the way.

I got out of the way and he started his movie playing.

I walked to the hall, stopped.

—Hey, man.

He held up a hand.

—I want to watch this.

I nodded.

—OK. Tomorrow?

He nodded.

—Tomorrow.

I cracked my bedroom door and looked in and saw Soledad under the blankets, her clothes tossed over the floor. I went in and dropped the towel and took off my shirt and kicked off my shoes and peeled the crusty socks from my feet and got into bed with her and opened the book I'd brought with me.

She rolled over and looked at what I was reading.

—Cute kids.

I turned another page of the Hollywoodland Elementary yearbook.

—Yeah. Cute kids.

TOO TIRED TO BE ALONE

I took a loaf of 99-grain whole wheat that Dot had bought out of the fridge and put a couple slices in the toaster oven.

—Which toothbrush is yours?

I looked at Soledad standing in the hall.

—The yellow one.

—I'm gonna use it.

—Sure.

I watched her go into the bathroom, and found some grapes and rinsed them off and put them in a bowl and got a couple small plates and a butter knife and took it all to the table. I looked at the table, remembered wiping it down, sponging away Talbot's blood, and changed course and took the breakfast things into the livingroom and set them out on the floor in front of the couch and threw a couple cushions down.

Soledad came out of the bathroom and went into my bedroom and closed the door. The coffeemaker gurgled and I took the pot off and filled two cups. Behind the door Soledad was talking to herself. The toaster oven dinged and I grabbed the two pieces of hot toast by their corners and carried them into the livingroom and set one on each plate. The bedroom door opened as I went back to the kitchen for the cups.

—Got coffee. Milk in yours?

—I called a cab.

I looked at her, face washed, hair pulled back, sunglasses on.

—I need to get going.

I set the cups down.

—Sure.

I looked around the apartment.

—I mean, considering the alternative is Malibu, why stay around here.

She nodded.

—Especially with all the exciting conversations with law enforcement officials I have to look forward to out at the beach.

She pointed at the couch.

—Where's?

—Don't know. Probably having brunch somewhere. Organic berries and egg whites for Dot, organic espresso and tobacco for Chev.

—Interesting couple, they seemed.

—I'd swear it won't last, but I don't know shit about relationships.

She cocked her head.

—A girl'd never know.

We stood there.

She put her hand on the doorknob.

—So.

—Hang on, I'll walk you out.

I went and grabbed something from my room and we walked down to the curb, the voices of the homeless couple drifting down the street as they worked their way from garbage can to garbage can, removing the recyclables.

—Fuckhead.

—Bitch.

—Asswipe.

—Cocksucker.

Soledad nodded.

—It must be love.

—Sounds like it, doesn't it?

A cab rounded the corner and pulled up.

—This is me.

I took the roll of bills from my pocket.

—Do me a favor, give this to Jaime.

She looked at the money.

—Web. You don't really have to.

I held the money out.

—I told him I'd pay him. I promised. I.

—He'll just.

—I don't care. It's his. Maybe it'll help. Maybe it'll keep him out of trouble for a while.

She shrugged.

—It won't.

She took the money.

—But it's a nice thing to do.

She put the money in her handbag.

—OK. So. OK.

She opened the door.

—So look.

She tossed her bag into the cab and looked at the driver.

—Just one more minute, that cool?

He nodded.

She looked at me, pushed her sunglasses firmly against the bridge of her nose.

—Web. Just so we're clear. I'm. I'm a mess.

—Really? Wow, you hide it so well.

—Yes, don't I? But. This isn't, you know, this isn't the normal me. This isn't the way my life normally goes. I'm an even-keel girl, you know. But. My dad. My dad. I'm not on steady ground. And the way I feel now, I just, I mean, look at the decisions I've been making the last few days. It's just. My emotions. I, I don't trust them. I don't trust myself to make the right, to make smart choices now. Especially with someone as spectacularly fucked up as you.

I looked at the ground.

—Thanks. Coming from you, that really means something.

—Thought you'd appreciate the sentiment.

—Oh, I do, I do.

She picked at the rubber seal along the edge of the cab door.

—Anyway. I'm in no shape to get into. Anything. Like. You know. I can't.

—Sure.

—But.

She raised her shoulders and dropped them.

—I'm just too tired to be alone with all the crap I'm going to have to go through. I don't want to do all this, the police, whatever kind of press, the estate. Jesus, the estate, when my mom starts sniffing around for her cut? That's gonna be a shit storm. And I don't want to be alone with all that. I don't want to sleep alone. I want someone to call. I want a friend. I want a lover. I don't want to do this alone. I want help.

She took my little finger and squeezed it.

—And I think you're the nice guy. I mean, I know you have a huge asshole in permanent residence inside, but I think you're the nice guy.

She leaned over the top of the door and kissed me.

—So I'm just gonna have to hope I'm right about that.

She got in the cab.

—'Cause I'm too tired to do anything else.

I put my hands in my pockets.

—Your flattery knows no bounds.

—Yeah. I'm a sweet talker.

—Right. So this means?

The cabby turned and gave her a look and she nodded and looked up at me.

—I'll see you tonight, Web.

She closed the door. The cab pulled away. The window rolled down and she stuck her head out.

—If I'm not in jail.

I watched the cab to the end of the street, standing on the curb, still there a couple minutes later when Chev pulled into his spot.

I wandered over.

—Hey.

He climbed out, ran a hand over the freshly washed door.

—Lucky you didn't fuck her up.

—I was careful.

He closed the door and sat on the running board.

—Beautiful day.

I looked at the utterly typical, stunning blue sky hovering relentlessly above.

—Yeah.

I sat next to him.

—Some things.

He stretched his legs, crossed his ankles.

—Like?

I leaned forward, put my elbows on my knees.

—I saw L.L. again. Last night.

I looked at him, looked away.

—He's, not that it matters, but he's in sorryass shape. And I'm gonna, I don't know, I need to see if I can. Help? I guess. And I don't want to sneak around doing it.

He uncrossed his ankles, recrossed them the other way.

—He's your dad. Do what you have to.

—And I took some money from him. For a guy I know. To pay a debt.

He slipped the smokes from his T sleeve and knocked one from the pack.

—'Kay.

—Just so you know.

—Now I know.

He lit up, tilted his face to the sun and closed his eyes and blew smoke.

I leaned my back against the hot steel of the door.

—I want to do better, Chev. I. I want to try and do better. Shit, man, I want to just, I want to try. I'm tired of. Things. I'm not saying. I don't *feel* any better. About it. I still can't think. About it. Too clearly. It still makes me want to fall asleep. But I know. It. Happened. I know I was there and the girl. I know. It. Happened. And I don't want to be him. I don't want to be L.L. I don't want this one fucked up thing to be who I am and that's it, this is the end of my life. I do not want to feel like this, be like this forever. I mean, I'm not sure, but I think I used to be kind of a nice guy.

He took the cigarette from his lips, opened his eyes and slid them my way.

—Web, man, you have never in your life been a nice guy.

He closed his eyes again.

—But you used to be pretty damn cool. You used to be a guy a friend could count on. And it'd be nice if you were that way again.

I nodded.

—See, that's it. That's it. I want to be that guy, I want to be the guy people can count on. That sounds great. I don't exactly remember how that worked, but I want to try and be that again. Really, man.

He nodded, worked a hand into his pocket.

—Cool.

He took his hand from his pocket.

—So why don't you start by telling me where you took my truck.

He opened his hand and showed me the nine-millimeter bullet inside.

—And how this got in there.

—The phone?

—Yeah.

—Jesus. I think we need to get rid of it.

We both sat on the couch, staring at the phone in the middle of the living-room floor.

I nodded.

—Yeah. Without a doubt.

　He pointed at the kitchen table.

—There was stuff on it?

—Um, yeah.

—Lots?

—Not really.

—On the top?

—Yeah.

　He shook his head.

—We got to get rid of it.

　He put his face in his hands.

—With the fucking phone. That is so. Oh man.

　He took his face from his hands and looked at me.

—Was the guy a dick?

—Chev, he beat his nephew to death with a fucking phone! Yes, he was a dick.

—No, the nephew, was he a?

—I don't know. Probably. Why do you?

　He stood up.

—I don't know. I'm just trying to deal and. Jesus. With the phone. Awwww, man. I used it after that. Awwww, shit!

　He sat back down.

—That's fucked.

—Sorry.

—What sorry? Fucked up inbred kills someone with the phone, what are you sorry about?

—I don't know. Feels like it's my fault.

　We stared at the phone.

　Chev cupped his chin in his hand, clicked his thumb ring against one of his earrings.

—No way I can look at that kitchen every day.

　He stood.

—We got to move out of here, man.

　I nodded.

—Do you *think*?

　He looked at me.

—Are you being a smartass? Are you being a smartass about a guy getting bludgeoned with a phone in my apartment?

I held my thumb and forefinger an inch apart.

—Little bit?

He shook his head.

—Looks like someone's feeling better.

He started for the door.

—Long as you're all chipper, you call the landlady and tell her we're out at the end of the month.

I stood.

—Where you going?

—The shop.

—Hang on, I'll come with.

He opened the door.

—Uh-uh, fuckwit, you have some disturbing shit to dispose of before I get home.

He pointed at the phone and the table.

—Those. Gone. And anything else that got. *Stuff* on it.

He looked at the kitchen.

—Telling you, Web, a weaker man than me, he'd have quit your shit long ago.

I shrugged.

—Must be my abundant charm.

SECRET SKELETONS

—So what now?

—I don't know for sure.

Po Sin stirred the ice cubes at the bottom of his glass.

—You gonna go back to teaching?

I thought about the classroom. The kids. How much fun they could be. How much of a pain. I thought about trying to walk back in there and be a normal teacher. Be a person without all these things clinging to him. Deaths like barnacles. They felt visible. And a burden. I didn't want to have them around kids.

And there were other things.

—I don't think I can really teach anymore.

—So?

—So I.

—Round two.

Gabe came back from the bar with two bottles of beer and another gin and juice for Po Sin.

I took my beer.

—Thanks.

Gabe nodded.

We all drank.

—Po Sin.

—My name. Means Grandfather Elephant. Speak it and I will answer.

—Po Sin.

I drank again.

—What'd you do with them?

Po Sin stared into his glass.

—Web, in all honesty, I have no idea what you're talking about.

I nodded.

—Sure, I get that. But. I called you. And I think, I think I need to know. I'm trying, this is new for me, but I'm trying to be kind of a grown-up. But, hey, not too many examples of that in my life, so I'm flying a little blind. Anyway. Part of. I think I need to know what I'm responsible for. What things I do that make other things happen.

I picked at my beer label.

—I think I really need to know what you did to them.

Po Sin looked at Gabe.

Gabe lifted his bottle, took a drink.

—It doesn't work like that, Web.

—I know. But.

—I said, *It doesn't work like that, Web.*

I looked at him.

He nodded.

—This is how it works. You ask someone for a favor.

He pointed at himself and Po Sin.

—And they come and do you a favor.

He moved his beer over the surface of the table, leaving a smear of moisture.

—They swing their weight behind you and give your actions gravity. They do things.

He wiped the smear away with the edge of his hand.

—You left the room. You could have stayed. You chose not to. Now you have to live with the consequences of leaving that room. The biggest of those is, you don't know what happened. After you leave the room, it's no longer your business. You want to know what price is paid in this world, you need to be there when the deal goes down.

He trained his lenses on me.

—That shit, whatever it is we may think we're taking about, it never even happened.

He got up.

—I'm gonna go shoot a rack.

He walked to the pool table at the back of the Monday night empty bar and started dropping quarters in.

Po Sin rattled the ice in his glass.

—He has a way of summing shit up.

He sipped, swallowed, looked over his shoulder at Gabe, and leaned close.

—Shit needs to be done sometimes, Web. I'm not saying it's the way the world should be, not saying it's the world I want my kids to be in, but this life we're in, you don't end up doing this kind of work because everything went the way it was supposed to. You're doing work like we do, it's because some shit got fucked up. That means things behind you, you don't always want them coming to the light. Further you go into this kind of job, more people you meet, more of them you find just like you. Secrets. Skeletons. Coworkers. Competitors. Clients. Secrets start cropping up. Know what I mean?

Did I know what he meant? Shit yes. I was hip deep in what he meant. Which he already knew.

So he kept talking without me giving an answer.

—What no one wants is for the secrets to start coming out into the open. Guys like we were just talking about, they can make things come to light. Just by being around and getting involved in your life, they can cause all kinds of shit to unnecessarily become unhinged. So we did what we do.

He gulped the last of his drink.

—We cleaned shit up.

He set the empty glass in front of me.

—Like the man said, you wanted to know, all you had to do was stay in the room.

I looked at the glass.

—That's the thing.

I looked at him.

—I don't want to leave the room. Po Sin, man, honestly, even if I did want to, I'm not sure I could find the door. But. That doesn't even matter. Because.

I shook my head.

—I love this shit.

I raised a hand.

—I liked teaching. I did. But I *love* this shit. It's like, man, it's like I found my calling. It's like if I took one of those employment placement tests we gave the kids in junior high. *You should be a scientist, an insurance adjuster, a flight attendant.* When I took that test, it said I should be a structural engineer. But this, this is like if that test said, *You shall be a crime scene cleaner, Webster Fillmore Goodhue, and you shall like it well.* It just fits. It fits me. This is what I want to do, man.

I lifted my beer.

—I want to clean up after dead people.

—Hey yo.

We looked at the bartender.

—You guys come over in that van?

Po Sin started to rise.

—It getting a ticket?

—No.

Po Sin started to sit.

—Good. That would have been a pisser.

The bartender pointed out the swinging saloon door.

—But looks like it's on fire.

The Lost and Found is in a strip mall at the corner of National and South Barrington. That far west, that close to their place of business, it was probably a provocation. But that wasn't the kind of thing I could be expected to know. Po Sin and Gabe, I guess they just wanted to go to one of their favorite bars.

We came out the swinging door into a small parking lot illuminated by the flames pouring from the shattered windows of the van. Morton's crew was already piling back into a silver Pathfinder. Morton was on the sidewalk with an ax handle. Dingbang just behind him, jumping up and down, jabbing a finger at us as we came out.

—'Bout that shit? Huh, motherfuckers? 'Bout that shit?

Morton raised the ax handle and pointed it at Po Sin.

—Had it coming. We were under truce, you pulled that shit. Had this coming.

Gabe started across the lot.

Po Sin grabbed him.

—Cool it. He's right.

He pulled Gabe back to his side.

—Deal with this later.

Dingbang bounced higher.

—'Bout that? Fuck with the best, get fucked in the ass like the rest.

Po Sin raised his voice over the flames.

—Shut up, Dingbang.

—Bang! Bang!

Morton raised the ax handle over his head.

—You are done, Chinaman. You and your nigger. Gonna squeeze you right out of business.

Dingbang pumped a fist.

—Right out of business!

—Motherfucker!

Po Sin started toward them.

—You're a disgrace, Dingbang!

—Bang!

—A wart. Your dad is a jailbird, but at least he has half a brain. At least he never let himself get used against his own family by some whiteass motherfucker.

He pointed at Morton.

—Fuck this midget. I'm gonna kill you. I'm gonna take the stain off my family. If I got dead ancestors watching, they are gonna be laughing their asses off tonight. I'm gonna improve the gene pool, Dingbang.

—*Bangbangbang!*

—*Motherfuckermotherfuckermotherfucker!*

He charged, Morton and Dingbang reeling back from him as his shadow fell over them.

Then he stopped, a monster in silhouette against the fire, and his hand came up and he grabbed his left shoulder.

—Oh. Motherfucker.

And he was falling.

Gabe got there first. Then me. Then Dingbang. The Pathfinder squealed away.

Dingbang kneeled and cried.

—Uncle. Uncleuncleuncle.

Sirens on National Boulevard.

EPILOGUE

The ghetto birds are buzzing over Hollywood.

I look up from under the hood and watch two of them as they cut diagonals against the grid of streets below. I set the socket wrench on the fender and walk down to the foot of the driveway and shade my eyes.

One of the LAPD copters freezes. The other tilts slightly into the wind and zips west. Sirens break out on Highland. Glancing down the street, I can see two squad cars run the light several blocks away. I take my new cell from my pocket and make sure it's on. More sirens on Sunset. I look up to where the first copter hovers. Not too far away, no more than a mile. I think about walking over, take out my wallet and look inside and find I have no cards. Crap. I walk back up the driveway. If it's something I should know about, I'll get a call. Deputy Mercer will give me a ring and give the victims a referral. Right now the starter is more important than drumming up business.

I get my head back under the hood and pull the last plug and wipe it clean. I squat and find the gapper in Chev's toolbox and fit the proper hoop of steel into the plug's spark gap. Too wide. Like the others. I press the top of the plug against the pavement, closing the gap, and check it again. The gapper passes in and out of the gap with a slight tug. I rise and replace the plug.

The tone of the helicopter's chop shifts, and I look up again and watch it through a screen of ficus branches as it wheels and heads east toward K-town or Rampart or Boil Heights or Skid Row, where it no doubt has more pressing business than sitting watch on a Hollywood crime scene in the middle of the day.

I mark its path, trace it back to where it had hovered.

There's a ninety-nine-cent store over there. I could take a look. Stop at the store and pick up the stuff we'll need tonight.

I bend and start picking up tools, making a mental shopping list as I go.

Scotch-Brite pads.

Wire brushes.

Paint scrapers.

Large sponges.

And those little nylon scrubbies.

Those are great, the ones that are like little wads of netting. Great for cracks and corners, perfect for snagging bits of skull and brain. Perfect for a shotgun job.

Next day I take the Datsun over the Hollywood Hills.

Just got it running and it's still a little balky, the way only a thirty-six-year-old 510 can be, but I'm not getting on any more fucking buses. Getting better is one thing, but there's a limit to how much healing I'm interested in doing. I was willing to deal with it. Too much to be done to wait for a ride all the time. But it was a white-knuckle job. Sweats. Nausea. Passed out once. That was charming. Passing out on public transportation is like begging the LAPD to give you all kinds of crap.

But riding the bus, I did start to see certain things.

Like the fact that I'm never going to be well. I'm never going to get over it. That there are things you don't get over. And why should you want to? I don't want to. Ride the bus enough, it might make me numb, but it won't make me better.

I don't want to be numb.

I drive up the Canyon, past the turnoff for L.L.'s place. Once every couple weeks over there is plenty. Place is clean enough now. Well, not clean, but not a death trap. As if L.L. gives a damn.

By all means, Web, whatever form of therapy you wish to indulge in, feel free. Yes, yes, certainly, come to your father's house and take away all traces of individuality. Do what you must to abnegate his personality and create a new reality where that man no longer exists. I can't wait to see how you fare with this effort, sweet child. By the way, I had a call from the dear bitch. She seemed to think I wasn't at my best. I wonder where she may have gotten that idea. Asked if I'd like some pies. Suggested I should perhaps drink a little less. All of this accompanied by the gurgle of a hookah. I don't suppose, no, I must be wrong, but I don't suppose you had anything to do with that, you little fucker?

My mistake.

I hadn't meant to tell Mom anything about L.L., but she'd been lucid enough one evening to ask what I was up to, and kept asking more questions, and I kept answering. It took me a half hour to realize it was a hit of X that was making her so avid. I never expected her to remember enough of the conversation to act on it.

She actually did send him a couple pies though.

He refused to eat them.

She'll have baked them full of hash. Or arsenic. In either case I don't care for the effects. Hand me that bottle, Web.

I took them home to Chev. He liked them. So did Dot. That's still going on. God knows why.

North of the Canyon, I hop on the Ventura going east and jump off in Burbank and drive to the far end of Flower and park in front of a long low house with a waist-high stucco wall closing off a yard that's half lawn and half patio.

I get out of the car and walk over and swing my legs over the wall and start across the grass.

Xing looks up from her dolls.

—You have to use the *gate* and walk on the *path*.

—I'm in a hurry, Xing.

She stands up and plants her fists on her hips and opens her mouth and emits a sustained shriek that just barely misses shattering every window in the neighborhood.

—You have to use the *gate* and walk on the *path*!

I go back out to the sidewalk, use the gate and walk on the path.

—Better?

She shakes her head at me.

—You suck. You can't do *anything* right.

I reach in the bag I'm carrying and show her the fuzzy white kitty I brought for her.

—See this, Xing.

She claps her hands and her eyes get big and she nods.

—For me for me for me?

I drop it back in the bag.

—Nope. Not this trip. Maybe if you're nice next visit you can have it.

I walk past her and she kicks me hard in the back of my leg.

—You suck! Yousuckyousuckyousuck!

I knock on the door and open it and walk in.

Lei is coming down the hall.

—You sure?

—Yeah, but just two hours, right?

—Yeah. Yes.

She grabs her purse from a hook next to the door.

—I'll be back. I just have to take Yong to his speech therapist or.

—Yeah.

—Yong!

Yong wanders down the hall, zipping his backpack. I reach in the bag and take out a fire engine Lego set and hold it low where he can see it. It catches his eyes and he comes toward it in a daze.

I shake the box.

He looks up at me and I nod and he grabs the box and runs out the front door.

Lei follows him.

—Thanks. Back in two hours. Xing needs a bath and dinner then a half hour of TV and then bed.

She squeezes Xing's shoulder as she goes by.

—Try not to kill Web.

Xing sticks her tongue out.

I take the kitty from the bag and toss it out the open door and it hits her in the back of the head.

She looks at it and turns up her nose.

—I don't *like* kitties.

I push the door closed.

—Some other little girl will find it, then.

Before the door closes she has the kitty in her arms.

I go down the hall, following the sound of the TV, the blare of a late-afternoon talk show; couples fighting, a conversation made up almost entirely of *bleeps*.

I raise my chin as I come into the room. Po Sin lifts his cane at me, reaches for the remote and hits mute.

—I love that shit. This one, those two there, they're sisters, they both married the same guy, but he's not a guy, he's a transsexual. Used to be a girl. Got a fake dick. Funny thing, the two who married him, both of them trannies, too. Both used to be guys. Brothers.

He goes to push himself from his chair and I wave him down.

—Sit. No, don't get up.

He gets up.

—Need to move around. They want me getting exercise. Took a walk yesterday.

—Yeah?

—Around the block. Thought my lungs would explode. Give me that shit.

   I hand him the bag and he takes out the invoices.

—What's this?

   I look.

—Decomp.

—You bill this?

—That my handwriting?

—Don't fuck around.

—I billed it.

—You underbilled for materials.

—You want it out of my pocket?

—No. I want it out of your hide. What's this expense?

—Day labor.

—For what?

—We had to do the job at night. Gabe was doing accommodations. I needed to pay someone.

—Who?

   I look at the families fighting on the TV.

—Dingbang.

   He grunts.

—He show up on time?

—Pretty much.

   He looks at another invoice.

—Shotgun job?

—Gabe did the invoice.

—I know.

   His eyes go over it.

—What was it?

   I sit on the edge of the bed.

—Guy put it to his chest. Knew his wife was the open-casket type, didn't want to blow his own head off. Maybe, I don't know, upset someone. Did it out in the backyard in their drained swimming pool. Blew out half his lung, missed his heart. He flopped around, actually tried to climb out of the pool, pumped blood over the whole thing. Handprints on the tile all the way around.

—How'd you?

—There was pathology on the side of the house from the blast. I did the detail work there while Gabe got the chunks out of the pool. We couldn't just hose those.

—Yeah, clog the drains.

—Yeah. Had to cover that. Ended up.

—I know.

—Filled the pool partway.

—Chlorinated the shit out of it. Scrubbed and pumped it out.

He runs a finger over the invoice.

—That's a good one.

We sit there till I stand up.

—You gonna eat? Want me to?

He shakes his head.

—The stuff I'm allowed to eat, I'd rather fast. Lost fifty pounds. I'd known I could do that, I'd have had a stroke ten years ago.

—Start a diet craze.

—Man, it's sweeping the nation.

I go to the door.

—I'm gonna see if I can get Xing in the bath.

He puts his hands together in prayer.

—Best thing about this whole deal, not having to wrestle with her. You want to borrow my cane to beat her?

—No, I brought a belt.

—Good man.

He picks up the remote.

—You know Lei won't make it back in two hours.

—She never does.

—Woman can't be on time for shit. You got something going tonight, you take off. I can handle Xing once she's run down a little.

—No, I'm cool. Hooking up with Soledad later. See a movie. Try to distract her a little. Tomorrow we have to get the last of her stuff out of the Malibu place and into her apartment. Fed will have it up for auction next week.

—Fucking Fed.

—Well. Her dad did the crimes. So. Anyway.

I go out in the hall.

—Web.

I go back to the door.

He looks at the TV, looks at me.

—I'll be back at it soon enough, and I'll forget how much help you've been and I'll just push you around on the job like the peon you are. So. Thanks for all this.

I touch the nearly healed cut on my forehead. It's going to scar bad because I never bothered to have it stitched.

—Yeah, sure. After all, not like you ever did anything for me.

Po Sin nods.

—Nothing I can remember.

He aims the remote at the TV and unmutes the escalating melee on the screen.

—These people, they're living proof that a human being can live with any old stupid shit they can dream up.

I look out the window and watch Xing on the front lawn, kicking her new kitty around like a soccer ball.

—No argument here, Grandfather Elephant.

He waves the remote.

—Holy! This chick is gonna claw that asshole's eyes out.

He bumps the volume up, and I turn and leave the room, the raised voices of brawling families following me down the hall as I go to bathe his daughter.

ABOUT THE AUTHOR

CHARLIE HUSTON is the author of *The Shotgun Rule;* the Henry Thompson trilogy, which includes the Edgar Award–nominated *Six Bad Things;* and The Joe Pitt casebooks. For Marvel Comics he has written *Moon Knight,* as well as special annual issues of *The Ultimates* and *X-Force.* He lives in Los Angeles with his wife, the actress Virginia Louise Smith. Visit him at www.pulpnoir.com

ABOUT THE TYPE

This book was set in Fairfield, the first typeface from the hand of the distinguished American artist and engraver Rudolph Ruzicka (1883–1978). Ruzicka was born in Bohemia and came to America in 1894. He set up his own shop, devoted to wood engraving and printing, in New York in 1913 after a varied career working as a wood engraver, in photoengraving and banknote printing plants, and as an art director and freelance artist. He designed and illustrated many books, and was the creator of a considerable list of individual prints—wood engravings, line engravings on copper, and aquatints.